THE HOPEFUL HEARTS SERIES ◊ BOOK ONE

PERFECTLY ARRANGED

Liana George
Prov 16:9

LIANA GEORGE

©2021 Liana George

Published by Scrivenings Press LLC
15 Lucky Lane
Morrilton, Arkansas 72110
https://ScriveningsPress.com

Printed in the United States of America

All rights reserved. No part of this publication may be reproduced, stored in a retrieval system, or transmitted in any form or by any means—for example, electronic, photocopy and recording— without the prior written permission of the publisher. The only exception is brief quotation in printed reviews.

Paperback ISBN 978-1-64917-155-9

eBook ISBN 978-1-64917-156-6

Library of Congress Control Number: 2021945604

Editors: Shannon Taylor Vannatter and K. Banks

Cover by Linda Fulkerson, www.bookmarketinggraphics.com.

All characters are fictional, and any resemblance to real people, either factual or historical, is purely coincidental.

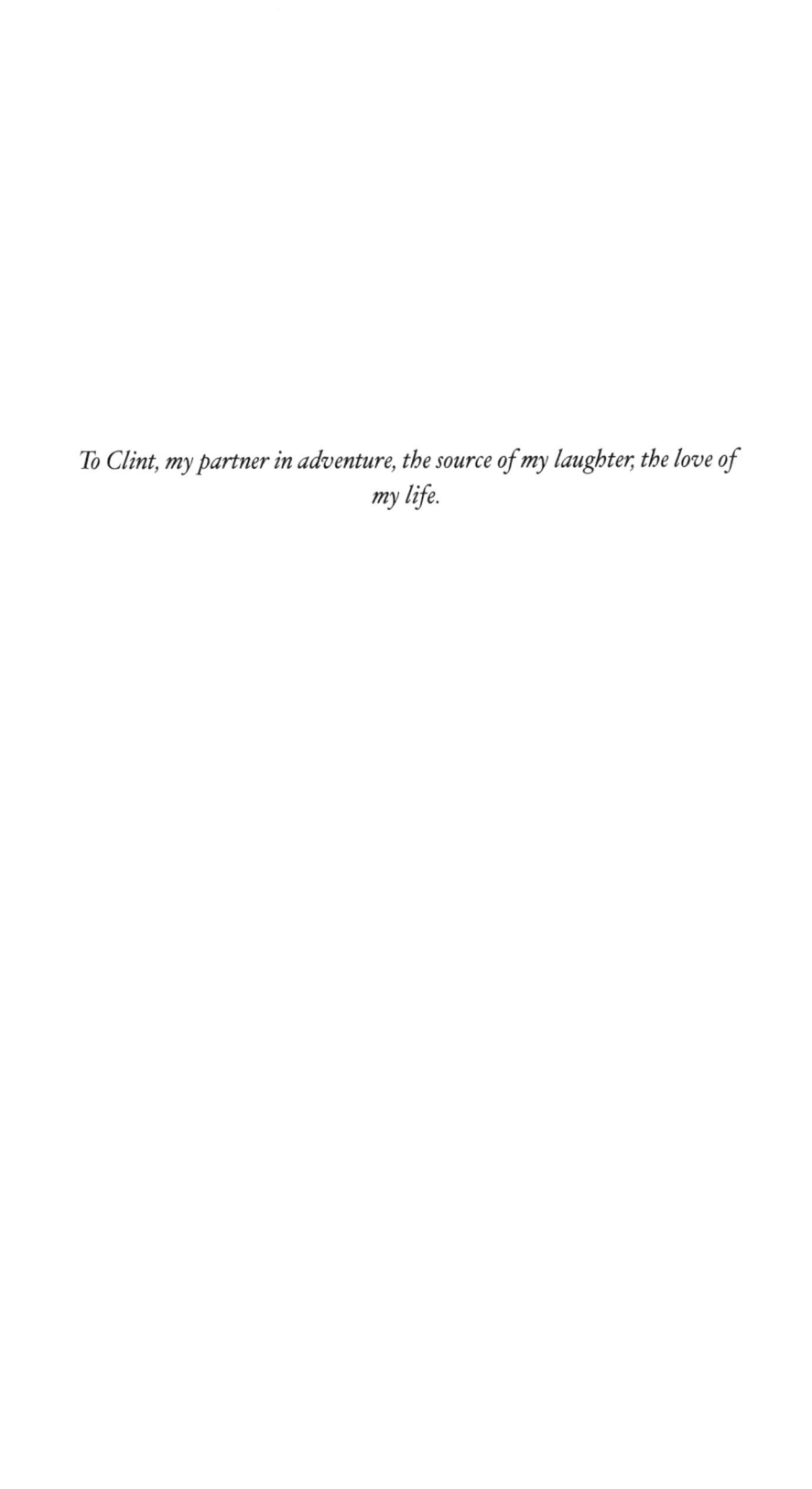

To Clint, my partner in adventure, the source of my laughter, the love of my life.

ACKNOWLEDGMENTS

As any author will tell you, writing a book is not a solo job. Yes, writers are notorious for spending lots of time alone creating and polishing their stories, but others assist, encourage, and pray for them on the sidelines and behind the scenes.

I'm no exception.

I've been blessed to have wonderful family and friends who've been with me every step of the way, and to them, I owe an immense debt of gratitude.

For the organizing business aspects and hoarding issues, I relied on professional organizer Hazel Thornton and hoarding specialist Ann Zanon for their expertise and knowledge. I consulted my former Mandarin teacher, Sally Kidwell, to ensure I had my Chinese words, foods, and settings correct. When I needed questions answered about the ins and outs of Hopeful Hearts, I deferred to Claudia Schuenemann, who continues to support the organization even from Germany! Finally, since I have no understanding of medical terminology or issues, I leaned on my dear friend, Lisa Alpeter, RN, for translating my Google research.

A special thanks to my early beta readers for their feedback, which allowed me to improve upon the story in ways I couldn't have done without their input, and to my hard-working Launch Team for their efforts to let as many people as possible know about this novel.

To Marisa Deshaies, editor extraordinaire, for making my words much better than they really are.

Editors Shannon Vannatter and Kaci Banks, Graphic Designer/Publisher Linda Fulkerson (and the rest of the Scrivenings Press Team). Not only did you believe in and love my story as much as I did, but you also did a fantastic job making it be the best story it could be. I appreciate each of your efforts to send this book out into the world. I'm thrilled to be part of the Scrivenings family!

Some extraordinary friends who have gone above and beyond rooting for me: Elizabeth Barbour, Kathy Brammer, Danielle Hoover, Jon and Regina Mortimer, and Brenda Nyberg. A girl couldn't ask for a better cheering section!

My prayer team - Lisa Alpeter, Lisa Rodriguez, Melanie Sharp, and Teresa Wells - you ladies have stood in the gap for me from the first day I sent you my prayer list to all the other days I called, texted, or emailed you and asked for emergency intercession.

My friend, mentor, and writing coach, Sandra Byrd. I have no doubt God brought you into my life, not once but twice, to guide my writing journey. I am so blessed by you, your wisdom, and your belief in me and my crazy ideas! I appreciate you helping me birth this book, and I look forward to us working together for many more years to come.

My family - first, to my dad, Bobby Bowman, without whom this book would have never been possible if he hadn't called and asked me to look up a mysterious address in Shanghai all those years ago. Next, my two amazing daughters, Kayley and Abbey, I hope my journey is proof that you're never too old to make your dreams come true. I'm so proud of the women you have become and of all that you've accomplished. Finally, to my "Wheel of Fortune" husband, Clint, your love and support mean more than you'll ever know. I hope we'll continue dreaming big dreams together for a very long time.

Above all else, to God. That you would entrust me with the skills, abilities, and opportunities to share this story with the world is humbling and beyond my understanding. I pray that those who read will draw closer to You and that You, and You, alone are glorified.

1

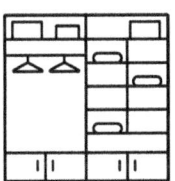

The tide must reach its lowest before turning.
~ Chinese Proverb

I'm hanging up my label maker.

While I'd been certain I would be the next Marie Kondo, organizing superstar, the lack of clients and shortage of funds in my bank account tells a different story. I grab another moving box and glide the packing tape across the bottom to secure it. The screech of the gun as it connects the two flaps resounds as the truth flashes in front of me.

After three years of blood, sweat, and tears, I've failed at the one thing I'd believed I was meant to do.

When I open a side desk drawer that holds a rainbow assortment of alphabetically arranged files, my heart flutters at the sight of everything in perfect order - just the kind of thing that would make my mother anxious.

I wince. Mom. Without a job, I have no other choice but to move back home with her.

As if on cue, her familiar blue Honda pulls up outside my window.

Seriously, what else could go wrong today?

Plowing my way through the heap of boxes, I grab my coat and purse from the chair and dash toward the door. Before I can step outside and hide my career woes, my mother walks in.

"Nicki, I ..." Mom closes the office door and studies the room. "What's going on in here?"

I survey the boxes scattered around the tiny cubicle. "Packing?"

"I see that, but why?"

"I'm closing up shop." I dig my shoe into the stained beige carpet. "Bridgeport's Organizing Business of the Year is no longer."

"What?" Her curly brown hair, which she'd passed on to me, shakes from side to side as she maneuvers her way across the room. "Why am I just now learning about this?"

"I didn't want to disappoint you." I retreat to my desk and set down my stuff. "I was going to tell you at dinner later this week."

"Honey, I could never be disappointed in you." She reaches for me and cups my chin. Her watered-down rose-scented perfume tickles my nostrils. "I'm sure whatever happened isn't as bad as you think."

"It is." I lower my eyes, too ashamed to match her gaze. The ashen look on my client's face as her cherished treasure shattered into tiny shards still haunts me, six months later.

"Let me turn on some lights in here and then you can tell me all about it." She heads back toward the door.

Uh-oh!

I lunge for the light switch, but Mom beats me to it.

"Mom, don't." I hold my hand out to stop her.

She clicks the switch on and off. On and off.

Nothing. I lean against the door and close my eyes. My failures continue to pile as high as the snow during our Connecticut winters.

"Why aren't the lights working?" Mom keeps flipping the switch as if she can make them magically turn on.

"They cut off my electricity." I drag myself back to my desk.

"Because?" The incessant clicking stops.

I flop down in my desk chair. "Because I didn't pay the bill." Rather than dwell on my shortcomings, I dump pens, paper clips, and label maker cartridges from my desktop into the flimsy brown cardboard.

"Oh, Nicki, why didn't you say something sooner?" My mom traipses back toward me. "Maybe I could have helped."

"I appreciate the offer, but I have to clean up my own messes."

She furrows her brow. "I know you like to think you have to handle everything on your own, but I could have at least shared some ideas that might have made a difference."

I bite my lip. My mother is the last person I'd seek advice from about my organizing business. I love her, but she is clueless when it comes to running things in an orderly and efficient manner. Plus, it was my carelessness that caused me to be in this predicament in the first place. No amount of glue could fix the damage I caused that day. The fewer people I had to confess that to, the better.

"Don't take this the wrong way, honey." My mother scans the boxes. "But did you try everything you could think of to get more clients?"

"Of course, I did." I pull a stack of business cards out of a box and hold them up to her like a deck of cards splayed out across a casino table. "I even made cold calls last week and still ended up with an empty calendar." I drop the pile of leads onto my desk and free the tears that I'd been forcing back.

"I'm sorry, Nicki, I didn't mean to upset you. Is there anything I can do to make this better?" Mom wraps my trembling body in her arms.

"No, but thanks for asking." I wiggle out of her embrace and search for the tissue pack buried at the bottom of my purse.

Once I've composed myself, I turn back to her, only to find

her poking around the box I'd allocated for donations. "What are you doing?"

Like a little kid caught stealing from the cookie jar, she quickly steps away from the mound of unwanted items. "Browsing." Dismissing her guilt, she pulls a book from the pile and flashes it at me. Marie Kondo's *The Life-Changing Magic of Tidying Up.* "Are you getting rid of this? I thought you idolized the woman."

Wary of her intentions, I bolt across the room and rescue the book from her hands. "To be honest, I've never been a big fan of her methods, but I'm not getting rid of it. I'm... blessing someone else with her knowledge." I place the bestseller back on top of the pile. I knew better than to admit to getting rid of anything.

"You're giving all this away?" She eyes the discards. "There's a lot of good stuff. I could use those manila folders. Oh, and those cute clip holders."

"You and I both know you don't need them," I say, my voice firm.

Resistant, she plops down into the shabby chic chair I bought at the flea market when I first rented my office space. "That's not true," she says with a pout.

I refuse to argue with her. "I'm glad to see you, Mom, but why are you here?"

She pulls on her tattered orange coat. "I—I wanted to see if it would be all right with you if I invited someone to join us for dinner this week, and I thought it would be best if I asked you in person."

"Bring someone to dinner?" I balk. It's been almost ten years since my dad suddenly died from a stroke, but I just can't imagine that she'd start dating again. "Like a man?"

"Yes!" She smiles, her face glowing. "I'm so glad you're open to the idea, Nicki."

"Uh, I don't know what to say, Mom," I stutter. "You've caught me off guard." I lean against my desk and clench my fingers around the edge. "Have you been seeing someone?"

My mom's mouth hangs open. "Of course not, Nicki. I could never replace your father!"

Relieved, I loosen my grip. "Then who do you want to bring with you?"

"Eleanor's son, Drew. Remember I told you about him? He's a doctor, good-looking, and single." She fidgets. "She told me at work this morning that he's considering going on one of those online dating apps, and I just figured since you were both unattached, why not skip all that digital mumbo-jumbo and introduce you to each other?"

I sigh. "Mom, we've talked about this."

"But, Nicki, you're twenty-six and not even dating. How will I ever have grandchildren if you aren't interested in spending time with someone?"

Someone? I lean over and place my hand on her shoulders. "I don't need a man right now, and I certainly don't want children." I raise my eyebrows. "Not today and not anytime in the future, either. You know that."

She waves a hand at me. "Don't start that nonsense about kids and the mess they make. Find and fall in love with your prince charming, and you'll see things differently. I'm sure of it."

"I appreciate your efforts, but I'm not looking for someone in shining armor to save me, a fairy tale romance to sweep me off my feet, or the ooey, gooey slobber of a baby right now." I spread my hands out and whirl around. "As you can see, I've got bigger things to be worried about."

When I've stopped being dramatic and turn back towards her, she's staring at me with laser focus.

"Never say never, dear. But you're right. Now probably isn't the best time for me to bring this up." She stands. "I'll let you get back to it." She shuffles to the door, occasionally stopping to peruse a box's contents and pull an item out.

"Mom ..." I growl.

"All right, all right."

"Thank you."

She opens the door allowing the frigid fall weather to seep into my office. "Oh, do you need a place to store your boxes? I'm not sure your tiny apartment can hold all this stuff."

"Where do you suggest I put them?"

"You can always leave them at my house." Her smile widens, and I know she's mentally calculating all the goodies she'd discover foraging through my stuff.

"That's okay. I'll figure something out. You don't need to worry yourself." I wave goodbye. "See you Thursday. Same place, same time?"

"Same," she says. Blowing me a kiss, she quickly closes the door.

I stare at the ceiling. I've got to find a job and fast. Otherwise, I'll be back under the same roof with her, her clutter, and the constant threat of her interfering in my romantic life. I definitely can't have that.

I'm not sure she wants that, either. She didn't suggest I move in. Her only concern was my boxes. Go figure.

Bolstered by this truth, I pull my phone from my back pocket to recheck my email inbox. Empty. No one seems willing to take a chance on me because there are zero responses to the applications and CVs I've submitted. I exhale and pray for something to come through soon. It has to.

I rub my hands together to get the blood flowing and resume my packing. Before I can, though, I glance over at my donation pile. Something is missing. I search high and low for the item I know was just there. After a few minutes of fruitless digging, I surrender and accept the facts. Somehow my mom managed to sneak off with my Marie Kondo book.

Chuckling, I reach for another box. It would be an act of God if my mother cracked open the book and actually followed the Japanese guru's organizing advice. Heaven knows Mom won't listen to mine.

Perfectly Arranged

TWO HOURS LATER, I've emptied my office and loaded all the boxes into my dilapidated Toyota Yaris, officially bringing my business to an end. There's barely room for me to sit and drive, but I squeeze in. Pulling out of the strip mall parking lot, I glance at all the boxes piled up around me.

Maybe Mom was right – how can I possibly fit all of this stuff in the shoebox apartment I call home without suffocating? I have to store these boxes elsewhere.

Instead of turning left on to the I-95 toward my place, I reluctantly drive to Mom's house. While I love my mother dearly and enjoy her company, I don't go there often. Better for us to meet at a location that isn't packed with unnecessary clearance items and stuff even antique collectors consider junk. It's just easier that way.

As the sun sets on familiar sights, my heart pounds faster. It's been at least three months since I last trekked through the neighborhood where I grew up. I reduce my NASCAR speed as I approach my old street and Mr. Davidson's house, where a classic red Ford pickup sits in the driveway.

Across the road, Mrs. Collins's garden of breath-taking gold, red, and orange foliage trickles from the front door to the street. Stopping in front of her mailbox, I roll down my window and inhale the sweet aroma that lingers over her lush fall nursery. I only wish she would work her magic in our yard next door.

Unable to avoid reality forever, I pull my car into my mom's driveway and turn off the engine. Her yard is a neglected jungle of flora and junk.

Over the years, she acquired stuff to ease the pain of losing my father, while I'd found solace in having things tidy. It was as if her disorganization made my desire for order even stronger. Unable to stomach the clutter she coddled and craved, I purposely created space between us for the sake of our relationship and moved out. Otherwise, I risked losing another parent.

As I contemplate what might happen if I were to live with her again, my phone blares, "Let It Go"—every professional organizer's favorite theme song—from the deep recesses of my purse. Happy for the distraction, I answer it without hesitation. "Hello?"

"Is this Nicki Mayfield with Save My Space Organizing?"

My pulse quickens at the unfamiliar female voice and her inquiry into my now-defunct company. "This is Nicki. How can I help you?"

"Nicki, hello! I'm so glad I was able to reach you," the sweet voice continues. "My name is Heather Campbell. You called and left a message for me last week."

Oh, the cold calls.

"Yes, Mrs. Campbell, about that—"

"Please, call me Heather," she interrupts.

"Okay, Heather." I squirm in my seat. "I appreciate you calling me back."

"It was perfect timing, really. My boss, Katherine O'Connor, needs your organizing services right away."

Woefully aware of the unfortunate timing, I press my forehead against the steering wheel.

"I'm sorry, Heather, but I'm afraid I'm not in a position to help you right now." I don't have the guts to tell her I've kissed my organizing days goodbye.

"Oh, I'm sure you're quite busy, but I'd love it if you'd reconsider."

I suppress a laugh at her incorrect assumption. She couldn't be more wrong about my workload. And now that the door to my business is officially closed, I'm not certain I want to re-open it either. "I'm so sorry, but I can't."

"Please, Nicki, I'm desperate," she pleads. "I made a mistake, and there aren't any other organizers who can assist me on such short notice." Her voice cracks. "I'm willing to pay double your rate for your services."

At her confession, my chest tightens. I'm all too familiar with costly mistakes. They caused my downfall.

I glance up from the steering wheel and survey the chaos that is my mother's front yard. Between the overgrown trees, knee-high grass, and mishmash of debris, it's hard to tell where the yard stops and the sidewalk starts. If this is what the outside looks like, I cringe to think what's inside.

The reality is, while there's a place for me in my mother's heart, there isn't any in her home.

Perhaps one more organizing job could hold me over until the next job, pay my rent, and keep me from sleeping under the freakishly scary dolls my mom stored in my old bedroom the last time I ventured inside.

Quietly questioning my decision, I rescind before I can change my mind. "I'd be more than happy to help you, Heather."

"You're a life-saver, Nicki!" Her voice rises a notch. "I can't thank you enough. I'll text you the address and meeting details in a bit."

"Perfect." A warm feeling washes over me. *Maybe there's hope.*

"Oh, one more thing, and I'll let you go," Heather says. "Are you familiar with Marie Kondo's methods? My boss is a big fan, and it would be a bonus if she knew you used them."

2

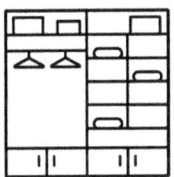

You can't expect to catch a cub without venturing into the tigress's den.
~ Chinese Proverb

The next morning, I drive to the address Heather had provided for my interview with Ms. O'Connor. This house is in Westport, a swanky little town along the Connecticut side of Long Island Sound. My family didn't put on the Ritz, so this is new territory for me.

After Googling the area, I'd gathered it was fancy, but I wasn't prepared for what's in front of me. Every house on the spacious tree-lined street is as large or larger than the White House. I'm nervous my car's dented door, cracked windshield, and hubcaps held on by zip ties might encourage someone to call the police. I grip the steering wheel.

Just because I am *in* trouble doesn't mean I *am* trouble.

My insecurities rise another level as I observe the O'Connor estate. The driveway to the house is as long as a football field and surrounded by large fountains, each the size of a playground pool. With a gabled roof, embellished doorways and windows, and a turret fit for a castle, the mansion takes my breath away.

Once I finish fawning over the house's intricate details, I ring the doorbell. In a matter of seconds, the large wooden door creaks open, and a middle-aged woman dressed in a dark navy uniform greets me.

"Yes?" She holds the door slightly ajar.

"Hi, I'm Nicki Mayfield with Save My Space Organizing. I'm here to see Ms. O'Connor."

"Do you have an appointment?"

"Heather asked me to come."

Satisfied by my name-dropping, she pushes the door open enough for me to enter. "Please, come in."

"Thank you." I step inside.

"Follow me."

I fall into step behind her down a dimly lit hallway covered with paintings that look like they belong in the Louvre. I only wish my guide would slow down so I could enjoy them. When we pass by an entire wall of windows leading to the backyard, I stop and take in the beautiful scenery.

The manicured lawn, ancient statues, and cobbled pathways remind me of a luxurious English garden straight out of a magazine. I smile, imagining myself wandering about out there, lost in my own little world.

"Miss Mayfield?" A voice snaps me out of my daydream.

I peel my gaze away from the scenic spot and back to the woman. "Oh, sorry, I'm coming." I quicken my pace and rejoin her.

We pause at a mahogany stained door. From the far side, I hear another woman's voice.

"That's a good girl, Princess! That's how to use the bathroom."

Princess? Bathroom? She must be in the middle of a potty-training session.

The woman taps on the bathroom door. "Ms. O'Connor? A Miss Mayfield is here to see you."

Without a word, my escort darts back down the hallway

from which we came, leaving me alone.

I turn back toward the bathroom, and the door thrusts open. Ms. O'Connor glares. Her short, silver-blue hair, crisply pressed khaki ankle pants, and white top reminds me of the prim and proper grandmother from *Gilmore Girls*. Even her black sweater lays perfectly on her shoulders.

"And who are you?"

"Hi, I'm Nicki Mayfield." I extend my hand. "Heather asked me to come discuss my organizing services with you."

The wealthy socialite gives me the once-over, keeping her perfectly manicured fingers affixed to the door.

I pull my hand back. "Is this not a good time?"

"Not really." Ms. O'Connor wipes away the small bead of sweat that has formed along her hairline. "I'm not sure why Lucinda brought you back here, but—"

A loud wail erupts from the bathroom.

Spinning back toward the cry, Ms. O'Connor rushes back inside. "No, no, no! You bad little girl! Now look at what you've done!"

With my ear against the door, I listen to the rush of scrambling feet and high-pitched howling.

"Ms. O'Connor," I say through the thick wood. "Do you need some help?"

"No, Princess, no!"

"Really, I'd be more than happy to assist," I call out again, this time a little louder. "I'm not great with kids, but I can try."

Ms. O'Connor yanks open the door. "Then get in here and help me."

Following her, I search for the right words to assure her that potty training young children is a difficult process. But when I catch sight of the toilet, it's not a toddler sitting on the seat.

I gasp. "What in the world?"

"I give up." Ms. O'Connor throws her arms in the air. "I've tried for almost an hour to get Princess to potty in the toilet, but she's stubborn."

"That—that's a cat!" I jump back. "You're potty training your cat?"

"Of course I am. Persians are so persnickety."

My eyes dart back and forth between Ms. O'Connor and the fluffy white cat straddling the adapted toilet seat. While it's rude to stare, I can't help myself. "I assumed you were potty training your grandchild."

"Don't be silly. I don't have, nor do I need, children or grandchildren." She rolls her eyes at me and runs her fingers through the cat's fur. "I don't like the smell or mess of cat litter, so this is a more suitable option."

Princess leaps off the toilet and onto the floor. Her pink diamond-encrusted collar jingles as she dashes out of the bathroom and down the hallway.

For a moment, I wish I could run away too.

After brushing off cat hair from her clothes and washing her hands, Ms. O'Connor struts out of the bathroom, leaving me alone. I'm tempted to go after her but decide that, like a lost child, it's probably best if I stay in place.

As sweat clings damply to my back, Ms. O'Connor pops her head in. "Well, don't just stand there. Come with me," she barks like a drill sergeant.

Being the rule-follower that I am, I fall in line behind her. A rogue organizer I am not.

We trek through the house in silence. I keep one eye on the back of Ms. O'Connor's perfectly coiffed hair and one on my surroundings. If I want to make a good impression on this woman, I need to understand more about her. Unfortunately, the sparse décor and minimalist design don't offer me many clues.

After a lengthy walk to another wing of the mansion, we arrive at a small room. Unlike the rest of the house, this space is cozy and warm, with floor-to-ceiling bookshelves all lined with beautifully bound tomes, an antique writing desk, and two wing back chairs situated in front of a toasty fireplace. I assumed these types of settings only existed in books or movies.

"This is gorgeous." I enter the room, awestruck by its ambiance. "You must love being in here."

"Yes, it's one of my favorite rooms." Ms. O'Connor settles into one of the chairs then points to the chair next to her. "Please, have a seat." She studies me like a science sample under a microscope. "So," she finally says, "tell me about yourself."

"My name is Nicki Mayfield, and I'm a professional organizer."

"Is Nicki short for something?" She places her forearms on the armrests and crosses her legs. "I don't care much for nicknames."

"Nicole is fine ... I guess."

"Good. Tell me then, Nicole, why should I hire you?"

For such an easy question, I have trouble responding. "Well, I ... I like order, and I think I can help you."

"You *think* you can?" She arches her left eyebrow. "Don't you believe in yourself and your abilities as an organizer?"

I rub my thumbs together. I *used* to think I was a good organizer. But with everything that happened over the last few months, doubt was my constant companion, always reminding me of my mistakes and failures.

As the bills piled up and the requests for help dwindled, I found myself questioning my talent more and more. I certainly couldn't share that with Ms. O'Connor, though. It's unlikely someone of her status would place much confidence in an employee who acted carelessly with her business and her client's keepsakes.

Ms. O'Connor lets out a heavy sigh. "Nicole, I'm not sure you're what I need. I've had other organizers work for me in the past, and I sense you aren't on their level." She rises from her chair. "This interview is over."

I watch her cross the room towards the door. Her words set my mind reeling with the thoughts of living with my mother and all her clutter again. *I can't go back there. My relationship with my mother would be destroyed, and she's all I have left.*

Ignoring the sour taste in my mouth, I stand. "Ms. O'Connor, wait."

She halts at the doorway and faces me.

"I understand why you'd be hesitant to hire me. Listening to my answers, or lack of them, I would be, too." I take a deep breath. "But I can assure you that hiring me will be a great decision." I inch closer to her. "I specialize in bringing order to nearly any cluttered space, and I can handle whatever you throw my way. If you're not satisfied with my work, I'll give you your money back. But I promise you, that won't happen."

Ms. O'Connor walks back into the room and glares at me, the lines around her eyes resembling cracked pottery. I stand as tall as possible and match her stare. My goal is to convey a strong and brave façade, but on the inside, I'm melting faster than Frosty the Snowman in Hawaii.

"You can start tomorrow at 10:00 a.m. Don't be late."

Restraining myself from hugging her, I smile. "Perfect. I'll email you my contracts and prep checklists later this evening."

Without as much as a goodbye, she leaves. When I'm sure she's gone, I slump into the chair. Thanks to my courage, I don't have to start packing.

But had I just sold my soul to the devil with a money-back guarantee?

THE NEXT DAY, adhering to Ms. O'Connor's imperative not to be late, I park my car in her driveway ten minutes early and do something that causes me to squirm in my seat.

I pray.

Fumbling for the right words, I spout the first thing that comes to mind. *Lord, thank you for this opportunity. It's not what I was looking for, but I'm grateful for the money to help me out of the mess I'm in. Give me patience to deal with Ms. O'Connor. Based on yesterday's experience, I'm going to need a lot of it.*

Hopefully, that will carry me through the workday.

I ring the doorbell precisely on time. Lucinda once again ushers me inside, where she takes my coat and hangs it up. "Follow me," she says, before heading down the hallway.

Please don't let her lead me to another potty-training session for Princess.

Walking in silence, I focus my attention on the back of her shirt and the tightly rolled bun that lies just above her neckline. Watching her head bob up and down, I have so many questions. *Does Ms. O'Connor require you to wear a uniform? What's it like working for the socialite? Do you like your job?* My mind was running so quickly I almost collide with Lucinda when she stops.

"This is the space Ms. O'Connor would like you to organize today." After unlocking the door, she steps aside to let me in.

I peek around the doorframe. The room is triple the size of my bedroom and lined with custom-made slanted shoe shelving similar to those I've seen in glossy fashion magazines or the high-end boutiques I've passed by in the city. "What's this room used for?"

"It's to be Ms. O'Connor's new shoe room."

My eyes widen. "You're kidding, right? This whole room is just for shoes?" I wait for a smile to break out across Lucinda's face, but the forlorn look she's worn since I arrived remains intact.

"It's not a joke, Miss Mayfield. This room is solely dedicated to Ms. O'Connor's vast number of shoes."

"Uh, okay." I have no clue how anyone could have so much footwear or why they would need a separate room just to store them, but what do I know about high society living? I glance back down the hallway. "So, where is Ms. O'Connor?"

"Not available."

"What? She's supposed to be here with me."

Lucinda sighs. "Not today. Now, if you'll excuse me—"

She takes a step to leave, but I pull on her arm.

"When will she be back?"

"This afternoon. I really must be going now." She removes my hand from her sleeve.

"How am I supposed to organize the shoes? By color? By type? By season?" I rake my hand through my hair as I realize the terrible position I've been put in. While I'm confident in my ability to bring order to any mess, I like to customize the organizing system to my client's preferences. How am I supposed to guess Ms. O'Connor's? Or is this why Heather asked about Marie Kondo? Ugh, how am I to know?

"The shoes will be delivered shortly. Just make sure you do your absolute best for her. Otherwise ..." Her voice trails off as she slinks away.

I close my eyes and imagine Ms. O'Connor having an outburst similar to what I've seen on *Hell's Kitchen*.

Dropping my workbag and purse onto the floor, I run my hand over the smooth shelving and inhale the smell of fresh paint and wood. The space is nothing more than a blank canvas waiting for the artist. Normally a room like this would be putty in my hands, but without Ms. O'Connor's input, it's like I'm carving a piece of stone with a dull knife.

Within minutes, a three-person crew arrives with the boxes. Like a game of Tetris, the workers carefully stack different-sized boxes in the middle of the room. I can only stand to the side and stare at the vast amount of footwear they bring in. Counting them all would be pointless and daunting, so I stop calculating how many pairs I'm going to be organizing and wait for the workers to finish.

Then I roll up my sleeves, pull my hair back into a ponytail, and turn on my shoe organizing playlist. I decide to sort and order the shoes by color from darkest to lightest to make it easier for Ms. O'Connor to find what she needs.

It will also provide a colorful aesthetic to the room, something that's missing from the rest of her house. Starting with her black shoes in the far right corner, I line up all her boots, flats, heels, wedges, and sandals in an orderly fashion.

Progressing through the color wheel, I can't help but admire Ms. O'Connor's great taste. Who would have guessed that a woman who cared so little about accessorizing her home would be such a fashionista?

As I'm about to place a pair of blue studded Versace heels into their new home, Princess meows and jumps out at me. I scream and drop the aquamarine beauties onto the floor. Realizing it's just Ms. O'Connor's pet-child, I catch my breath and swat my hand at the fluffy troublemaker. Chasing her around the room, the white ball of fur races into the hallway to escape my wrath.

There, I run smack-dab into a young woman dressed in gray dress slacks and a green cable knit sweater that matches the color of her eyes. Her strawberry-blonde bob frames her face and reminds me of Taylor Swift a few haircuts past.

"I'm so sorry I didn't see you there," I say to her, panting.

"Oh, don't worry. Princess has that effect on people." She laughs. "Nicki, right?"

I nod. "Yes. And you are?"

"I'm Heather Campbell." She beams. Her smile is a pleasant change from Ms. O'Connor's pinched face and Lucinda's worried expression.

"Oh, Heather." I hold out my hand to her. "It's so nice to meet you in person."

Heather bypasses my hand and wraps me in a bear hug. For a small woman, she's quite strong. "I'm so glad you called the other day." She holds me tighter. "I had gotten the dates mixed up for the completion of the shoe room and had to have it ready for Ms. O'Connor ASAP. You were the only one willing to help me. Thank you so much!"

"You're welcome," I say, gasping for air.

She releases me and steps inside the room. "Wow, this looks great. Katherine will be impressed."

"I hope so." I shake my arms to get the blood pumping

through them again. "I'm worried I didn't make a great first impression on her yesterday."

"Don't worry." She waves off my comment. "She liked you. If I recall, she described you to me as young, smart, and surprisingly bold."

"Well, that's a shock."

Heather chuckles. "Katherine has a hard exterior, and she's guarded, but once she's in your corner she'll fight for you like a mother bear. Do a good job, and she can connect you to all the right people." She picks up the abandoned Versaces. "She's a bit obsessed, wouldn't you say?"

"Uh-huh."

"According to Katherine, she's competing with Imelda Marcos—whomever that is—for the title of largest shoe collection." She sets the heels on the shelf. Her phone dings and she pulls it from her pocket. "Sorry, Nicki, but I need to reply to this. Let me know if you need anything or have any questions." She disappears into the hallway.

I take a deep breath and look back at the half-finished shoe room. If Ms. O'Connor could connect me to all the right people, it might be just the thing I need to get a stable job.

After seven hours of intense work, I finally finish organizing all of Ms. O'Connor's shoes. The kaleidoscope effect of the room fills my heart to bursting. "Not too bad," I say, patting myself on the back.

"Um ..." A voice behind me speaks over the clearing of a throat. I spin around to see my client in the doorway.

"Ms. O'Connor, hi! I didn't hear you come in." I stretch out my hand like a model introducing prize items on *The Price is Right*. "So, what do you think?"

Ms. O'Connor sets down three shopping bags and surveys the room. She taps her finger across her mouth as she takes in my work. "Well, it's not the KonMari method I was expecting, but I guess it will do."

I frown. "If you aren't happy with the way I've set things up,

I can always change it. Had Marie Kondo had her way with this space, she would have gotten rid of half of your collection and organized everything by category." I chuckle. "To me, doing it this way just seemed like the best way to handle the large quantity of shoes you have. Plus, I thought the rainbow effect it gave the room was a nice touch."

"It will be fine." She scans the room again. "However, it makes me realize I don't have enough yellow and green shoes."

My pulse races. I want to remind her that she has more than enough, but there's no point in wasting my breath. She won't listen to me. I'm just hired help.

"I'm glad you're pleased with what I've done," I say through clenched teeth.

"As I said, it will do." She retrieves the bags she abandoned at the door and hands them to me. "Please take care of these."

I open the bags to find four more boxes of brand-name shoes. A foul taste fills my mouth. How much does one woman need to be content? I'm not a sage, but I'm certain acquiring more shoes is not the answer.

When I look back up, Ms. O'Connor is gone. Blowing through my lips, I add the new footwear to her overflowing inventory. I scan the room one last time. Just think of how all the money spent on these shoes could have made a difference in the world! Confused by the ways of the wealthy, I close the door and make a beeline for the front entrance.

Once I'm situated in my car, I take deep breaths to regain my composure. I'm meeting my mom for our weekly dinner, and I don't want to show up in a sour mood. It wouldn't be fair to her. I crank the ignition and head down the driveway at full speed.

Watching the estate shrink in my rearview mirror, I question what's truly bothering me: Ms. O'Connor's extravagant materialism, the fact that I don't have her in my corner yet, or that her shoe obsession is eerily reminiscent of my mother's hoarding.

Perhaps it's a mix of all three.

3

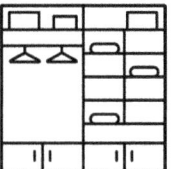

The heart never speaks, but you have to listen to it to understand.
~ Chinese Proverb

My attitude has improved by the time I slide into my favorite booth at Luigi's Italian Cocina. It's hard to be upset in a charming establishment like Luigi's. For two years, it has become a sanctuary not only for my stomach but also for my soul. After the Container Store and the library, it rounds out the top three of my happy places.

"Nicki, it's so good to see you, *bella*." Luigi, the restaurant's namesake, races towards me. One of the reasons why my mom and I love this place so much—besides the tasty food, checkered tablecloths, and true Italian ambiance—is its endearing owner. He calls all his customers by their first name and insists on waiting tables himself.

"Luigi, how are you today?" I hold out my hands, and Luigi takes them, kissing each as part of his traditional greeting.

"I'm good, *bella,* now that you're back in my *ristorante*. I don't know what I'd do if you and your *madre* stopped visiting me each week." He pouts like a little kid, and I can't help but smile. A man of about sixty-five, he is still handsome. If you didn't love the food, you'd come just to spend time with Luigi. He's adorable.

"Oh, you don't have to worry about that. Thanks to your warm hospitality and your delicious cuisine, we'll be customers for life."

"That's what I like to hear!" He claps. "Do you want me to bring your usual, or do you want to look at a menu?"

"The usual, please."

"Wonderful, I'll be back with your drinks and some bread." He nods and disappears.

I glance at my watch and notice Mom is running late. I'm sure she's fine, I just hope she's not out shopping. Rather than rush to judgment, I purge the thought from my mind and try to think positively.

Pulling out my phone, I click on social media and scroll through my feed. A memory from several years ago pops up on my screen—an old photo of my dad. I choke back the tears as I read the caption, *First snow of the season!* and gaze at my father building a snowman in our front yard when that was still possible.

From the wrinkled corners of his eyes and the huge smile on his face, he was doing what he loved—finding joy in the simple things of life. I set my phone on the table and rub my hands over my face.

My dad was the center of my world. Without his boisterous laugh and larger-than-life personality, an eerie silence ruled our home. No amount of noise blaring from the radio or television could fill the void he'd left behind. I'd tried. Yet nothing could have prepared me for the changes his absence would bring. Tears spatter onto the red and white tablecloth. I reach for a napkin and wipe my cheeks.

"Nicki?" My mother's voice pulls me back to reality.

I hide the tissue under the table. "Mom, I didn't see you." I climb out of the booth and hug her. "I'm glad you're here."

Rather than coming together, my mother and I each found

our own way to grieve. For me, it was simply trying to navigate my teenage years without him. He'd always been the one to help me with my homework, cheer me on at my soccer games, and play chess with me on the weekends. Without his constant support, I retreated to my room and isolated myself from everyone. It was easier that way.

"Are you okay?" She slides into the bench opposite me.

"I'm fine," I lie, sitting back down. "How are you?"

"I'm good. Sorry I'm late." She peels her coat and hat off, revealing an oversized sweater and messy hair. Sadly, neither look recently washed.

For mom, it was hoarding. Over time, it became increasingly obvious that her need for stuff wasn't healthy. When it became too difficult to walk in our house without tripping over something, I knew it was time to intervene.

"Now that Halloween's over, people are in full holiday-shopping mode. It was crazy at work, and I just couldn't get out on time."

I sigh in relief. "No problem."

Many times, when she was at work, I used to sneak bags out of the house, relocating them to the trash, certain she'd never miss them. Once, she caught me tossing some of the precious things she'd abandoned in my room into the dumpster and had been utterly undone.

Shaking the memory away, I say, "I was just scrolling through social media."

"Oh, looking for a job?" She unrolls the napkin and places it in her lap.

"I've had a change of plans." I scoot closer to the table. "I got a temporary organizing gig that should hold me over financially until I'm able to find another job from the applications and résumés I sent out."

"Wonderful! Maybe then you'll be able to restart your business."

"That's a nice thought, Mom, but I think it's time for me to move on from organizing. As they say, when God closes one door, He opens another. Maybe it's time for me to walk through a new door."

"Who says that?" Her forehead wrinkles. "I don't remember reading that in the Bible."

I chuckle. There are some things you can joke about with my mom, but the veracity of the Holy Scriptures isn't one of them. "Calm down, it's just a saying."

Just then, my stomach growls. "I guess I'm hungrier than I realized." I scan the restaurant for my favorite waiter. "Where's Luigi?"

"Did someone say my name?" Luigi arrives at our table with the appetizers.

The smell of warm breadsticks and olive oil wafts through the air. "Just in time, Luigi." I take the breadsticks out of his hands and set them on the table. "I'm starving."

"Not in my ristorante, *bella*!" He wags his finger at me then places two glasses of water and a small plate of oil next to the bread.

I take a quick bite. "*Delizioso!*" I pinch my fingers together in front of my puckered lips, and Luigi's eyes sparkle.

"*Grazie*! Eat, and I'll be back with your entrees, *pronto*." He speeds back off towards the kitchen.

Once Luigi has left, Mom and I devour the garlic bread.

"So, tell me about this temporary job." My mother dabs her mouth with a napkin. "How did it come about?"

"Remember how I told you I made those cold calls last week?" I lick the garlic off my fingers.

She nods then bites off another piece of her breadstick.

"One of them called back. She desperately needed someone to work with her boss, so I agreed to help."

"It's just like you to help those in need. You've always been an inspiration in that way."

"I'm not sure how inspiring I am, considering the circumstances." I grab another breadstick and dip it into the oil.

"My client is a handful, and it's going to take an act of God for me to get on her good side."

"Oh?"

Before I can reply, Luigi returns with our meals. "*Buon appetito*, ladies!" Placing the spaghetti and tortellini bowls on the table, he winks at each of us before dashing off again.

After we pray and settle in with our food, my mother circles back to our earlier conversation. "So, tell me more about this lady you're working for."

I slurp a noodle into my mouth and swallow. "Her name is Katherine O'Connor. According to the Internet, she's a Connecticut socialite and CEO. But if you ask me, I'd say she's difficult to work for and extremely eccentric."

My mother picks up the parmesan cheese and sprinkles some onto her dish. "What makes her eccentric?"

Despite my need for food, I push my plate away from me. "You're not going to believe me when I tell you." Without missing a beat, I fill my mother in on Princess's potty training, Ms. O'Connor's sterile decorating style, and her unbelievable shoe addiction.

"And after seven hours of work, her only comment was 'It will do'! Can you believe that?" My voice rises a notch as my cheeks flush. "And then she had the nerve to declare she needed more shoes!"

"Nic, I think you're the one who needs to calm down now." My mother reaches over and pats my hand. "Why are you letting yourself get so worked up over this woman?"

I exhale in an attempt to let out all my frustrations. "Because she's exasperating and hard to please. And her shoe issues remind me of —" I stop myself before saying something I'll regret later.

"Reminds you of what?" she asks innocently.

Twirling my napkin around my thumb, I don't have the heart to tell her that working with Ms. O'Connor stirs up memories of our tumultuous times together in the past. And the decision I made to ensure we didn't grow apart again.

Despite all my efforts to bring order to our lives, I couldn't. Nor could I handle the chaos that constantly surrounded me inside the four walls of our home. Eventually, a chasm grew between us. Like a game of tug-of-war that no one ever won, our relationship deteriorated to the point that we were simply two former shells of ourselves living under the same roof.

Ultimately, I decided that I'd live on my own when I graduated from college because putting space between us was the only way I knew how to salvage what little family I had left. In doing so, my mother and I have a happier and healthier relationship today.

"Nothing. Forget I said anything." I toss my napkin on the table. "I just need this job to go well with her because she has connections that might help me get a permanent position somewhere."

A smile forms on my mom's lips. "This O'Connor woman may be rich and have connections, but never forget that God is the one who perfectly arranges all the details of your life."

I shrug. While I'm a believer, my faith isn't as strong as my mother's, and I'm not a hundred percent sure God is working out anything on my behalf right now. It certainly doesn't feel like it.

"Nic," my mom says softly, "maybe this is God's way of refining you and teaching you to have patience and love for people who aren't so easy to get along with. And who knows, maybe there's more to Ms. O'Connor than you realize."

"Let's talk about something else." I steer our conversation in another direction. "I shouldn't be discussing her with you in the first place, and since I have to go back to the estate tomorrow, I'd rather not give work any more of my time and energy right now. They belong to you."

She cups her chin in her hand and tilts her head. "What else do you want to talk about?"

"I don't know. Something interesting that happened at work? What you want to do for Thanksgiving? What you learned at church last night?"

My mom's face lights up at the mention of her weekly Wednesday night worship service. "Oh, Nic, you should have heard Pastor Jeff last night. It's perfect for what you're dealing with."

"How so?" I raise my eyebrows. I seriously doubt that Pastor Jeff has any words of wisdom to share with me on the current situations of my life, but I'm open to listening.

"Well, he spoke about not storing up treasures here on earth and instead storing up treasures in heaven, which have eternal significance." She pulls out her phone from her purse. "I'm sure you can find the sermon on iTunes or the church website. After you listen to it, maybe you could bring it up with your client and talk to her about how God doesn't want us tied down to earthly things, like a room full of shoes, that don't really bring much value to our lives."

I balk. She's not serious, is she? Mom's entire house is full of treasures that have no value! I shake my head. *Does she hear herself or see the irony in what she's telling me?*

Pausing to find the right words, I purse my lips. "Umm, Mom, did *you* listen to what Pastor Jeff was saying?"

"Of course I did—"

"Ladies," Luigi interrupts us. "Do you want dessert or to-go boxes?"

"To-go boxes, please," I reply without giving my mom a chance to respond. "Thanks, Luigi. Everything was great, but it's getting late, so it's probably best if we skip dessert this week."

My mom nods.

"Okay, I'll be back with your boxes and your check, *un momento.*" Like the Flash, he darts off again.

When I'm certain Luigi is far enough from the table, I confront my mom. "Do you think maybe what Pastor Jeff was talking about last night is something you might want to take to heart?"

She picks at the sleeve of her sweater and grows quiet. I'm not sure if she's avoiding me or contemplating what I'm saying. I pray it's the latter. I've tried everything I can think of to get her to stop collecting things and stockpiling them for years now, but it's fallen on deaf ears.

Maybe a wake-up call from God will get her to change her ways. I'm not sure how many miracles I can ask for in one day, but I'll press my luck and see, because that's what it's going to take to cure my mother of her hoarding.

After a few minutes of awkward silence, she finally speaks up. "Nic, I think you're right."

I perk up. "Really?"

"Yes, I do." She pauses. "I don't know how I missed it before, but I realize now that I've been wrong."

My heart pounds so hard inside my chest I'm sure she can hear it across the table. *Stay calm!* I don't want to embarrass or cause her any sort of shame. I'm just grateful her eyes have been opened, and she's willing to finally get the help and healing she needs.

"Thank you for pointing out this to me." Her voice trembles. "I've been in the wrong, but not anymore."

Tears pool in the corner of my eyes. "Mom, I'm so glad you see this too. No matter what happens, I'll be by your side the entire time."

"That is so sweet, Nic, but I know you have your own volunteer activities. However, I'd be happy to look and see if there's something we can do together."

"Wait, what?" I blink and shake my head. "Why are you talking about volunteering?"

"Because you made me realize that perhaps I need to be doing more work that has eternal significance. You know, just as Pastor Jeff was saying."

I pinch the bridge of my nose. "Mom, that's not what I was—"

"For my two favorite ladies." Luigi returns with our to-go bags and the check.

"Thank you, *Signore*," my mother giggles. "We'll be back again next week. Right, Nic?"

Shell-shocked by the day's events and my mother's misunderstanding of what I was trying to help her see, I'm rendered speechless. I simply grin and wave at my favorite waiter.

After we pay the bill and gather our belongings, I quickly scoot out of the booth. At this point, I'm desperate for a long hot bath and a good night's sleep.

"Nic," my mom calls out after me. "You forgot your food."

Exhausted, I turn around and stare at the white plastic bag. "Just leave it. I'm full."

"Well, we certainly can't let it go to waste." She picks up the container of food and chases after me. "If you don't want it, I'll gladly take it."

Rather than argue with her, I let her have her way. There's nothing I can say that will change her mind.

BY THE TIME I arrive at my apartment, I'm mentally, emotionally, and physically drained. I forgo the bath, slip into pajamas, and faceplant onto my bed.

I'm almost in a deep sleep when I remember I never asked Ms. O'Connor or Heather what time I should arrive at the estate in the morning. Pushing myself up off the lumpy mattress, I reach for my phone. When I open it, I see a missed call and voicemail. My fingers tremble as I press the button and listen to the message.

"Nicki, it's Heather."

Her sharp tone causes my back to stiffen.

"I wanted to let you know that you don't need to come to the estate tomorrow after all. Thanks. Bye."

Listening to the succinct recording again, I search for clues but can only come to one conclusion. Ms. O'Connor wasn't as satisfied as she'd said.

Between the false hope of my mom getting help *and* being fired on the same day, I slink down under my bedding. I thought I had all the answers for Ms. O'Connor and my mom, but clearly, I was wrong. I don't even have them for myself.

Now, what am I going to do?

4

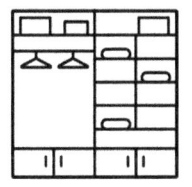

It's hard to plumb the depths of the water in the ocean.
~ Chinese Proverb

It's been three weeks since I was fired from the O'Connor estate job. Rather than binge-watch another TV show on Netflix or sink into a deep depression, I've managed to be productive, personally and professionally. I deep cleaned my apartment and volunteered at a soup kitchen, then updated my LinkedIn profile and CV before applying for five more positions with high-profile companies.

While none of this has added to my bank account, it offers a glimmer of hope that something good is just around the corner.

If anyone needs some good, it's me.

Shuffling through my unpaid bills, I pray it comes soon. I've used the funds Ms. O'Connor paid me to keep afloat these past few weeks, but I won't last much longer on the little that is left.

Deflated by that reality and the need to work off the food I'd consumed at the all-you-can-eat Thanksgiving buffet last week, I muster the strength to throw on exercise gear and head out for a run. While I'm lacing up my holey Nikes, my phone rings. I cautiously hit the button.

"H—hello?" I stutter.

"May I speak with Nicki Mayfield, please?" a male voice asks.

"This is she."

"Miss Mayfield, I'm with the human resource department at Emerson Technologies. We received your application and would like to schedule an interview with you to discuss the project management position we have open. Would you be available to meet with us next week?"

I jump up from my seat, almost falling over my untied laces. "Uh, yes, I can do that." I try to sound calm and not like someone tripping over herself.

"Wonderful," he says. "I'll email you a list of times and dates. Select the one that works best for you, and we'll make the arrangements."

"Great!" I squeal a bit too loudly. *Slow down, Nicki*. I lower my voice. "I mean, thank you."

"You're welcome. We are quite impressed with your organizational skills and feel that it might be a good fit for our position. That's why we'd like to visit with you as soon as possible."

"That sounds great."

"There's just one more thing, Miss Mayfield," he says. "Please bring the names and numbers of your last five clients so we can verify your recent work experience. This is standard procedure when we hire those who've been self-employed."

My stomach flips. "Sure, no problem."

"Good day," he says before promptly hanging up.

I set my phone down and pace around my living room.

They want a list of references.

I don't have any issues providing them with my clients from this past summer. It's just Ms. O'Connor who raises a red flag. How do I explain to the people at Emerson Technologies about my sudden dismissal after only one day of work? That certainly won't leave a favorable impression with them. It didn't with me.

I'd contacted Heather to see what I could have possibly done wrong. She'd never responded to my calls.

Pulling the vacuum cleaner out of the closet, I start pushing it back and forth over the ratty carpet. Although the place is squeaky clean, my shoulders relax a bit with the constant motion. It's not until I turn the hefty machine off that I realize there's another problem. Ms. O'Connor hadn't returned the contracts I'd emailed to her after our interview. Without her signed consent, I can't divulge any of her information to Emerson.

Which means I'd have to use my client Mrs. Jacobson as my fifth reference.

I shiver as my mind replays the moment her keepsake plate slipped out of my hand and shattered into tiny shards on the rich hardwood floor. The shock that covered her face and the despair that filled my heart when our eyes locked. I'd known I was doomed.

I rub my hands over my face.

Reaching out to either of these two clients will not help me gain stable employment, but I have no other options. It's just a matter of which one will help me most. I rearrange the pillows on my couch and organize my shoe rack by the front door as I contemplate my best course of action.

While I know Mrs. Jacobson would be kind, I don't want anyone to know I was so negligent with my business. But being fired for not using the KonMari method? That I can explain and justify.

Certain of my decision, I pick up my phone and dial Heather's number. Thankfully, she answers after only two rings.

"Hello, this is Heather."

Heavy static fills the line. "Uh, Heather, hi. It's Nicki Mayfield. Can you hear me?"

"Oh, Nicki! It's so good to hear from you."

"Really?" I try to hide my surprise. "After the message you left me a few weeks ago, I wasn't sure. I tried following up."

"My apologies." Her voice sounds like it's in a blender. "Things have been crazy here at the estate. We had an emergency come up shortly after you ... left that last day."

I open the patio door and step out onto the balcony for better reception. "An emergency?"

"Yes. Sadly, Mr. O'Connor passed away a few hours after you left."

I lean over the rail and the irritating noise stops. "I'm sorry, Heather, did you say Ms. O'Connor died?" While I wasn't fond of the woman, I certainly didn't wish her dead. "That's terrible!"

"No, not Katherine," Heather corrects me. "It was *Mr.* O'Connor, her father, who passed."

"Her father?" I breathe a sigh of relief. "Well, that's good news." I hit myself on the forehead with the palm of my hand. "I mean, not good news for him, but good news for Ms. O'Connor." *Ugh! I did it again.* "No, that's not right, either I mean—"

"It's okay, Nicki." Heather's calm voice somewhat settles my nerves. "I know what you mean."

"Sorry about that. I got a little tongue-tied there for a minute."

"No problem. In fact, I was going to call you later today."

"You were?" My pulse races.

"Yes. With Mr. O'Connor's passing, we're going to need help dealing with his personal items. Katherine is too overwhelmed to make any decisions about his stuff by herself, and I'm too busy overseeing the business to assist her. I thought perhaps you might be able to help her with the process."

"When were you needing my help?"

"The sooner the better, perhaps even tomorrow?"

I gulp. If I agree to help Ms. O'Connor with her father's things, I won't be able to schedule my interview anytime soon since I have no clue how much time it could take to sort through all her father's belongings. He might have as much or more than

Perfectly Arranged

his daughter. But can I afford to hold off on a new position that long?

Every part of me wants to decline Heather's request, but they had given me a large advance, without which I'd have been sunk. The Bible verse I'd read this morning as part of my new daily routine comes to mind. *"But even if you should suffer for what is right, you are blessed."* Working with Ms. O'Connor will likely cause me to suffer *a lot*, but I know in my heart it's the right thing to do.

"Uh, let me check my calendar." I race back inside, grab my planner and flip through the pages pretending to look for an open slot. I know full well it's empty, but I can't let Heather know that.

After a few more page turns, I speak up. "I think I can rearrange a few things and clear my calendar for tomorrow. What time?"

"Wonderful." She proceeds to rattle off a time and location of where I should go.

"I'll be there."

THE ADDRESS HEATHER gave me was for Mr. O'Connor's residence, five miles down the road from his daughter's house.

His home is a miniature version of hers, just as elaborate but on a smaller scale. The only other difference between the two buildings is the dozen marble lion statues guarding the main courtyard of his home, rather than the wading pool-size fountains dominating her landscape.

I pause when I get to the front door. While I shouldn't be nervous about meeting with Ms. O'Connor again, I can't help but wonder what type of mood she'll be in. I rub my sweaty palms against my pants before ringing the doorbell.

When the door opens, I catch my breath. The lady standing in front of me is nothing like the one I met a few weeks ago. Her normally coiffed hair is unkempt, dark circles shadow her eyes, and her intimidating posture has an edge of frailty. I actually feel sorry for her.

"Hello, Ms. O'Connor. It's nice to see you again." I'd offer her a hug or touch on the shoulder but based on our previous encounters, I keep my hands to myself and grip my workbag tighter.

"Nicole, come in." She steps aside to let me enter. Once inside, I see that Princess is standing faithfully next to her owner, as if on guard. I reach down and rub the soft white fur. She emits a soft purr, and I take that as a sign that she remembers me.

Straightening, I look Ms. O'Connor in the eyes. "I'm so sorry for your loss."

"Thank you, but there's no need. My father and I weren't close."

"Well, uh, I know how hard it is to lose a parent and to have to go through their things while you're grieving."

Ms. O'Connor's eyes narrow. "You've lost a parent?"

"Yes. My father died when I was fifteen." I look at the white tile floor. Even after all these years, it's still hard to talk about it.

"That must have been difficult at such a young age." Our eyes meet, and my client flashes a sympathetic look at me. For a moment, I believe that perhaps, like the Grinch, she's grown a heart amid her loss.

"Well, we could stand here and trade sob stories, but we have a lot of work to do."

I was wrong.

"Let's get started." She walks down a short hallway and disappears through a door on the right. Princess follows suit.

As I sprint down the hallway after the pair, I can't help but notice how aesthetically different this house is from Ms. O'Connor's. There's plush carpeting on the floor, vibrant colors on the walls, and a decent amount of décor perfectly staged throughout. The house gives off a cozy, lived-in vibe, unlike Ms. O'Connor's cold and sterile abode.

Funny how a child and parent can be so different despite sharing the same DNA.

When I finally catch up with Ms. O'Connor, she's staring at one of the many paintings lining the room's walls. I quietly enter and glance at the artwork that's captured her attention—a piece depicting a father explaining the Bible to his children. She's so engrossed in her thoughts that I'm not sure she's aware of my presence.

Placing my bag and coat next to Princess, who's curled up in a chair in the corner, I wait for my client to acknowledge me.

It doesn't take long.

"For reasons I will never understand, my father loved this piece," she says, her voice barely above a whisper.

Unsure how to reply, I remain silent. I let my eyes wander between Ms. O'Connor and the painting while my mind considers her comment. After a few moments, she turns her gaze away from the artwork and toward me, her eyebrows arched high.

How should I know? I have no knowledge of ancient paintings, nor did I know her father or understand his taste in artwork.

I shrug. "Maybe he appreciated the importance of fathers training their children in spiritual matters?"

"My father?" She snickers. "He wasn't overly interested in any aspect of my life, much less my spiritual upbringing."

From her sharp response, it's obvious I've hit a sore spot. Yet I can't help but feel sorry for her. Although my mom and I just recently came to faith in Jesus, I appreciate the efforts she's made to encourage me on my spiritual journey. I treasure that aspect of our relationship.

I shift my weight from side to side. "Why don't we discuss what you need my help with?"

Ms. O'Connor sighs and makes her way to the center of the room. "As you can see, my father was a collector of eighteenth-century French art and furniture." She spreads her arms open wide as if putting the room on display. "We'll need to inventory all the pieces so we can determine whether they need to be auctioned, donated, or placed in one of the museums we support."

"Okay. Just the items in this room?" I scan the space, mostly taken up with paintings.

"Of course not, Nicole," she snaps. "I've designated this room as a staging area where we can bring in the smaller pieces to photograph and catalog. The larger pieces we'll leave where they are."

Heat rushes to my face. "We?"

"Yes, we. You and I will be working together on this. Is that a problem?"

"Oh, no, of course not." A lump forms in my throat. "It's just that last time, you weren't interested in working alongside me."

She squints her eyes at me as if she was throwing darts in my direction and straightens her back. "This is different. If having me work with you is a problem, I'm sure I can find someone else who won't mind."

I tug at the hem of my sweater. I'm willing to do what's needed. Who knows, I might even learn a thing or two about genuine antiques as opposed to the junk my mom refers to as collector's items.

"No, it's not a problem at all," I tell her. "Like the Bible says, 'Two are better than one for they get a good return on their work.'"

She rolls her eyes at me. "You're not going to preach too, are you?"

"Of course not." I laugh. "I'm the last person to be preaching to anyone."

"Good. Now let's get to work."

We spend the rest of the morning inventorying the paintings in the room and other parts of the house. While we don't engage in any deep discussion, Ms. O'Connor shares her extensive knowledge about French art, and I'm surprised to find myself so intrigued by the paintings.

Growing up, I never truly appreciated art. Now, I find myself mesmerized by the intricate details of the artists' work, their unique subjects, and the mediums they used to create their masterpieces. Just like Jasmine in Aladdin, a whole new world has opened to me, and I'm absorbing it like dry ground soaking up water.

Shortly after one, a loud rumble fills the room, and my face turns red. My stomach always betrays me. Ms. O'Connor notices the sound of my body's demands and suggests we take a lunch break. I follow her to the kitchen, where a small buffet has been set up.

"Help yourself, Nicole." She hands me a plate. "I wasn't sure what you'd like, so I had Heather select a variety of options."

"Thank you." I take the plate and open the first chafing pan. Once I've filled my plate with an assortment of vegetables, salad, chicken, and rice, I join Ms. O'Connor in the formal dining room.

We eat without talking, the only noise the clanking of silverware against our dishes.

Normally I can handle dining in silence, but the profound quiet that looms over us is unnerving. It reminds me of the stillness that penetrated my house when my father died. I wonder if all houses endure this type of quiet when someone has passed away, a sadness that creeps inside the walls indicating that something is wrong or missing. My spine tingles at the thought.

Batting away a morsel of rice from my sweater, I attempt to lighten the mood by making small talk. "So, what was your father like?"

Ms. O'Connor pinches her lips. From beneath her creased forehead, the veins bulge in her neck. She doesn't answer me but continues to move food around on her plate.

"Ms. O'Connor?" I raise my voice to ensure she hears me this time.

Still no reply.

Wanting to respect her privacy, I push my chair back slightly from the table. It's clear she's not in the mood for chitchat. "Thanks for lunch. It was delicious." I stand. "I'll wait for you in the staging area."

As I'm placing my silverware on my plate and readying to leave, she hits the table with the flat of her hand. "He wasn't a loving father." Her bottom lip wobbles.

I freeze.

The color drains from her face as she pushes her plate from the edge of the table. When she looks at me, her eyes are clouded with tears.

"You asked me what my father was like, and I'm telling you he wasn't fond of me."

Tongue-tied, I fall back into my seat. *How do I even respond to that?* It's not possible. I stay mute and allow her to continue sharing what's on her mind. Maybe even her heart.

"I was born with a heart condition that required surgery." She rolls her thumb over the linen tablecloth. "I guess having an imperfect daughter was an embarrassment to him. So rather than finding joy in his only child, he escaped me by obsessing over work and money. In his eyes, I didn't hold much value since I was broken."

A pang of familiarity hits me as I think about my mother. I know exactly what Ms. O'Connor is talking about because most days, it seems that my mother values her expired food cans, collection of telephone books, and broken microwaves more than she does me.

"I'm so sorry. I know how difficult that can be too. Really, I do."

She grins. "Don't be sorry. He always ran away from things that scared him, and it was his choice to push me away. Unfortunately, I suffered the consequences.

"We moved to Bridgeport when I was seven. Even though the doctors said I would be fine, my father thought I was too fragile to participate in outdoor activities. So, I was confined inside and forced to learn French and Italian and read all the classics. But no matter how hard I worked, it seemed nothing was ever good enough for him."

I nod in sympathy. My heart is torn as I think about the similarities this supposedly aloof woman and I share despite our vastly different living situations.

"When I was eighteen, I went off to college and fell in love. But my boyfriend was drafted into the military and died in the war. I was heartbroken. My father, however, refused to allow me to go to the funeral. He never liked John and didn't want us together. After he died, I resented my father and wanted nothing to do with him, his money, or his business."

Trembling, she wipes her nose with her napkin before taking a sip of water. When she doesn't continue, my curiosity gets the best of me.

"But you did stay because you're here, and you run part of the company."

"Yes." She sighs. "My mother, whom I adored, convinced me to change my mind. Plus, when you get used to a certain lifestyle of money and privilege ... Well, it's not that easy to walk away from. So, I buried my resentment and anger and did what was expected of me.

"But that's enough of that." She throws her napkin on her plate and pushes away from the table. "We should get back to work." She rises from her chair and leans on the table. Her steel-blue eyes bore into me. "I don't think I need to remind you that none of what was discussed here should be shared with anyone or mentioned again."

I jut out my chin. "Don't worry. I have a professional code of ethics I would never breach."

She nods at me and skitters towards the kitchen, leaving her plate untouched.

Glued to my seat, I replay what just happened. That Ms. O'Connor would confide in me floods me with happiness. I never dreamed the two of us would share a meal, much less forge a secret alliance. *God definitely works in mysterious ways.*

I pick up our plates and chuckle. A few weeks ago, I couldn't stand being in the same room with this woman. Now the ice around my heart has thawed, and I have a new understanding and respect for her. Funny how time changes things. And people.

As we trek back to the staging area, it dawns on me that Ms. O'Connor isn't who I thought she is. The scary truth is she and I are a lot alike. But that realization also makes me aware I don't want to end up anything like her—alone and miserable.

5

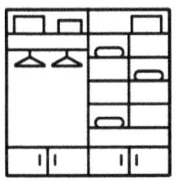

Wishes of mind and heart are as hard to control as a horse and an ape.
~ Chinese Proverb

After two weeks of working around the clock, Ms. O'Connor and I inventoried and cataloged all her father's belongings. Whatever wasn't donated or placed in a museum will be auctioned off at his home this afternoon.

I've been so busy assisting Ms. O'Connor I haven't had time to internalize the significance of the day's events. Not only does it mean that my time with Ms. O'Connor is complete, but it also signals the official end of my organizing business. Under normal circumstances, I'd be wallowing in sadness, but there's no time for that now. There's still work to do, and Ms. O'Connor is expecting me at my best for the finale.

As auction employees run through last-minute details, I observe Ms. O'Connor withdraw to one of the folding chairs in the main room where the auction will take place. I assumed she'd be doling out marching orders. Instead, she stares vacantly into space, oblivious to the people bustling around her.

Watching my client, I realize my mom was right. There's

more to Ms. O'Connor than meets the eye. My stomach turns with guilt knowing I judged her so harshly at the beginning of our working relationship.

A lesson I'll take with me as I move into my next job is not making assumptions about people based on first impressions. I'm grateful I've gotten to know her better.

The auctioneer taps me on the shoulder and lets me know he's ready to begin.

I join Ms. O'Connor on the front row. "They're ready to start."

When she doesn't look at me or acknowledge my presence, I worry she may have changed her mind about the auction. I wouldn't blame her if she had. In all my years of organizing, I've learned letting go of family heirlooms is one of the most difficult things for people to do. I lean over to mention this to her.

But she gets up out of her chair and straightens her white-trimmed navy blazer. "Well, let's get to it."

A few minutes later, Heather opens the front doors, and the fifty well-dressed, sophisticated socialites personally invited to the event are ushered in. They quietly roam the halls and rooms, eyeing items they may want to adorn their own mansions. Ms. O'Connor, Heather, and I patrol the rooms, answering questions interested buyers have about the furniture, artwork, and décor included in the auction.

Once the preview period ends, it doesn't take long for the bidding wars to start.

The amount of money offered for the pieces is staggering as I eavesdrop on a couple discussing the price they're willing to pay for a painting. I had no clue people could throw around money so easily.

Heather taps me on the shoulder. "Nicki, things are moving well enough that I'm going to run home and check on my girls before the Giving Gown charity event starts later this evening. Can you make sure everything finishes smoothly?"

"Yes, of course," I say, delighted by her trust in me. "But what's the Giving Gown charity event?"

Heather's face lights up. "Oh, it's my favorite time of year at the O'Connor estate!" She draws closer as if sharing a highly classified secret. "Every December, Katherine opens her closets and allows select underprivileged teens to choose a gown and shoes from her collection for their spring formals, or if they don't fit, she buys them new ones.

"It's a tradition she and her mother started several years ago after they heard about two local teens who were unable to attend their high school proms because finances wouldn't allow them to go. Now we bring in more than fifty girls so they can have the prom dresses of their dreams."

"Wow." I'm shocked by Ms. O'Connor's generous spirit. Who knew? "That's amazing. I wish someone had done that for me when I was in school." I pause, remembering the trauma. "My mom spent our money on jun—on other things. I ended up wearing the fanciest dress I could find at the local resale shop. As you can guess, the selections were meager."

"I'm so sorry, Nicki." Heather puts her hand on my arm. "As a young girl, that must have been difficult for you."

"It was. But as they say, you can't change the past." I look over to where Ms. O'Connor waits for the auction to start. "Thanks to Ms. O'Connor, those girls will never have to know that feeling."

"Yes, she has a big heart for the less fortunate. Whenever she hears of or sees someone in need, she does whatever she can to help them. Quietly. That's just one of the many things I adore about her." Heather looks at her beeping phone. "Look, I'd love to visit about this more, but I've got to go. You'll take care of Katherine for me, right?"

I nod in assurance. "Yeah, don't worry. I'll make sure she's okay."

Heather gives me a quick hug and rushes out the front door.

Keeping my promise, I join my boss in the back row of the auction room.

"I just learned about the Giving Gown charity event. That's so nice of you to do that for those girls," I whisper.

From the stage up front, the auctioneer calls out the price for a pair of Louis XV French gilt armchairs. "Twelve thousand. Do I hear fifteen?" Bidding cards wave through the air.

"Who told you about that?" Ms. O'Connor keeps her eyes on the action in the room.

"Heather." My cheeks pink at the confession. "As someone who didn't have the best prom experience in high school, I admire what you're doing."

"Do I hear 17,000?" The auctioneer's voice booms around the room.

Ms. O'Connor glances away from the stage and looks at me. "I'm sorry you didn't have a positive experience, Nicole. When I see children suffering because of their parents' neglect or personal issues, I can't help but step in. I too know firsthand what that feels like, and I wouldn't wish it on anyone."

Her words pierce my heart and once again remind me how alike we are.

"Well, I think it's wonderful that you open your heart and your closet like that. I have no doubt these girls will treasure tonight's event for a long time."

"Going once. Going twice. Sold for $22,000 to the gentleman in the third row." The auctioneer pounds his gavel on the podium for the final sale.

My mouth drops open. "Did he just say $22,000?"

Ms. O'Connor notices my shock. "Don't be so surprised, Nicole. That's not a large amount of money for the gentleman who purchased them. He's getting quite a good deal, actually, and I'm getting more funds to expand the Giving Gown charity."

I shake my head. "I can't imagine ever spending that kind of money on furniture, even if I had it, which I don't."

"Are you saying professional organizing isn't that lucrative of a business?" She looks at me, and a faint smile lifts her lips.

"Not *that* lucrative." I snicker. "Some people do well, though."

"You're not one of them?"

The auctioneer rings a bell. "The last item up for auction is the eighteenth-century French painting *White Hat* by Jean-Baptiste Greuze. It is considered one of the greatest portrait paintings of the Rococo age."

Ignoring Ms. O'Connor's question, I crane my neck to look at the picture of the beautiful young girl donning a white feathered hat.

"I'll start the bidding at $75,000."

"Wow," I say while leaning closer to Ms. O'Connor. "It would take a lot of messy clients for me to make that much money."

"You never answered my question," she says, redirecting my attention. "Do you consider yourself to be successful?"

I'm not sure how to respond, but I take a deep breath and decide the truth is always the best answer. "Well, I know I'm good at helping people bring order to their chaos, but honestly, as a business owner, I struggled. I didn't always make the best decisions about stuff like insurance and savings. So when I accidentally dropped a client's very expensive plate, that was the end of my company. Repaying her for the loss took everything I had."

"I can see how that would cause a problem." She frowns. "I'm sorry things ended that way for you, Nicole."

"Me too, but I've learned my lesson. Now it's time for me to move on." I pause. "That's why I've been applying for jobs with different companies—project manager, administrative assistant, anything that will allow me to use my organizing skills."

This information seems to pique her interest. "Which companies have you applied with?"

"Well, I've submitted applications to Hunter, Williams and Taylor, Invista, and Allied Resourcing, but I haven't heard back from any of them yet. I did get a call from Emerson Technology, though. They're completing their search but want to set up an interview with me soon. I need to get back with them."

"What are you waiting for?"

I hesitate before answering. "I wanted to finish helping you first. It seemed the responsible thing to do."

"Oh, I see." She taps her manicured red nails against her leg. "I know quite a few people at Emerson Technology."

"Sold for $250,000 to the lady in the fourth row," the auctioneer shouts before pounding his gavel on the podium, ending the auction.

As the bidders rush to leave, I begin collecting my things. "Well, I guess this is the end of the road for us." Not wanting my shaking hands or teary eyes to be on display for everyone, I turn my back. I've always hated goodbyes.

"Nicole, wait," Ms. O'Connor demands.

"Sorry." I fall back against my seat. My ears and cheeks burn, so I pull my hair over my ears and across my face to hide the redness. And sorrow. This is officially the end of my organizing career. For some reason, this hits me harder than packing up my office.

Once the room is empty, Ms. O'Connor turns to address me. "I just want to say ... to say thank you." She looks down at her lap. "I honestly don't know how I would have sorted through all of my father's belongings without your help."

"Oh, Ms. O'Connor." I reach over and place my hands on top of hers. "I'm glad I could be here for you."

When she looks up at me, our eyes meet. My client may wear a heavy armor of elegance, strength, and poise to hide from the rest of the world, but with those words, there is a small chink in it now.

She clears her throat. "Yes, well, as an additional act of gratitude, I'd like to help you with your next job. I'd be happy to speak to my contacts at Emerson on your behalf. One word from me, and I'm sure they'd be happy to hire you."

My jaw drops, and I want to pinch myself to make sure I'm not dreaming. Did Ms. O'Connor really just offer to help me get another job? I'm flabbergasted.

While I'm tempted to do a happy dance or even hug her, I'm not sure she'd be open to such emotion. My fingers pulse with the need to do something, and my feet long to launch me forward, but I restrain myself. "That would be amazing! Thank you!"

"You're quite welcome. It's much deserved." She flicks her eyes away, scanning the room again. "Before you go, though, there's one more thing I'd like your help with."

Puzzled by her statement, my brow lifts. What else is left?

She reaches inside her purse and pulls out a small mahogany box engraved with the letters *TGO* on it. A small golden key plate covers the front.

Not having seen the item before, I lean forward for a closer look.

"This contains my father's most personal items. It was given to me by his lawyer at the reading of his will last month." She places her palms on top of the box. "I haven't had the courage to open it yet. Now that we're finished going through all his belongings, the time seems right."

My mind whirrs with possibilities of what's inside. *Gold? Diamonds? The lost map to Atlantis?*

It doesn't matter.

Whatever secrets are hidden in there are none of my business. This is an intimate moment for Ms. O'Connor, and an outsider shouldn't intrude even if invited.

I look up at Ms. O'Connor. "I don't think I should be here when you open it."

"Why not?" A pained expression covers her face. "You've helped me with everything else."

"Yes, but this seems like a private moment, and since I just work for you, I don't think it's appropriate for me to be part of that."

The corners of her mouth draw downward. I can't tell if she's upset by the circumstances or displeased with my answer. She stares at the box for a while before saying anything.

"I understand your reasoning, but"—she swallows hard before continuing—"I don't think I can do this alone."

"What about Heather?" I place my hand on her shoulder. "She's like family to you and seems like the right person to be here when you open it."

Ms. O'Connor shakes her head and keeps her eyes focused on the box. "Heather is busy handling my charity event, and I don't want to wait any longer. I promised myself I would open it when the auction finished." She brushes her hand over the lid. "I need to do this now."

Speechless, I rack my brain for ways to convince her otherwise. Yet, how can I possibly refuse to help her just because I'm uncomfortable? *Never walk away from someone who deserves help; your hand is God's hand for that person.* My heart squeezes at my mother's words. While I don't agree with all her mantras, in this case, she's right.

"I'd be honored to sit with you, Ms. O'Connor."

Without hesitation, Ms. O'Connor pulls a small key from her blazer pocket and slides it into the plate. With shaking hands, she turns the key to the right with a soft click.

Neither of us makes a sound as she slowly lifts the lid and peeks inside. From my viewpoint, all I see is green velvet lining. While I'm curious to know what's hidden in there, I don't want to gawk.

After scrutinizing the contents, Ms. O'Connor sweeps them up with one hand. Cradled inside her palm are a platinum wedding band, a gold-encased money clip, and a small white business card with unfamiliar writing on it. She deposits the three items on her lap with the utmost care.

Moments laced with heaviness linger over us before she closes the lid and sets the box down next to her. She reaches for the wedding band and spins it around on her index finger.

"While he didn't do a good job of showing it, my father loved my mother. That was one of the few things he and I had in common—our love for her."

She removes the ring from her finger and reads aloud the inscription on the inside of the band. "To a lifetime of love." She shakes her head as she places the ring back in the box. "Why she loved him so much, I'll never understand. I guess love truly is blind sometimes."

Next, she scoops up the money clip.

"This," she murmurs, twirling the clip through her fingers like a magician with a playing card, "was his true love. He put money before everything, including his wife and daughter. I remember he always had this clip loaded with bills. Not to flaunt his wealth, mind you, but to keep a tight hold on it." She stops twirling the clip.

"He rarely donated money to worthwhile causes unless he could get a tax break or a business advantage," she says. "That's why philanthropy is so important to me. I can do good for the less fortunate that my father would never consider doing. He mostly collected colorful art."

She tosses the clip back into the box. "You had to have an excellent reason for him to give you any money from that thing."

When the clip lands with a *thud* on the velvet, she throws back her head and lets out a high-pitched laugh. Startled by her expressiveness, I jump. In all the time I've spent with her, I've never heard her laugh.

"I just remembered when I was about nine or ten and asked my father for some money." She wraps her arms around herself. "I didn't tell him what it was for, so of course, a great inquisition followed. When I finally revealed to him that I wanted the money to send to starving children in Africa, he said no. I tried to explain how important it was to me, but he said he already gave enough to charity and sent me to my room."

She shrugs her shoulders, sighs, and bows her head. "It was then I realized my father loved his money more than anything in this world. Including his only child." She wipes a tear from her eye.

Staring at the remaining item, she picks up the card and holds it before her with both hands. She doesn't comment on the strange writing at first but intently studies both sides of it for a few minutes.

Finally, she looks at me with a dazed look in her eyes. "I don't understand this," she says, her voice laced with confusion.

I inch closer to her to get a better look. "May I?" I take the card from her and examine it myself. Unfamiliar symbols label its front and back. "I'm not an expert in Asian linguistics," I say as I continue studying the card, "but if I had to guess, I'd say the writing was Chinese."

Plucking the card from my hand, she holds it close to her face as if proximity would offer an explanation. "But that doesn't make sense."

"Your father was a businessman. Could he have done business in China?"

"No ... well, yes." She fidgets in her seat. "Maybe he did, but that doesn't explain why the card would be included among his most valuable possessions."

She taps the card against her knee and grows silent. From her narrowed eyes and downturned mouth, I can tell the card bothers her, but I don't understand why.

"There could be a million reasons why that card was left in the box." I try to ease her worries by offering some possible scenarios. "Maybe the card was placed there by mistake. Or maybe it was his favorite Chinese restaurant or hotel when he worked in Asia."

"I doubt any of those hold true, Nicole." Ms. O'Connor gets up from the chair and paces down the aisle. "I have no clue why he counted this among his treasured items, but ... " She stops at the end of the row, and her words linger in the air.

Eager for her to continue, I scoot along the chairs closer to her. "But what?"

"I don't know why my father would have this in his box, but I know how I can figure it out." Her eyes twinkle.

"How? I ... I'd really like to know." *I would?* Perhaps this woman's gotten to me more than I realized.

Without answering, she turns and heads out of the room.

"Where are you going?" I call out after her. "You have the Giving Gown event in a few hours, remember?"

She stops in the doorway and looks at me. "I won't forget. It's my event." Her tone turns serious. "Be at my house tomorrow at 11:00 a.m. By the time you arrive, I'll have solved this mystery."

Before I can respond or change her mind, Ms. O'Connor vanishes down the hallway.

6

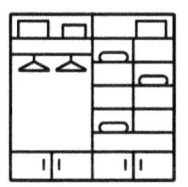

A journey of a thousand miles begins with the first step.
~ Chinese Proverb

Curious, crazy, or obedient. I'm unsure which one best describes me as I pause before ringing Ms. O'Connor's doorbell the next morning.

I had been sure Ms. O'Connor would call to tell me she was going to forget about the unknown business card and move on. But during my insomnia-filled night, I began to suspect her fierce determination to uncover her father's connection to it wouldn't let her. She won't stop until she learns the truth.

A flush of adrenaline courses through my body as I ring the doorbell. I honestly believed yesterday was the final curtain call on my working relationship with Ms. O'Connor. Yet, as I stand and wait for Lucinda to answer the door, I'm torn. Part of me wants to ask my client for her recommendation of my professional organizing skills, leave, and put all this behind me.

Yet, something stronger is drawing me here. My mother calls that being nosy. I think there's more to it. And, I have to admit, I am intrigued.

When the front door creaks open, it's not Lucinda who

greets me. Instead, it's a young Asian man. His unexpected presence and appearance startle me, and I momentarily question whether I'm at the right house.

His sleek black hair, black suit, and round glasses are reminiscent of a fifties flashback, but I remind myself first impressions aren't always what they seem. Still, I wonder why he's answering Ms. O'Connor's door rather than Lucinda.

I flash a smile. "Uh, hi. I'm here to see Ms. O'Connor."

Before he can answer, Ms. O'Connor rushes to his side and ushers him out the door.

"Mr. Hei, thank you for coming." She bows to him then he responds in kind. "I'll be in touch soon." She waves me in.

Upon his departure, I look at her, hands upon my hips. "Who was that?"

"Mr. Hei." She closes the door behind me.

I suppress my irritation. "I got that. But *why* was he here?"

Without answering me, Ms. O'Connor saunters to the sitting room just off the foyer. I have no choice but to follow her.

Taking a seat on the sofa, she pours herself a cup of coffee from a carafe on the table. "Would you like some?" She lifts her cup and saucer toward me before taking a sip.

"No, thanks, I don't drink coffee." I sit down and wait for her to finish. Scanning the room for any traces of her father's box or its contents, I spot the faded white business card lying next to the carafe.

"Was Mr. Hei here to translate the writing for you?" I pick up the card and study it as if it's the missing clue to an unsolved murder.

"Yes, I hired him to decipher it."

"So, what does it say?"

"According to him, it's an address on the outskirts of Beijing."

"An address to what?"

Ms. O'Connor lets out a heavy sigh. "He's not sure."

I blink in disbelief. "That doesn't make sense. In this day and age, we can look up any address with Google and the click of a button." I snap my fingers for extra emphasis.

"Yes, but Mr. Hei says the card and writing are old and perhaps imprecise. He'll have to conduct more research to pinpoint the exact location for me." She takes another sip of coffee.

"So, when will he let you know more about the address and what's there?"

She sets her cup down then crosses and uncrosses her legs. "When I arrive in China."

A flicker of shock courses through me. I must have misheard. She can't possibly be so invested in figuring out the connection between this obscure address and her father that she'd jet off across the world. "China? By yourself? Isn't that a bit hasty?"

"No." She shakes her head.

Okay, now I know she's unstable. No one just picks up and goes to China on a whim. *Or do they?*

"I'm not hasty, and I don't plan on going alone." She pauses and looks me square in the eyes. "I'd like you to go with me."

My eyebrows raise without my consent, yet I can't seem to pull them back down. "You want me to go to China ... with you?"

"Yes, I was hoping you would. I'd rather not go alone." She props herself up on the couch in a defensive position, ready for battle.

"I—I appreciate the offer, Ms. O'Connor, but I can't go with you to China." Although my knees are knocking, I somehow manage to rise from the sofa. I need to put as much distance as I can between the two of us in case her crazy behavior tries to rub off on me.

"Why not?"

"Because, because—" I rack my brain for a suitable reply but remain quiet. *Because I don't have a passport. Because I need to nail down a stable job rather than rush off to a foreign country at a moment's notice. Because joining you on this last-minute adventure would make me hasty and unstable too.*

While all those seem like perfectly valid reasons to me, I know she'll punch holes in every one. I offer her the two most logical reasons I can muster under this kind of pressure. "Well, one, because it's almost Christmas. And two, if anyone should accompany you on a trip like this, it should be Heather."

Ms. O'Connor stands up and draws so close to me I'm sure she can hear my heart pounding in my chest.

"First of all, Heather has young children she cannot leave." She crosses her arms. "Secondly, you never mentioned any Christmas plans in the past few weeks we've been working together. I assumed you had none."

"You have no idea how I intend to celebrate Christmas," I say smugly.

"Then tell me, what do your holiday activities include?" she scoffs.

I shift from side to side. Christmas for the Mayfields will be a quiet evening at the diner, just like Thanksgiving. *Nothing to write home about, that's for sure.*

Rather than admit the sad truth, I divert the conversation. "You know you can't prance into a Communist country unannounced, right? It takes time to get the paperwork completed."

I'm grasping at straws, and she knows it.

"You've forgotten that money talks, my dear, and I have plenty of it." She fingers her pearl necklace. "So much so that I'm willing to pay you upfront to join me. Quite handsomely, I may add, and as a bonus, I'll call my friends at Emerson before we leave. As I mentioned to you before, a good word from me practically *guarantees* you'll have a job."

Like a wild animal trapped in a noose, I'm stuck.

If I tell her no, I can kiss her recommendation goodbye. If I agree to go with her, I'll have money as well as job security, but who knows what could happen while we're there? I bite my lip. I've never been one to take risks, and I'm not sure I want to start now. But if I do take the leap, who knows what I might discover?

Perfectly Arranged

It may be an adventure.

Ms. O'Connor taps her foot. "Nicole, I know it's a lot to ask on such short notice, but I don't have a lot of time, and there's a considerable amount of work that has to be done. I need your answer. Would you ... please come with me?" She looks vulnerable.

Despite the frustration and doubt that engulf me, she needs me, and how could I withhold my help? Plus, traveling to foreign lands has always been on my bucket list, and I'm just as curious as she is as to what her father's card might lead us to. A long-lost sibling, perhaps? Whatever may happen, either at home or abroad, going on this expedition might be what I need to turn my life around. She'd said she'd see to that.

I hand the card back to her. "Yes, I'll go with you."

"Wonderful!" Her eyes light up, and she claps her hands. "I'll get the paperwork started right away." She picks up her phone from the coffee table. Before dialing, though, she looks at me once more. "You're certain you want to do this?"

Ignoring the butterflies in my stomach, I nod at her. "I'm not changing my mind. I'm in."

As she makes her phone call, I tilt my head toward the ceiling. *Lord, I'm going, but I just want to confirm—You'll be with me, right?*

AFTER LEAVING MS. O'CONNOR'S, I return home to soak in a warm bubble bath. I need time to process what I just got myself into.

I add cocoa-scented bubbles to the water, bring up my meditation playlist, and slip into the tub. Leaning my head back against the edge, I close my eyes and replay the events from earlier. *Did I actually agree to travel to the land of red dragons to locate some strange address?* How could I be so rash? It's as if Ms.

O'Connor's eccentric personality rubbed off on me and took possession of my brain.

I admit, though, the thought of traveling to an exotic destination fills me with excitement. I can't wait to tell my mom, although I'm afraid she might think I've lost it. She may not be wrong.

The pull of sweet slumber is tugging me into its fog when the shrill of my ringtone disrupts the silence. Reluctantly, I push the green button.

"Hello?" The word tumbles out of my mouth slowly.

"Nicole Mayfield, please," the business-like voice requests. Other than Ms. O'Connor, no one else refers to me by that name. I sit up in the tub, my heart racing.

"This is Nicole," I reply. My irritation turns to anxiety. "Who is this?" The sound of shuffling papers comes across the phone line, and even though I'm soaking in a tub of chocolate, I'm anything but calm.

"My name is Lisa, and I'm calling on behalf of Ms. O'Connor and Asia Tiger Travel Services. I'm in charge of all the arrangements and documentation for your upcoming trip to Beijing. There are a few items I need to discuss with you if you're available."

I lean back and chuckle. Bubble baths were supposed to ease stress. Obviously, I need to soak longer.

"Sure," I tell her as I pop a bubble floating in front of me.

Without missing a beat, Lisa gets right to business. "Since you'll be leaving in four days, I'll need the following information faxed or emailed to me by six o'clock tonight—your birth certificate, a list of your most recent shots or immunizations, a recent photo—"

"Wait, what?" The panic sets back in. "That soon? I thought I'd have a little more time to prepare."

Irritated by my interruption, she repeats her laundry list of requests. "I need the following sent to me by six o'clock tonight —your birth—"

"I heard what you needed, but did you say we're leaving for Beijing in four days?"

"Yes, that is correct. "

My head swirls in confusion. "How is that possible? I don't even have a passport!"

"I understand that, Nicole." Lisa huffs. "That's why I'm trying to get the paperwork processed as quickly as possible. Now, if you could please take note of what I need from you."

"But four days?" That doesn't give me much time to pack, tell my family and friends, or prepare to leave for an unknown amount of time. *Who acts that hastily?* Clearly, Ms. O'Connor does. And now so do I.

"Miss Mayfield," she snaps, oblivious to my dilemma. "I don't have much time to complete everything, so could you please write these things down?"

I realize my issues are not her problem and leap out of the tub to take down the information. "Sure, hold on a minute and let me get something to write with."

With no time to go to the kitchen for a pen and paper, I scan the bathroom for a possible writing instrument. I rifle through one of the vanity drawers. *Success!* Eyeliner pencil in hand, time to find something to write on.

"Miss Mayfield?"

I unroll some toilet paper squares and lay them on the counter.

"Uh, yes, I'm ready."

Lisa rapidly unleashes her list of demands as I scribble the information on the paper as best as I can. The dull tip isn't doing me any favors, and before I can write any more, the toilet paper rips. *Great, now what am I supposed to do?*

"Finally," Lisa continues, "these are the items you'll need to have with you when you arrive at the airport."

"Uh, okay," I stammer as I hunt for something else to write with. "Just a minute ..." I open another drawer and spot my favorite lipstick. Lisa's heavy breathing propels my inner turmoil at using Revlon's fire-engine red lipstick for anything other than beauty into motion. I jump onto the counter and lean in close to the mirror. "Okay, go ahead."

As Lisa continues dispensing information like a cash register receipt, I push the cherry-colored stick against the mirror and pray it doesn't crumble to pieces before she finishes.

"That's everything," she says. "Do you have any questions?"

"Not right now." I come down from my perch, toss my ruined lipstick tube back into the drawer, and plop down onto the toilet seat.

"All right. I'll be expecting those documents in the next few hours."

Before I can say anything else, she hangs up. I set my phone on the counter and look at the mess in my bathroom. Water puddles and clothes cover the floor, ragged toilet paper lines the counter, and flashy chicken scratch splatters the mirror.

My blissful retreat resembles a war zone.

While such a sight would usually send me into a panic, it's the least of my problems. With only a few days until I head out on this wild adventure, I need to let the world know what I've gotten myself into.

AFTER I FINISH SUPPLYING Lisa with all the necessary paperwork, I drive over to my mom's house to inform her of my plans, a task that takes all the courage I can summon.

My stomach tightens as I park next to her car. The back and front seats are littered with books, plastic bags, all types of clothes, and trash.

I lean against the hood and gain my composure. I can only handle so much clutter, and my mom's house exceeds my threshold. After knocking on the front door, I wait and pray for the strength to step inside.

The door opens just as I finish. "Nicki, what a surprise! I

wasn't expecting you." My mom's wearing a floral-patterned nightgown and house slippers whose fuzz is long gone. Except for a few strands poking out from the edges, her Shirley Temple curls are wrapped tightly in a battered blue towel.

"Mom, it's only five-thirty. Why are you ready for bed?"

She giggles like a little girl while closing the door behind me. "Just like you, I like being prepared, Nicki. Where do you think you got it from?" She loops her arm in mine, leading me down the narrow entryway. "Oh, now that you're here, I have so many new things I want to show you."

We snake our way through the musty hallway filled with telephone books and paperbacks toward the kitchen. When we arrive, it looks pretty much the same as when I visited the last time. The counter surfaces are covered by unopened mail and loose papers, kitchen appliances line up on the floor like soldiers in an army, and open shelving crammed with mostly expired canned goods litter the shelves.

If my mother has managed to purchase anything new, the long-term residents that claimed their stake of her home years ago have swallowed it up.

"Not much has changed, Mom." I pull out a rusty metal chair from under the kitchen table situated in the center of the room. I check my seat to make sure no tiny creature is crawling on it, or me, before sitting down. My mom sits in a slatted wooden chair next to me.

"Oh, but it has, Nicki!" She points to a small pile in the corner next to the hallway. "I bought those beautiful gloves just last week. They were on sale at the ninety-nine-cent store. You won't believe how much I paid for all twenty pairs."

I turn my head and notice a brown plastic bag overflowing with canvas garden gloves in every imaginable color and pattern. "Mom, you don't even have a garden. Why do you need twenty pairs of gloves?" I ask, despite knowing that she'll have a *reasonable* explanation for her purchase.

"Didn't I tell you? I'm going to start a vegetable garden in the spring." She gets up and opens a drawer next to the table. "I ordered a bunch of seeds after watching this cable special. Now, where did I put them?" I watch her frantically search for the seed packets and marvel at how such a witty and intelligent woman had morphed into a forgetful and obsessive collector of undesirable junk.

While I don't blame her for what has happened to her—it's a mental issue, I know—the toll it's taken on our relationship has been difficult to handle. When I needed her most, she wasn't there for me, and regardless of how hard I tried to help her, she wouldn't let me. We're on better terms now, but we have to take it day by day.

I get up and follow her around the kitchen. "Mom, it's okay. I don't need to see the seeds. I believe you." I close a drawer and spin her toward me. "Look, I don't have much time, and I want to tell you something." Holding her hand, I lead her back to the table and mismatched seating.

"So, you know how I told you I was working for that wealthy woman, Ms. O'Connor?"

Her eyes light up in recollection. "The eccentric one?"

"Yes, that one." I lean over and take her hands. "Well, she invited me to accompany her on a trip to China to help her find something. I've agreed to go with her."

"Oh, that sounds fun," she says. "I've always wanted to travel to an interesting destination like that."

I don't recall my mother ever voicing a desire to travel, but I don't remember ever asking her, either. Now that our relationship is in a better place, maybe it's time for us to get to know one another again. Like normal mothers and daughters do.

"Well, now I get to go for the two of us." I pause and gather my courage before sharing the rest of the story. "The only problem is that we leave soon, and I won't be home for Christmas."

Despite the bombshell I just dropped on her, my mother remains calm. Her face doesn't show any signs of anger or disappointment. In fact, she seems a million miles away. I wave my hand in front of her. "Mom, did you hear me?"

She jerks back against her chair. "Sorry, dear. Yes, I heard you."

"So, it's okay with you that I won't be home for Christmas?"

Reaching for me, she cups my cheeks in the palms of her hands and smiles. "I'll miss you, but I'll be fine. I can go next door and eat lunch with Cathy and her husband. They're always inviting me to join them."

"I hate not being with you, but I'm glad you understand." Relief washes over me. I wasn't expecting her to react so positively, but her response lightens the load of guilt I've been carrying.

"Of course, dear." She drops her hands from my face. "You have a job to do. I'll miss you terribly, though."

My chest tightens. "You know what they say, Mom," I joke. "Absence makes the heart grow fonder."

"That it does." Her words float toward me on a whisper. "After all these years of him being gone, I love your father even more."

"I know." I wipe the tear from her cheek. "I miss him too and would give anything to bring him back to you."

"Oh, speaking of bringing back …" The rapid and unexpected change in subject draws my attention back to the present. "Could you bring a few things back from China for me?"

Seriously? I drop my head in dismay. She's surrounded by more stuff than is needed or healthy, and she wants me to bring her more?

With no energy or desire to tell her no, I resign myself to the lie. "Sure, Mom, I'll see what I can find for you while I'm there."

Her eyes sparkle. "That would be wonderful! I'd love to have some chopsticks, a traditional Chinese robe, and maybe one of those cute straw hats?" She claps her hands, and I'm certain she's reverted in age at least forty years.

"I'll see what I can do," I tell her, knowing full well I won't bring back half of what she's asking for. Pushing away from the table, I get up and wrap my arms around her from behind. "I love you, Mom."

She pats my arms. "I love you too. And I'll look forward to seeing you and those wonderful trinkets when you return."

Suppressing my anger, I quickly pull away from her. It's not surprising my mother would await my return only to see what I bring back. That's been the story of my life since my dad died, and this terrible disease overtook her home and mind. I may never be able to fix it or understand it, but I hope one day I'll be able to fully accept the reality of the situation. I have to for both of us.

"Okay, I need to head home and pack." I make my way toward the hallway.

My mother jumps out of her chair. "Wait, I have something for you." She retreats into her bedroom. I await her return, worrying that she's going to offer me some of the broken luggage she's stockpiled.

When she comes back, she's carrying a book.

"Here, I want you to take this with you." She places a well-used Bible into my hands. I'm not sure if this is just another of her second-hand purchases or if she's read and studied the Bible more than I ever realized, but it has definitely been loved on by someone.

"Mom," I say softly, the worry shifting into sadness, "I have a Bible. I don't need another one. Plus, what will you do without it while I'm gone?" I give it back to her, but she refuses to accept it.

"Oh, I have lots more but this one is my favorite." She eyes the worn, leather bound book. "But I want you to have something of mine with you while you're gone. It's kind of like I'll be there with you that way."

My heart squeezes at her thoughtfulness. Letting go of things is difficult for hoarders, so for my mom to give me such a valuable possession stretches my ability to keep it together.

Fighting back tears, I put the Bible in my purse and give her one last hug.

"I'll call you when I get there and email you as much as I can," I assure her as I open the door.

She grips my arm and plants a kiss on my cheek. While I'm not used to so much emotion between the two of us, her sweet gesture conveys more than words could ever express.

7

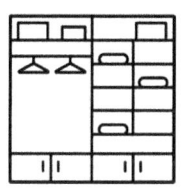

Either do not begin or, having begun, do not give up.
~ Chinese Proverb

Who knew time could pass so quickly? While I'm typically organized and efficient with my time, I spend the four days before my departure on the Internet learning as much as I can about Chinese customs, practicing a few words in Mandarin, and scoping out the tourist attractions I want to visit.

Other than packing my suitcase and retrieving my documents from the travel agency, I wasn't able to do much else. So, when it's time to leave, I spend the morning tidying up my apartment, watering my plants, and sorting through the paperwork on my desk.

I quickly sort the mail into piles of *to keep* and *to trash*. I toss the junk mail into the recycling bin and stuff the bills and other legal types of correspondence into my backpack to review later. Thanks to Ms. O'Connor and her advance on this trip, I've been able to pay my bills in a timely manner. I'm not out of trouble yet, but at least I don't have bill collectors hounding me.

While checking my email one last time before shutting down

my computer, a new notification flashes in my inbox. Emerson Technologies has responded!

Miss Mayfield,

We have it on good authority that you would make a valuable addition to our company as a Project Manager. Based on this, we look forward to speaking with you after the new year for an interview—merely a formality—to discuss your training and start date.

Best wishes for a wonderful holiday season.

I sit back in my chair, my mouth falling open. Ms. O'Connor is a woman who wields more power than I'd realized, with money and friends in high places. She'd promised to call Emerson before we left, and I appreciate that she kept her word.

While I'd love to break out in a happy dance over my newfound employment, I slam my computer shut and dash out the door to meet my Uber driver. I'll have plenty to celebrate when I return home.

Forty-five minutes later, my ride pulls into the international departures terminal at the airport. We'd made good time despite the traffic, and I'm grateful for the few minutes to spare. The added pressure of being late would push me over the edge, with the range of emotions coursing through me right now.

I don't know whether to throw up, sing from the rafters, or curl up in a fetal position and cry. With my timely arrival, I won't have to find out.

After retrieving my suitcase and pulling my backpack onto my shoulders, I lean over the passenger window and look my driver in the eye. "Thanks for the ride, and Merry Christmas."

"Merry Christmas, honey!" The older woman offers me a huge smile, her pearly whites on full display. Shaking her beaded black hair, she holds out a card for me. "I give this to all my airport passengers as my way of pouring a little bit of light and truth into their days."

"Thank you." I take the card from her and jam it into my pocket.

A loud whistle wails in my direction. Not wanting to violate the allotted time for unloading, I grab my bags and quickly move away from the pea-green Volkswagen. Slithering through the jungle of cars eager to empty their cargo, I spy a young couple lip-locked in a romantic goodbye. My heart unexpectedly lurches.

I flick my eyes and ball my fists as I walk towards the sidewalk past them. While I have little interest in dating right now, something about their intimate embrace rattles me. I glance over my shoulder at them one last time before entering the airport terminal.

Am I missing something trying to be independent and self-sufficient, not needing a relationship? I shake my head. I was never the kind of girl who wanted to find Prince Charming, and he certainly hadn't found me.

Dismissing the thought, and the couple, I proceed through the sliding glass doors and into the terminal, which hums with activity. People race from one place to the next. Suitcases screech along the tile floors. Loudspeakers blast announcements for flight departures, gate changes, and forgotten items at security. I quickly scan the area for my airline check-in and join the long queue.

After a ten-minute wait, the desk attendant waves me over. "Next, please."

I push my suitcase out in front of me, but the rest of my body remains stuck in place. My legs wobble. I try to shuffle closer to the desk, but it's as if my feet are laden with steel.

"Next." The attendant growls in my direction.

Move, Nic!

Hunched over, I turn to the person behind me. "Go ahead."

She mutters under her breath as she passes me.

Trying not to make a scene, I take three deep breaths and stand up straight. The room spins faster than the Tilt-A-Whirl at the local amusement park. I reach into my purse for my phone.

I have to call Ms. O'Connor and tell her I've changed my mind. Although I believed going on this journey would allow me to step out of my comfort zone and explore the unknown, the last few minutes have shown me I'm not ready to plunge into uncharted waters. Ms. O'Connor will understand that, right?

As I type in the passcode, a notification pops up on my screen. It's a new text message from my boss:

Where are you? I'm waiting for you.

My insides quiver. I can't abandon her. *I can't*. But how can I be there for her when I can't even help myself right now?

Trembling, I slide the phone into my pocket. As I do, my fingers brush against the card my enthusiastic Bohemian driver gave me. I retrieve the crumpled paper and read the bold writing.

"Be strong and courageous. Do not be terrified; do not be discouraged, for the Lord your God will be with you wherever you go."

I hang my head and choke back the tears. Only God.

Encouraged by the timely message, I fight the panic that's settled in my body and get back in the queue. I gave Ms. O'Connor my word, and no matter how uncertain I am about what's waiting for us on the other side of the world, I'm going to honor that.

AFTER CHECKING in my luggage and suffering through security, I locate Ms. O'Connor, who is pacing rapidly back and forth at our gate.

Perfectly Arranged

"I was starting to get worried." Her eyebrows crease. "Was there a problem?"

I gulp. While I don't want to mislead this woman, I don't want to disappoint her either.

"No." I shake my head. "The check-in line was really long, and it took more time than I anticipated. Sorry about that."

"I'm glad you made it." Ms. O'Connor leads me to a pair of chairs secluded from the other passengers and sits down. "You have all the paperwork from Lisa, correct?"

"Signed, sealed, and delivered." I wave my passport and a large manila envelope in front of her.

"Good." She tugs on the collar of her shirt. "I don't want any problems on this trip."

"You didn't forget to pack the one item that's responsible for this little adventure in the first place, did you?" I chuckle.

"It's haunted my dreams since the day we found it." She removes the Asian business card from a side pocket of her purse and holds it up to the light. "Whatever secret it's keeping, I'm going to uncover it." Her mouth twists as she twirls it through her fingers.

I watch as she scrutinizes the thin piece of paper, lost in her thoughts. Although I've only worked for her for a few weeks, I know that she is a determined woman who sees things through, regardless of the outcome. It's that last part that worries me most. There's no telling what's waiting for us on the other side of the world.

"Ms. O'Connor?" I tuck a loose curl behind my ear.

She steers her gaze away from the card to me. "Yes?"

"What if you were never meant to discover the truth?"

"I don't understand." She tilts her head and studies me as she would an ancient artifact.

"It's just ..." I stammer to find the right way to explain this to her. "Well, we all carry secrets we never want anyone else to know about. Secrets that would hurt them, or us, if the truth ever came out." My heart rate quickens. I can only hope my next words will not fall on deaf ears. "What if your father never intended for you to know why he had that card?"

"It doesn't matter," her voice quivers. "I have to know regardless of what I find out."

"I get that. But I once read that wanting to know everything is the worst of follies. Maybe there's some wisdom to that."

She grimaces. "You're probably right, but I've come too far to stop now. Plus, aren't you the least bit curious to know?"

"I'm dying to know. I'm just worried about you and how you're going to react to whatever it is that we find."

"I appreciate your concern, Nicole, but this is something I have to do."

I reach across the seat and pat her hand. There's no point in fighting her. "Then I guess we'll find out shortly."

She pulls her hand away from mine. "Yes, we will." She glances at her watch. "First-class should be boarding soon."

"First-class?" I ask, gobsmacked. "We're flying to Beijing first class?"

"Is there any other way to fly? Plus, it's a thirteen-hour flight—"

A bell dings in our gate area. "At this time, we would like to start boarding our first-class passengers," a voice booms over the intercom.

"That's us." Ms. O'Connor stands and picks up her carry-on bag. "It's time for us to learn how that card is connected to my father." She trots off towards the jetway.

The hair lifts on the back of my neck. *There's no turning back now.*

I sling my backpack over my shoulder and speed after Ms. O'Connor.

When we arrive in first-class, a young flight attendant greets me. "Miss Mayfield, welcome. Your seat is 3A." He points to a window seat a few rows up.

"Thank you."

"My pleasure." He smiles and hands me a small gift bag. "Please let me know if you need anything. I'm at your service."

I slink towards my seat, carefully taking in the classy compartment. It's like the Nordstrom of the air!

Before I can fully absorb my roomy accommodations, Ms. O'Connor sidles up next to me.

"Is there a problem, Nicole?"

"No," I tell her. "I've never flown first-class before, that's all."

"You'll like it, I promise." Without saying anything else, she retreats to her seat across the aisle.

After I place my backpack in the overhead compartment, I slide into my oversized seat. The plush leather chair and large TV screen remind me of the movie theater next to my house. Who knew flying could be so luxurious?

Curious about others' reactions to our state-of-the-art plane ride, I survey my fellow passengers to see if they're as awed by their seating arrangements as I am. *Nope, it seems I'm the only one fascinated by the fanciness of the aircraft.*

I glance over at Ms. O'Connor reclining in her chair, a pink mask covering her eyes.

"Ms. O'Connor?" I whisper in her direction.

She raises half of the mask from her face. "What is it, Nicole?" she asks through clenched teeth.

"Who is taking care of Princess while you're away?"

"Heather is. I trust her immensely." Her demeanor shifts at the mention of her cat, and her eyes twinkle. "Plus, she promised to text and send daily updates and pictures."

"Well, keep me posted on how Princess is faring without you." I chuckle at her concern over her feline baby.

"I shall. Now, if you'll excuse me, I'm off to sleep. Flying isn't my favorite way to travel, so I've taken a sleeping pill to help me pass the time." Her hand flutters as she replaces the mask over her eyes. "Relax. I'll see you when we get to China."

As much as I'd love to follow her instructions, I'm still slightly nervous. The flight attendant, however, puts me at ease with unlimited soft drinks and an appetizer. I wrap a blanket around me and reach for the movie guide buried in the seat pocket in front of me.

Despite my earlier misgivings, I'm glad I didn't cave into my fear. I guess I am ready to plunge into uncharted waters. Between the first-rate service and in-flight entertainment, this may be the most pampering I've ever indulged in.

My spirits soar as my movie starts playing, and I sink deeper into the seat. For now, comfort and indulgence win because Lord only knows what's going to happen when we land.

8

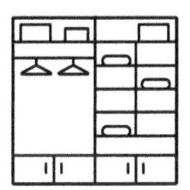

Paper can't wrap up a fire.
~ Chinese Proverb

After five movies, two short naps, and some decent airplane food, I watch as our plane makes a smooth landing at Beijing International Airport twenty minutes ahead of schedule.

Despite the carefree hours I've enjoyed, I'm anxious to deplane and uncover what secret Mr. O'Connor has been hiding all these years. My feet wiggle back and forth while I wait for the flight attendant to open the door. I look over at Ms. O'Connor, whose wrinkled forehead and tapping foot are setting my nerves on edge just as much as my own antsiness.

After passing through customs and immigration then retrieving our luggage, Ms. O'Connor and I are whisked away to the hotel by a private car. While the plane ride and landing were without drama, the ride to the hotel isn't.

Small cars, bicycles, and mopeds weave through the streets without any sense of order. Heavy exhaust fumes and blaring car horns fill the air. And mixed in between all the congestion, smells, and noise, crowds of people line the sidewalks and streets.

"Doesn't this chaos bother you?" I ask Ms. O'Connor as I watch our car narrowly avoid hitting a moped that has swerved in front of us.

"I'll admit it's extreme, but I guess that's just the way they do it here." She seems unfazed by the pandemonium.

"Honestly, I've never experienced anything like it. I mean, how do people get anywhere when there's so much confusion? Aren't there any rules to follow?" I jump as another car pulls into our lane without blinking its lights or waiting for enough space. "It's like a NASCAR race on steroids," I scream, without meaning to.

My words linger in the air without any response.

After a while, the constant stop-and-go of the traffic flow leaves me dizzy and nauseous. I'm reminded of when I was a little girl twirling on those cheap amusement park rides at the local fair. I was sure I'd lose my lunch every time I got on one of them. *Lord, please don't let there be a reappearance of my last meal anytime soon.*

I glance over to see if Ms. O'Connor is carsick as well, but she keeps her steady gaze focused out the window, no pallor or queasy expression crossing her face. She's lost in her own world and far more intent on her reason for being here. I keep my eyes closed and pray the ride will end soon.

Our car pulls into the hotel driveway a few minutes later, and I rush to exit and breathe fresh air. The beauty and opulence of our hotel arrest me as soon as my feet hit the ground. The combination of ancient and modern-day China is stunning.

There are sleek architectural aspects to the building that lend themselves to a contemporary style, but the furniture, décor, and color schemes remind me of the Asian culture I've only seen in books or on TV. Combined, they offer a breathtaking environment.

While I take in the scenery around me, Ms. O'Connor is all business. She traipses past me into the lobby. I pull myself from my reverie and fall into step behind her. The last thing I need is to get lost in a country where I don't even speak the language.

Without wasting time, Ms. O'Connor heads straight to the registration desk and inquiries about our liaison, Zhou Longchen. The desk attendant motions to an elderly gentleman sitting in one of the lobby chairs. He rises and makes his way towards us.

"Zhou Longchen," Ms. O'Connor says, extending her hand. "It's so nice to meet you in person. Mr. Hei has told me so much about you."

"The pleasure is mine, madam." He bows slightly. "But please, call me Longchen."

As I observe their exchange, I notice that Longchen, who's dressed in a black wool sweater, gray trousers, and shiny black loafers, reminds me more of a grandfather than a business professional. I assumed that, as our investigator, translator, and guide, he would resemble a young Jackie Chan, a suave man with an array of skills and talents.

Instead, the deep wrinkles in his forehead, as well as his salt and pepper hair and beard, designate him as a man of many years. But while he may be older than I'd expected, his demeanor is youthful.

As if he senses my analysis of him, his gaze falls on me. "And you must be Miss Mayfield. Welcome to Beijing. It's so nice of you to accompany Ms. O'Connor such a long way."

"Thank you. I'm happy to be here." I shake his hand. "But please call me Nicki." He bows slightly at me, and I reciprocate the greeting. When we're both face-to-face again, he winks at my efforts, settling my rapid heartbeat down just a bit.

When he releases my hand, he turns his attention back to Ms. O'Connor. "I've ensured everything is ready for you here at the hotel, per your instructions. I assumed you'd be tired from your travels, so rather than go out today, I've arranged for us to leave tomorrow after breakfast."

Ms. O'Connor frowns. "I was hoping to see the location today. It's only mid-afternoon. Surely we could still try?"

"You want to go right away?" There goes my heart rate again. "I thought we'd get some rest first."

"Of course, we should go now, Nicole." Her voice rises a level. "No point in wasting time."

Longchen interrupts our heated exchange. "I'm sorry, ladies, but with traffic and the long distance to get there, it would be too dark for us to see much. Plus, Miss Mayfield, I mean, Nicki, looks like she could use some rest before we venture out into the unknown."

Ms. O'Connor lets out a heavy sigh. "I guess I have no choice but to wait until tomorrow then." She plasters on a strained smile for Longchen, but I'm certain these arrangements aren't sitting well with her. She's much too urbane, however, to make an issue of it, especially in a foreign land.

"May I escort you to your rooms?" He motions in the direction of the elevators.

"That won't be necessary, Longchen, but thank you. Nicole and I can find our way." She looks at me

I nod my head. "Yes, we'll be fine."

He passes the room keys to Ms. O'Connor. "Very well. I'll meet you here for breakfast at eight. Rest well." He bows again and leaves us to speak with one of the hotel employees. I'm intrigued by the sound of his Mandarin and his ability to switch between two languages with ease.

When I turn back to Ms. O'Connor, she's already headed for the elevators. I dash to catch up with her, thankful that the attendant waits until I'm in before pressing the PH button on the panel.

"We're staying on the penthouse floor?" I ask.

She doesn't look at me. "Of course."

"Oh, okay." Well, perhaps it wasn't okay. I've never stayed at anything nicer than a Holiday Inn, so to leapfrog all the way to a penthouse suite causes my stomach to start doing somersaults.

Between the car ride here and this new piece of information, I'll be lucky if I can hold it all together until bedtime.

I don't have time to focus on it, though, as the elevator dings and the doors open. While Ms. O'Connor nods at the attendant and exits, I can only manage a smile, unsure if I should say something or tip him. I decide just to nod and leave the elevator before it gets awkward.

In the hallway, she hands me my room key. "Your room is over there." She points to a door on my left. "If you need anything, just call the front desk."

"I'll be fine." I take the key. "I didn't sleep much on the plane, so I'm going to take a shower, let my mom know we arrived, and head to bed. Would it be okay for me to order room service later, once my stomach settles down a bit?"

"Yes, feel free to order whatever you'd like." She turns to her right. Before inserting her key into the door that presumably leads to her room, she stops and casts a steely gaze at me. "And Nicole, please don't be late for breakfast. I'm anxious to see what's at that address."

"Of course." *Isn't that the only reason we're here on Christmas Eve rather than at church with our loved ones?*

I watch Ms. O'Connor enter the room and shut the door behind her. Knowing that she'd slept for the entire flight, I can't imagine what she's going to do all evening. I should probably check on her in a few hours and make sure she's okay, but my brain is too foggy from sleep deprivation to consider much more than that. Like Scarlett O'Hara, I'll think about it another time.

Opening the door to my room, I'm unprepared for the view in front of me. While I was expecting an upgrade from a standard hotel room, I am shocked to discover a tiny apartment waiting for me.

I set down my backpack and explore the room. There's a sitting area, a dining space, and two large bedrooms, each with king-sized beds and en-suite spa bathrooms. I grab my phone and start taking pictures. This place is nicer than my apartment, and possibly even bigger, so I want to document its lavishness to show everyone back home.

After salivating over my home away from home, I pull my suitcase into one of the bedrooms and plop onto the enormous bed, sink into the soft, plush comforter, and allow it to envelop me. Before I can even think about showering, changing clothes, or letting my mom know I've arrived safely, I'm fast asleep.

WHEN I FINALLY WAKE UP, I scan the room for a clock. I feel like I've slept for hours, but the red numbers on the nightstand clock reveal it's only eight o'clock. I open the curtains to take in the night lights of the capital, but instead, sunlight blinds me. Why is it so bright this late in the evening? I look out the window again, searching for answers, but the views outside don't offer me any.

I grab the phone next to my bed and press the button for the front desk. After one ring, a soft voice answers.

"Nǐ hǎo, Miss Mayfield. How may I assist you?"

"Uh, hello, I mean, nǐ hǎo. Is it possible for me to order some dinner?"

"I'm sorry, Miss Mayfield, but we discontinued dinner service quite a long time ago."

I'm startled that they stopped service so early, but maybe that's how they do things here. "Okay then, do you know where I can get some food?"

"But of course. The breakfast buffet downstairs is open until 10:00 a.m., or we can deliver the food to your room."

Breakfast for dinner? I'm confused. I pause and put all the pieces together, disbelief coloring my understanding. Strong sunlight, no dinner options, breakfast buffet. *Oh, no!* "Is it eight in the morning?"

"Yes, it is," the attendant confirms. "Is everything okay?"

No, it's not, but it's not her fault I overslept. "Uh, yes,

everything's fine. Thanks," I lie before rudely slamming down the phone. Great. My first day in China with Ms. O'Connor and I'm going to be late.

After a quick shower, I race down to the hotel restaurant. I spot Ms. O'Connor and Longchen at a table near the window and rush over to them.

"I'm so sorry I'm late," I pant. "I must have been more tired than I realized and overslept."

Eyes downcast and lips pinched, Ms. O'Connor glances at her watch. "Next time, you should set an alarm, Nicole. That way, you won't be twenty minutes late for breakfast."

"Yes, I'll do that," I reply.

"Don't worry, Nicki," Longchen chimes in. "We have plenty of time before the car arrives. Please have a seat and let me get you some coffee or tea." He lifts his hand to gain the waiter's attention.

"No, thank you," I tell him and wave the waiter away. "I'll just grab something from the buffet so we can get going." Before he can protest, I make a beeline for the food.

I quickly load some eggs, bacon, and toast onto my plate. While I'm tempted to sample the different Chinese food options, I decide to wait for a better time to indulge in the local cuisine. Thanks to my late arrival for breakfast and Ms. O'Connor's irritation with me, the pleasure of enjoying and savoring any food has disappeared.

When I return to the table, Longchen and Ms. O'Connor are in a serious discussion.

"Yes, I'm sure this is the correct location," he informs her. "However, because of the time constraints, I haven't been able to visit it to see what's there. The best I can tell from land surveys and computer images is that it's a large building complex surrounded by several acres of land."

"I appreciate the information and your help with this matter on such short notice," she says. Her hands grip her coffee cup. "I'll just have to wait until we get there to see exactly what it is."

Since I'm short on time, I inhale my food and chug my orange juice. "I'm ready whenever you are," I tell them after wiping my mouth on my napkin.

Ms. O'Connor doesn't waste any time placing her napkin on the table and pushing back her chair. "Well then," she picks up her purse, "let's get going."

THE THOUGHT of hurtling through the city streets again unsettles me, but I push down my unease and climb into the sleek black car. Rather than focus on the traffic, I decide it might be better for me and my stomach if I instead concentrate on the buildings and people I see through my car window. Fortunately, in a city like Beijing, there's plenty to distract me.

As the car pulls out of the hotel driveway, the sky grabs my attention. What should have been a backdrop of blue is a muted gray, giving off the impression of thick fog. My eyes shift from there to the tall buildings that define the city skyline. Each skyscraper is just a smidgen taller than the next, as if the architects were competing with one another to determine who could reach heaven first.

Bringing my view down to the street level, I concentrate on the buildings. Smaller apartment buildings fight for space among the businesses, and laundry hangs from almost every balcony of the crammed high rises as if shielding the windows from any sunrays that dare penetrate the hazy clouds guarding the city. Farther down the road, groups of men squatting on the curb smoke cigarettes while others gather around small tables to play games.

As we continue our drive out of the city, I encounter situations I've never experienced before—a young bicyclist slowly pulling twelve oversized fish tanks full of water and sealife down a crowded street, workers sweeping up piles of litter with handmade straw brooms, and a toddler flashing the world thanks to the large slit in the back of his pajamas. I cackle at the sight of his bare skin.

"What's so funny?" Ms. O'Connor snaps.

I tear my gaze away from the entertaining little boy and turn toward her. "Oh, just this kid on the street. For some reason, he's not wearing a diaper or underwear, so you have a clear view of his backside. See?" I point to where the boy and his mother are walking, but she doesn't bother to look.

Uninterested, she turns her face back out her window. Maybe she wasn't as okay with being here as she was trying to pass off. While I'd love to keep watching the people and scenery passing by, my attention seemed to be needed elsewhere.

"Have you seen anything interesting yet?"

"Not really," she says. I surmise she's not paying attention, because there's a world of fascinating things passing by us.

Despite her curt response, I keep the conversation going. "Ms. O'Connor, I'm going to ask you this one last time, and then I promise I won't ask you again." I take a deep breath. "Are you positive you're ready for whatever is waiting for us at this address?"

She spins her head toward me so fast I'm worried she might have whiplash. "I already told you, Nicole. Yes."

To avoid the daggers shooting from her eyes, I raise my hands in self-defense. "Okay."

"I apologize." She pushes back against the seat. "I'm just ready to figure all of this out. It doesn't make any sense to me, and I know I won't have any peace until I uncover the truth."

I nod to let her know I understand where she's coming from, but question if her desire to know the truth will offer her the peace she's longing for.

"And if the truth isn't what you thought it'd be, then what?"

"I haven't allowed myself to consider that option." She wrings her hands together.

"I hope you find what you've been looking for, Ms.

O'Connor. And regardless of what we discover, either good or bad, I'm here for you."

"Thank you, Nicole." Ms. O'Connor averts her eyes and gazes back out the car window, signaling the end of our conversation.

Respecting her wishes, I don my tourist hat again and observe the changing scenery. The smog, congestion, and noise that monopolized the city have been replaced by large fields, snow-capped mountains, and the clear skies of the countryside. Sparse communities of shacks, farmlands, and grazing animals dominate my view.

It's a stark contrast from the concrete landscape of Beijing, and I find it hard to believe that the two worlds coexist so close to each other. Definitely not the China I envisioned.

Five minutes later, we exit off the main highway and drive down a gravel road. Longchen looks back at us from the front seat. "This is it, ladies."

Ms. O'Connor and I crane our necks, but unfortunately, all I see out the front windshield is more of the gravel road.

As we drive a bit farther, a speck on the horizon comes into sight.

"I see something!" I point to a dot further in the distance. The driver speeds up, and within a few minutes, three large concrete buildings come into view. The car comes to a stop in front of the largest one.

Ms. O'Connor and I look at each other before opening our doors and stepping into the cold. I scan the area, trying to get an idea of what might be inside the giant structures. *A technology center? Sweat farm? Merchandise warehouse?* The tan brick façades with Chinese writing on the side don't reveal much.

Longchen walks ahead of us and waits for us to join him on the sidewalk. When we catch up with him, he takes a deep breath. "To the best of my knowledge, this is the address printed on your father's card."

"You're certain this is it?" Ms. O'Connor surveys the buildings, and he nods in confirmation.

Curious, I ask the question I've been dying to know since agreeing to come on this adventure. "What is this place?"

Reading the symbols written on the side of the building, Longchen hesitates before answering. "It's an orphanage."

9

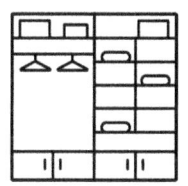

Fools who are in a hurry drink with chopsticks.
~ Chinese Proverb

"An orphanage?" Ms. O'Connor and I ask in unison.

"Yes." Longchen points at the writing. "The sign reads New Hope Orphanage."

Ms. O'Connor stares at the buildings. "You're certain this is the right address?"

"Yes. I've researched everything carefully, and this is the location written on the card."

"But this doesn't make sense." Ms. O'Connor lets out a heavy sigh, a look of dismay covering her face. "What would my father have to do with an orphanage? He wasn't an orphan, he didn't adopt anyone from here, and he didn't have any businesses related to children or orphanages."

"I'm sorry, madam, but I can't answer your question." Longchen looks from the building to her. "Perhaps we should go inside and see if we can find someone who can help you."

"Yes, perhaps we should."

We follow our guide to the front doors, where he ushers us into a small waiting room.

"Stay here while I talk to the receptionist." He points at the five empty metal chairs situated around the perimeter of the room, then proceeds to the reception desk, where a plump lady happily greets him.

While they converse, I scope out the room to see if I can learn more about the orphanage—if that's truly what it is. Nothing in the space indicates it's a home for children. The white walls, which would be ideal for photos or posters, are bare except for a red and gold Chinese calendar.

Other than the chairs, the only other furniture in the room is an ornate wooden table situated under a window. On one end of the table sits a small bonsai tree and on the other is a smiling golden Buddha. In front of him, a small flask filled with incense floods the room with an unusual aroma.

Taking one last look around, I'm reminded more of a funeral director's office than a place where you'd wait to meet your soon-to-be child. Plus, there are no children in sight. *Strange.*

Ms. O'Connor leans over to me with a puzzled expression crossing her impeccably made-up face. "I'm not sure this is the right place, Nicole."

"Me neither, but Longchen seems fairly certain it is."

"No, it can't be." She shakes her head. "There is no connection here between this place and my father or that card."

Carefully choosing my words, I shift in my chair and narrow my eyes at her. "Just because you don't want to believe it doesn't mean it's not true." I place my hands on top of hers. "Let's wait for Longchen to come back with more information before making any conclusions, okay?"

"Fine." Her stern tone cuts across my reasoning like a sharp blade chopping vegetables.

By the time Longchen returns, I'm fairly certain Ms. O'Connor has caused the metal chair to patina from all her fidgeting. It's not until he sits down next to her that she calms down.

"What did she say?" Ms. O'Connor sits up straight.

Perfectly Arranged

He rubs his jaw before answering. "She said that we should speak with the director. Unfortunately, Director Wu is on holiday for the next few days. So, she called for the assistant director, Ms. Chang. As soon as she's available, she'll meet with us."

Crossing her arms, Ms. O'Connor remains silent.

Not wanting to disregard Longchen's efforts, I step in on her behalf. "Thank you, Longchen, that's helpful." I glance at Ms. O'Connor, who keeps her eyes on the floor. "We've waited this long to know more. A little longer won't kill us."

He bows slightly and offers us some refreshments while we wait. I decline but inquire about using the restroom. He points to a door with the letters "W/C" on it.

Following his finger, I turn and look in that direction but don't see what he could be referring to. "W/C?"

"It means water closet." He belts out a boisterous laugh. "I believe you refer to it as the bathroom or restroom."

"Oh." I grin. "Well, excuse me while I go to the water closet then."

Amused by the cultural differences, even with something as simple as using a bathroom, I dash towards the door. Locking it behind me, I search for the toilet but don't see one. I spin around the room just to make sure I'm not missing anything. There are only a sink and a small, raised ledge on the opposite wall. I'm not expected to go in the sink, am I?

With uncertain steps, I walk across the cream-colored floor. I carefully place my right foot on the ledge and glance down. There, on the ground, is what looks like the top half of a ceramic toilet seat. I cover my hand over my mouth to stifle a scream.

Not a squatty potty!

I'd read about these in-ground toilets, but I hadn't expected I'd have to use one, what with our upscale accommodations. Rookie traveler mistake. They are, apparently, everywhere.

Taking one last look around the room, I pray for a regular toilet to appear like the burning bush did for Moses but have no such luck. I quickly debate whether or not to abandon my bathroom adventure, but since I'd gulped down my breakfast and neglected to take advantage of the Western-style restrooms at the hotel before we left, my bladder is not willing to wait.

I have no choice.

The squatty potty it is.

Maneuvering myself over the hole, I pull down my jeans and try to balance as best as I can. I take one last look at the toilet and realize I not only need to keep myself from falling over, but I also have to make sure I don't soak my pants too.

When I finally manage to position myself properly and take care of business, I crack up at the whole situation. A few weeks ago, I was worried about making ends meet. Now, my only concern is making sure I don't make a mess all over myself.

After surviving my first squatty potty experience, I return to the waiting room. I need to warn my boss that she might want to wait to use the restroom. I'm not as confident she could handle it.

Ms. O'Connor looks up at me as I sit back down. "I was beginning to wonder if I needed to send in a Navy SEAL team to extract you."

"I'm fine." I giggle. I don't want to hurt Longchen's feelings or insult his country's unique bathroom options, so I play it cool. "I just, uh, needed a little more time than I thought. The time change and new environment are wreaking havoc on me." Sweat trickles down the side of my face. I sneak a peek at Longchen, and by the faint smile on his face, I'm sure he's figured out what happened behind closed doors.

Twenty minutes later a door opens, and a petite woman with short black hair and wire-rimmed glasses comes into the room.

"Zhou Longchen?"

He promptly rises out of his chair and walks over to greet her. They begin talking in Mandarin, occasionally pausing in the conversation to look over at Ms. O'Connor and me. After a few more minutes, Longchen returns to his seat.

Perfectly Arranged

"Assistant Director Chang"—he points to the woman at the door—"will see us now."

"Good." Ms. O'Connor's clipped response showed no reservations about what could happen once we meet with the director. "Let's solve this mystery once and for all."

Without hesitating, we both rise from our chairs and greet Ms. Chang.

"*Nǐ hǎo*." Her warm tone belies the austerity of the building. "Please follow me this way."

"Your English is flawless," I tell her.

"Thank you. With so many foreigners visiting here, it's necessary to speak several languages."

Once inside the door, she leads us down a narrow hallway and into a small office. Like the waiting room, it's sparsely furnished with nothing more than a metal desk and two small cushioned chairs. With so little décor in this place, I'm curious if they keep things simple for financial reasons or if they're minimalists by nature. If it's the latter, I may have found my new home.

"Please have a seat," Assistant Director Chang says, offering the two chairs to us. Ms. O'Connor and I lower ourselves into the chairs while Longchen leans against the wall next to us. Once we're settled, she slips behind the desk and sits down.

"So, Ms. O'Connor, Zhou Longchen tells me that you're here because you have a card with our address on it."

Ms. O'Connor pulls the card out of her purse and hands it to the woman, who scans both sides of the card before placing it onto the desk.

"This is one of our older cards." Her short response does little to appease my curiosity.

"So, this is the correct location?" Ms. O'Connor's tone lifts with surprise.

"Yes." She pushes the card back toward my boss. "Longchen also tells me that the card belonged to your father."

"That's right," Ms. O'Connor says. "I found it in a box with his most valuable possessions after he passed away. I have no clue why he had it, and I came here hoping someone could help me figure out why he would. It doesn't make any sense."

Assistant Director Chang leans over the desk. "I'm sorry for your loss," she says, her voice low and soothing. "I can't get into the specifics with you, but know that here at the orphanage, we are mourning with you."

My interest in this story grows tenfold at her words, and I glance at Ms. O'Connor to gauge her reaction. If I'm surprised by the news, I can only imagine how puzzled she must be. Her wide eyes and partly open mouth confirm my suspicions.

"Did you know my father, Thomas O'Connor?"

She shakes her head. "No, not personally."

"Well then, why would you mourn him?" Anger laces her words.

Pursing her lips, Assistant Director Chang looks at Longchen. I glance in his direction and see him nod as if giving her permission to answer.

"As I said, I'm not able to share the specific details with you." She wrings her hands. "Only Director Wu can do that. However, I can tell you that your father was an integral part of the orphanage, and we're deeply saddened by his passing."

Like a lion on the attack, Ms. O'Connor jumps up from her chair and moves closer to the woman. "What do you mean he was an integral part of this orphanage? How is that possible?"

"I'm sorry." Assistant Director Chang pushes her chair away from her desk. "But I'm not the person who can speak to you about that. You'll have to wait until Director Wu returns in a few days."

"No." Ms. O'Connor's voice has risen along with a reddening of her cheeks. "I didn't come all this way to wait longer."

"I understand how frustrating it must be for you, but I don't have all the details you are looking for. Only Director Wu can—"

"No, you don't know how frustrating this is. I want answers—"

"Ms. O'Connor." I intercede before things escalate. Her cold stare, scowling mouth, and clenched fists don't scare me, but I don't relish being the object under her inspection either.

"Not now, Nicole."

I quickly leave my seat and stand next to her. "Yes, now." I place my hands on her arms to let her know I'm on her side. "I know you want answers, but getting upset with Ms. Chang is not going to help. We'll just have to be patient and wait for Director Wu to return."

"I don't want to wait."

"You don't have a choice," I say gently. "No one knew we were coming, so we can't expect them to accommodate us." I grin. "But on the bright side, at least we know we're on the right track."

Stepping away from the wall, Longchen clears his throat. "Nicki is right. We are on the right track. We need to be patient. If we push too hard, we may not get the answers we want."

Ms. O'Connor slumps her shoulders in resignation. "Fine." She picks up her purse from the chair and addresses Assistant Director Chang. "We'll be back. Please tell the director to expect us." She steps around the chairs and marches out of the office.

After she's gone, I look at Longchen and Assistant Director Chang. "I'm sorry about her outburst. She's extremely eager to know about the connection between her father and the orphanage. I appreciate your time today and look forward to seeing you and Director Wu soon."

Bowing, I leave the room then bolt out of the building. Back at the car, I find Ms. O'Connor waiting in the backseat.

Once I'm settled next to her, I find the courage to speak up. "Ms. O'Connor, I know you're upset and want answers, but getting angry and raising your voice isn't going to get them any faster. You may find that it works well for you back home, but I don't think that's the right tactic to use here. Please, just wait a few more days, and Director Wu will tell you everything you want to know."

She lets out a low, long sigh. "While I hate to admit it, you're right. I didn't handle that well, and I appreciate you stepping in and stopping me. I can't wrap my head around the fact that this place has some connection to my father. I get a headache just trying to figure it all out."

"I understand. And I'm sorry we didn't find what you were looking for today. But the good news is we made some progress, and after a few days of rest and sightseeing, we'll come back and get the full story."

"I suppose." She spins the card in her hand. "I was just hoping for a Christmas miracle, that's all." Her body slackens as she deposits the card back into her purse.

"Oh, my goodness," I exclaim. "Today is Christmas, isn't it? Between jetlag, the time difference, and the craziness of coming here, I completely forgot that today is the twenty-fifth. Merry Christmas, Ms. O'Connor!" Caught up in the excitement of the holiday moment, I lean over to hug her.

Although she looks uncomfortable, she lets me wrap my arms around her. "Merry Christmas, Nicole."

The car door opens, and Longchen gets inside. "Everything okay in here?"

I nod. "Yes, it is. Thank you, Longchen." I scoot closer to the front seat where he's sitting. "We were just talking about how it's Christmas Day. Could we find a nice place to eat and celebrate?" Maybe there's even a church service we could attend afterward.

"Of course, I know just the place."

"Wonderful." I sink back into my seat. We may not have received the answers we were expecting on Christmas, but at least we can rejoice in the hope the day offered. And the hope for what is yet to come.

THANKS TO JETLAG, I fall asleep on the way back to Beijing. I wanted to observe as many of the sights as I could on the drive back, but between the long journey to get here, our meeting at the orphanage, and the joy of celebrating Christmas, I couldn't keep my eyes open one minute longer.

When I wake up, we're back in the city and stuck in traffic. I check on Ms. O'Connor to see if she's resting, but she's busy typing something into her phone, her forehead wrinkled in concentration.

"Did you sleep?" I know full well she didn't.

"No, I don't have time for that right now." She keeps typing.

I want to remind her that she needs to take care of herself but decide against it. She brought me here to support her, not mother her. "Do you mind if I ask what you're doing?"

"Checking in on Princess, of course." She turns toward me and flashes her phone in my direction so I can see her cat-child's face plastered across the screen.

"Glad she's getting along without you." I resist the urge to laugh.

She glances at the picture and smiles before placing her phone onto the rich leather as she shifts in her seat toward me. "Nicole, may I ask you a question?"

"Sure, ask me anything." After the words tumble out of my mouth, my hands break out into a slight sweat. I might have been a bit rash. Do I really want my boss to ask me anything? That could be a frightening proposition.

"What's your secret?"

I freeze at the question. While I can guess why she's asking, I'm startled that she is. "My secret?"

"Yes, yesterday at the airport, you said that everyone has a secret. As we learned earlier today, my father had one. If what you say is true, then you must have one too."

With my heart hammering, I gulp and debate what to say. While our relationship has grown since our first meeting a few weeks ago, I'm not sure it's advanced enough to open myself up to her completely. Then again, maybe she'll find some comfort knowing we all have secrets we keep hidden from the world. *Plus, it's not like she's going to tell the National Enquirer.*

"My mother's a hoarder," I blurt out before I can change my mind.

Her eyes widen and her mouth opens. "A hoarder? Really?"

The muscle in my jaw tightens at her surprise, and I lower my head in shame.

"Well, I certainly was not expecting a professional organizer to admit that."

"Yeah, it's not generally something I tell my clients. Except you, I guess." We laugh in soft tones.

Grateful for the positive response, I can't help but wonder if now would be a good time to inquire about her secret. I mean, if she can ask, can't I? I contemplate making the request but don't think I'm ready to cross that bridge just yet.

Despite my reluctance, Ms. O'Connor continues the conversation. "I apologize if I was intrusive, but I do appreciate your honesty. For someone as passionate about having things in proper order as you are, I'm sure that is extremely difficult ..."

Before she can finish, she is wracked with heavy coughs.

"Ms. O'Connor, are you okay?" I move closer to her and put my arm around her.

She gasps for air, and I'm afraid something is terribly wrong. I want to pull the car over and call for help, but I doubt 9-1-1 works here. Longchen turns from the front seat to see what's going on. I'm about to tell him to take us to the closest hospital when her coughing subsides.

"I'm fine." She dismisses me with a wave of her hand. "I just got choked up." Longchen hands her a bottle of water. "Thank you." She opens it and takes a few sips.

"Are you sure you're okay? Would you rather go back to the hotel?"

"Really, I'm fine." She looks at me with intention before taking another drink from the bottle. "Plus, we need to eat."

"I'm glad you're okay, madam, and I'm pleased to hear you're hungry." Longchen's voice drifts toward us from the front seat. "We've arrived."

When we step into the restaurant, I'm surprised at the number of people filling the space. In the States, most people stay home or visit family for the holidays but eating out for Christmas must be a popular tradition in China.

Longchen guides us to a small table in the back of the restaurant. While it's secluded from the other customers since we're near the kitchen, we're privy to the banging pots, loud conversations between the waitstaff, and a variety of smells wafting in the air.

"What is this place?" I ask Longchen for the second time today.

"It's a local Chinese favorite called Gold and Silver."

"Great," I say, following after him, not sure that it is. I love Chinese food, but this local cuisine may not be the same Western Chinese I'm used to. "What do they serve here?"

"Don't worry, I called ahead and placed our order. You wouldn't be able to read the menu anyway." He pulls out each of our chairs and waits for us to be seated. "I've requested the best dishes for us to dine on this evening. They may be slightly different from the Chinese food you eat at home, but I think you'll enjoy them immensely."

"I'm sure I will." *Oh, Lord, please let it be just like the fried rice, dumplings, and noodles I get from the Chinese take-out place down the street from my apartment. Please!*

While Ms. O'Connor is busy on her phone, I scope out the restaurant. Other than a large number of people, chopsticks, and ducks hanging by the window, it seems like a typical holiday crowd to me.

"Do all Chinese people celebrate Christmas by eating out?" I'm curious why there are so many customers.

Longchen laughs. "They aren't celebrating anything. They're just having lunch like they do every day."

"They're not celebrating Christmas? But all the stores are decorated for the holidays like they are back home."

He looks at me with softness in his eyes. "The majority of people in this country are Buddhists, my dear. They don't celebrate Christian holidays."

"So, they recognize and promote the holiday, but not its spiritual significance?" I scratch my head.

"That's correct."

"Well, that's confusing," I tell him in all honesty. "I haven't traveled much, especially not at Christmas. I guess I live in my little bubble and forget that not everyone is just like me."

Longchen wrinkles into a grin. "What matters is that you're learning now."

Letting his words sink in, I realize how limited my knowledge is regarding different world religions. "What about the underground Christians and churches I've read about?"

He leans over the table, close enough that I can smell his woodsy cologne. "If I tell you what I know, we'll be killed."

Seriously? My body trembles at his words.

Before I can even grapple with the idea or verbalize any of my thoughts, Longchen belts a mischievous laugh. Even Ms. O'Connor looks up to see what's happening.

"It was a joke, Nicki," Lonchen says, clutching his stomach.

Delighted by the news, I let loose a deep sigh of relief. "Whoo, you had me going there for a minute, Longchen."

A waiter arrives as Longchen winks at me. Three dishes, one set in front of each of us, elicit distinctly Chinese aromas. The waiter removes the lids.

"Our first entrée is a special soup reserved for highly esteemed guests such as yourselves," Longchen explains.

I glance down at the bowl. It's a dark broth soup with green onions and a rubbery substance floating around. I lean closer to the bowl to see if I can smell anything familiar, but the only thing I recognize is a strong onion flavor. I poke at the rubbery substance but can't penetrate it.

A perplexed look crosses Ms. O'Connor's face as well. "What do you call this, Longchen?" she asks politely before taking a sip of the unusual liquid dish.

His face lights up in delight from the question. "It's fish lip soup."

"Fish lips?" I'm sure he's playing a prank on us. "That's just the name, not what's in the bowl, right?"

"Oh, no." He juts out his chin. "Fish lip soup is a delicacy here in China."

Reflecting on his words, my spoon slips from my hand and onto the table.

Concern etches Longchen's face. "Can I be of assistance, Nicki?"

"No, I'm fine. Just clumsy, that's all," I say, retrieving my utensil.

Shaking, I raise the murky water to my lips and try to imagine that I'm eating my mom's French onion soup instead of kissing a strange fish. I slurp a small portion from my spoon and swirl it around as if it were nothing more than mouthwash. When I finally swallow, I'm pleasantly surprised by the spiciness and warmth of the soup, though I can tell it's an acquired taste. I manage a few more courtesy sips, then quietly push my bowl to the side.

Thankfully, the rest of the meal is milder and more of what I'm used to—savory meats, sticky rice, and tangy vegetables. As we feast on our communal dinner, Longchen graciously answers my unending list of questions about Chinese life and culture.

"So if the Chinese don't celebrate Christmas, what do they celebrate?" I ask after devouring the last bite of my tangy beef dish.

Longchen sets his chopsticks sideways on his plate and beams. "We have several yearly celebrations, including Tomb Sweeping Day, the Dragon Boat Festival, and the Mid-Autumn Festival. But perhaps our most important holiday is Chinese New Year."

"On January first?"

"It depends."

"On what?" I cock my head.

"Well," he removes his napkin from his lap and sets it next to his plate, "our new year depends on the moon. It sounds strange, but the holiday is tied to the lunar calendar and begins with the first new moon between January and February. That's why it varies from year to year."

"Well, that makes sense then." I push my plate away and inch closer to him. "But what makes Chinese New Year so special?"

Longchen's eyes sparkle. "Traditionally, it was a time to honor household and heavenly deities as well as ancestors, but today it's about spending time with family and sharing blessings and abundance with loved ones. It's not unusual for everyone to flock back to their village homes to watch dazzling firework displays light up the sky, participate in a handful of special festivals, and eat every day until we can eat no more. Each day. For fifteen days straight."

"Fifteen days? That's a long time! Did you hear that, Ms. O'Connor?" I glance over to see if my boss is as captivated by the private culture lesson as much as I am, but her fingers fly furiously over her phone's keyboard. It must be essential if she's willing to miss out on all that Longchen is sharing.

I lean toward him once more and smile to encourage him to continue.

"Fifteen days," he reassures. "It's like your Western Christmas but without the tree, the large number of presents, and the holiday songs." He pulls out his phone and searches through it. After scrolling for a few minutes, he passes it to me. "Here is a short video I took last year. It should give you an idea of what it's like here during the holidays."

For the next two minutes, I'm enthralled as fireworks flood the screen with bright bursts of color, red dragons prance through the streets, and a flurry of Chinese sayings flow from everyone's lips.

When the video ends, I look at Longchen. "That was incredible! Are all those people in the video your family members?"

"Yes, they are." His mouth curves into a smile. "Family ties are extremely important to our people. It's expected that we spend the holidays together. Not only that, but it's not uncommon to see five generations living together under one roof."

The thought of so many people in one household makes my head spin. It's so different from life back in the States, and especially with my own family. Perhaps I didn't have much to complain about, potentially moving back in with my mom.

"Maybe you can come back someday and experience Chinese New Year for yourself," he continues. "My family and I would love for you to visit our home anytime."

His kind invitation causes me to blush. "That would be a dream, but I'm not sure when, if ever, I'll be able to visit your lovely country again."

"That would be a shame, but I know it's not the easiest trip to make." He rests his chin in his palm. "I apologize I've done all the talking. Why don't you tell me about your Christmas celebration? I'm sure the holidays with your family are just as wonderful."

I wrinkle my nose. "It's not as festive as yours, that's for sure."

"And why is that?"

"Well, it's just my mom and me now—"

"I'm so sorry." His happy demeanor evaporates. "I didn't mean to bring up any sad memories."

"Oh, no, you didn't." I press my hand across my chest. "I miss my dad terribly, but that's not why our holidays aren't the happy occasion yours is." I look down at my hands and hope he doesn't expect more. While I feel comfortable with Longchen, he doesn't need to hear about my family dysfunction.

Nor would he want to know how dreary it is with no colorful

décor splayed around our family home, no pine tree aroma drifting through the rooms, and no caroling around the blazing fireplace. We tried to bring the holidays to life at our home the first few years after my father died, including putting up a small tree, but between the clutter in the house and the void Dad left, it was more than I could handle.

So, we found a way to celebrate that wasn't shrouded in sad memories and unbridled mess. I'm not even sure I'd know what a normal Christmas with all the trimmings would be like, but to have one would be a wish come true. Instead, it's just the two of us at a local diner chomping on dry turkey and exchanging gifts across a cold metal table. That's what it's like when your mother's a hoarder and you can't visit her house.

"Ah, here comes dessert," Longchen says, his voice tinged with relief. "I think you'll like it."

My head pops up at the opportunity to indulge in more Chinese cuisine, as long as it doesn't include any body parts that belong to ocean animals. As the waiter strolls towards us with a large round tray sprinkled with an array of colorful foods poking out from the top, I lick my lips.

When the waiter places a fruit platter on our table—which Longchen informs us is traditional dessert—Ms. O'Connor finally sets down her phone and rejoins us. From her narrowed eyes and knit brows, I can tell she's flustered about something. I wait for her to make the first move towards the dessert.

"I'd like to return to the hotel now," she says, reaching for her purse rather than the juicy watermelon slices neatly arranged in front of her.

"So soon?" I whine like a child who doesn't want the fun to stop.

"Yes, I think it would be best." She rises from her chair. Her rapid movement indicates her statement is a directive rather than a suggestion.

"I'll pay the bill and meet you at the car." Without skipping a beat, Longchen pushes back from his chair and dashes off to find the waiter.

I try not to sulk as I pull my coat on and sling my purse over my shoulder, but I can't help feeling disappointed. Not only would the wide assortment of fresh fruit have been sweet to eat, but I was also enjoying my conversation with Longchen. Like a sponge, I was soaking up every word he shared about his motherland. Hopefully, we'll have another opportunity to visit. For now, duty calls, and I plod after Ms. O'Connor into the bitter cold.

After a short drive back to the hotel, we arrange our plans for the next day then head to our rooms.

"I hope you'll be able to get some rest this afternoon," I tell her after we enter the elevator.

"I'm not that tired." Her matter-of-fact, almost frustrated tone takes me by surprise.

"Then why did you want to come back so early?"

"I have work to do."

"Work? What could you possibly have to do on Christmas?" The elevator dings when we reach the penthouse floor.

She turns to me as the doors open. "I'm shutting down the orphanage."

10

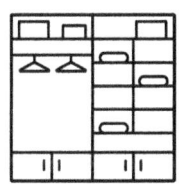

When your hair is in disarray, look for a comb,
when your heart is in disarray, look for a friend.
~ Chinese Proverb

Ms. O'Connor's words paralyze me. She's shutting down the orphanage? How can she do that?

Stuck in my spot, I watch as the elevator doors converge on one another. Before they can shut me in completely, I snap myself out of my shock and jump out of the elevator.

"Ms. O'Connor, wait!" I race down the hallway after her and reach her as she's opening the door to her room.

She turns toward me, a scowl lining her face. "What is it, Nicole?"

"You didn't mean it, did you? That you're going to close the orphanage?" I look at her with pleading eyes, hoping and praying that I misheard her. I know she could arrange for speedy passports and a job for me, but this? "I mean, how can you?"

She lets out a heavy sigh. "Not that it's your concern, but that's exactly what I plan to do." Without waiting for my reply, she steps inside the doorway.

"But why would you do that?" I call after her, blocking the door to keep it from closing on me.

From deep inside the room, she reasserts, "Because I can."

Although I wasn't invited inside, I shut the door behind me and traipse after her. My stomach is in knots as I make my way down the narrow hallway toward the living space. I'm not in any position to question her, but in my gut, I know I have to.

Why else would God give me the opportunity to accompany her on this trip, other than to be an advocate for these innocent children? I shudder at the thought that I could simply stand by and ignore such injustice.

When I catch up with her, she's pouring herself a drink. A pervasive silence fills the room as my boss refuses to acknowledge my presence. Fine. I can go on the offensive.

"What power do you have to do something like that?"

"A financial one." She smirks as she picks up her water glass and sits on the chenille sofa.

"How is that possible? You didn't even know this place existed until today."

"Have a seat, and I'll explain." She gestures to the chair across from her.

I trudge towards a black lacquer armchair, then lower myself onto the ubiquitous red fabric. It's a chair made for royalty, yet I feel more like the court jester than someone who wields power and confidence. Pushing aside my insecurities, I put on a courageous front. I can't fathom shutting down the orphanage is the solution. To do so would be cruel, and that's not the Ms. O'Connor I know.

As if we had all the time in the world, she slowly sips from her glass before delving into her explanation. "You're right, Nicole, that I had no clue the orphanage existed. Nor did I know that the O'Connor estate was involved with any of its operations. However, the only thing that could tie my family to the orphanage would be money."

I lean back against the seat cushion. "But that doesn't make sense."

"No, it doesn't," she says, her voice lowering a bit. "Honestly, I was shocked when the address led to an orphanage. And when I heard Assistant Director Chang talk about my father with such deep respect, I knew there had to be more to it." She pauses and takes another long drink of water.

"I was baffled that my father could be involved, so on the drive back to Beijing, I emailed my accountant, the CFO of our company, as well as my father's accountant and had them do some research for me."

"On Christmas?" Sadness settles over my heart. How can she pull people away from their families on such an important holiday?

"Of course. I expect all my employees to be available whenever I need them."

I make a mental note that if I ever work for Ms. O'Connor again, I need to prepare myself for unreasonable, middle-of-the-night requests.

"And what did they discover?"

Fingering the rim of her glass and staring out the large window across the room, she exhales. "My father's accountant confirmed that my father has been funding and supporting the orphanage out of his own pocket for more than thirty years."

"Wow, I wasn't expecting *that*." I shake my head in disbelief. My mind is racing with so many questions, but I refrain from bombarding her with them because I doubt she has the answers. Against my better judgment, I ask the question I know we're both pondering. "Why wouldn't he have told you about this? Or mention it in his will?"

"I have no clue. I'm hoping Director Wu will give me some insight into my father's motivation and thinking," she replies grimly. "I can only assume he was hoping I would somehow discover its existence and then continue what he so foolishly started."

An eerie quiet descends upon the room.

As she gazes out at the twinkling lights of the Beijing skyline, I see the toll today's events have taken on her. A mix of sadness, anger, and confusion washes over her, from her deeply wrinkled forehead to her taut mouth and clenched jawline. I can only imagine the emotional rollercoaster she must be riding. If I'm reeling from her announcement, I'm sure she's even more bewildered.

"Ms. O'Connor," I whisper to comfort her and gain her attention.

When she finally turns back toward me, her sullen eyes confirm the depths of her emotions. *Lord, give me the words to encourage her right now.*

"I know this must be a huge shock for you, and I completely understand why you're upset. But I'm not sure shutting down the orphanage is going to make you feel any better. Don't you think you should probably wait a few days, at least until we've spoken with Director Wu before you make a decision?"

"No, I don't." Her mouth curves into a frown. "Despite what you may think, I'm looking at this solely from a financial perspective. As the sole heir of the O'Connor estate, I have the right to do as I please, and I believe it is in my family's best interests to stop providing funds to the orphanage. Funds that haven't been stewarded well, in my opinion." She pauses. "If that results in it being shut down, so be it."

Her lack of compassion stuns me. Surely I misunderstood something. "But what about the children? Aren't you concerned about them? Your haste will cause those at the orphanage a lot of problems that could be avoided if you wait for a full explanation from the director. Who knows—once you've heard what she has to say, you may want to continue supporting it."

She rises from her seat and refills her glass. "I highly doubt anything will cause me to change my decision. When I make up my mind about something, I'm determined to see it through."

It takes all my energy not to belt out a laugh. Isn't that why we're here?

Leaning forward in my chair, I try to appease her. "Look, I know you're a smart and savvy businesswoman, and I have no doubt your intel is reason enough for you to pull out of this, but …" I trail off and bite my lip.

"But what, Nicole?" Her voice is laced with frustration.

"It's just that I don't think you're making this decision based on your business acumen. To be honest, I think you're making it from your heart and your emotions, which are in a state of shock and maybe, even, a little … hurt."

She slams her glass down on the counter, clear liquid sloshing onto the granite, and walks toward me. Her eyes are on fire, and despite being across the room from her, I begin to sweat from the heat of her anger. I jump up out of my seat and brace myself for the storm.

"Hurt?" She's so close to me that the smell of her perfume, still strong after a long day, overtakes my senses. "Of course, I'm hurt! Not only did my father keep a secret from me that concerns our family's finances, but he also chose to care for and nurture children he didn't even know. Why should those children continue receiving that level of devotion when his daughter, his flesh and blood, never got that from him? Explain that to me, Nicole!"

Dropping to the floor, Ms. O'Connor begins to cry. Her outburst catches me off guard. I didn't think she was capable of showing that much emotion. Falling to my knees, I place my hands over her shoulder.

"Ms. O'Connor, I'm so sorry. I didn't mean to upset you." I reach for the tissue box on the coffee table and hand her a Kleenex. She takes it from me and wipes the tears flowing down her face.

Once she's calmed down a bit, I summon the courage to say something I pray will reach her heart. "Ms. O'Connor, I know that you're hurt and upset by all of this, but please believe me when I tell you that making an emotional decision like this won't make you feel any better or take away your pain."

"You have no right to tell me what or how I'm feeling, Nicole, or to question my business decisions for that matter." She stands, returns to the bar, adds more ice to her drink. The chunks of frozen water clink against the glass. "And why should you care about this? You've never once mentioned the importance of caring for children. When did you become a child advocate?"

I stand back up. Brushing carpet threads off my pants, I debate whether I should even attempt to answer her question. To do so would mean divulging more of the life I've worked so hard to keep hidden. I grimace. While I know what I feel may not be the same kind of hurt she's experiencing right now, I hope my honesty will help her. And the children at the orphanage.

"My mother's hoarding."

"What about it?" Her eyebrows lift in interest.

I gulp and muster the strength to keep going. "Her hoarding has caused me a lot of hurt over the years. Spending my prom dress money on more junk was a drop in the bucket compared to some of the other things I've had to endure because of her illness. I've been overlooked, ignored, or forgotten due to my mother's obsession with material possessions.

"Because of that pain, I've made some personal decisions and closed myself up in ways that haunt me, even now." I pause to see if my words are piercing her armor, but from her cold stare, I don't think it's working. I soldier on. "Things were so bad between us that I vowed I'd never live with her again, nor would I have any children. Ever. It doesn't take much to wound a child for a lifetime. We both know that."

Tilting her head to one side, she glares at me. I'm sure she was just as surprised to hear my thoughts as I was to share them. Lines crease her forehead, and a softness has come over her eyes.

She understands how personal that truth was for me to reveal despite not knowing I'd never disclosed it to anyone else.

She takes a few steps towards me and clears her throat. "I can't imagine your life has been easy, and I'm sorry that you've been hurt like that. However, comparing our experiences is like comparing apples to oranges. It doesn't translate the same, so let's not continue this conversation any longer. I've had enough for today, so if you wouldn't mind leaving now, I'd like to be alone."

While I'm tempted to argue, I think better of it and head to the door. Once in the hallway, I turn. I want her to know I'm on her side, not the enemy.

"Ms. O'Connor, please reconsider your decision," I beg. This is not the woman I know or have come to admire, and I need to remind her of that. "This is not who you are. You just opened your closet to underprivileged girls so they could feel better about themselves. Deep down, I know you couldn't, you wouldn't, let innocent children suffer because you're—"

"Goodnight, Nicole." She closes the door before I can finish.

Staring at the grain of the mahogany wood, the urge to knock on the door until she lets me back in propels me forward. But no matter how hard or how long I banged, nothing would change. She's shut me out, and I'm not sure when I'll be able to enter again.

With a heavy heart, I plod back to my suite. Taking one last glance toward Ms. O'Connor's room, I look upward and close my eyes. *Lord, be with her. Heal her heart.*

FAILURE WASHES over me like a cold shower as I walk into my suite. I'm numb from head to toe.

Ms. O'Connor is hurt and upset right now, but to remove any funding that might cause the orphanage to close based on raw emotions is wrong. Since I was unable to convince her of that, I might as well have *Accessory to Crime* stamped on my forehead.

While a nice warm bath might allow me to relax and cleanse me of my guilt, I don't feel like slipping into the tub. Instead, I pace the floor of my bedroom, wracking my brain for a solution. After twenty minutes of wearing the carpet thin, I reach for my phone. Despite the time difference, I make the call.

My mom picks up on the third ring. "Nic, is everything okay?" She sounds groggy.

"Yes," I lie, surprised she's asking. "Why?" I hear her shuffling her bedsheets and realize I've woken her up.

"Well, it's still dark outside here, so if you're calling this early in the morning, something must be wrong."

"I knew you'd be sleeping, but I hoped you wouldn't mind. Would you rather I call back later?"

"No, that's okay. I'm awake now. What's wrong?"

I plop down on my bed and stare at the ceiling. "Um, well, it's just that something's come up, and I needed to talk to someone about it."

"I'm glad you called. What's wrong?"

I exhale and spend the next thirty minutes retelling the day's events, so engrossed in conveying every detail I barely pause to breathe. She listens without interrupting, allowing me the time and space I need to get everything off my chest.

When I finally get to the part about Ms. O'Connor closing the door in my face, I'm crying. "So, I came back to my suite to come up with a solution on my own. But after my brain started to hurt and I hadn't come up with anything, I thought I'd call you and see if you had any ideas."

"Well, I don't know what to say to all that, Nic." Mom clears her throat. "I'm honestly in a state of shock right now. Who would have guessed that card would lead to an orphanage that her father has been secretly funding."

"I know." A feeling of fatigue overtakes me. I'm not sure if it's the jetlag, the emotions of the day, or a combination of it all, but it all just feels like too much. I sit up against the headboard to stay awake. "I'm not sure what to do now. To shut down the orphanage would be wrong on so many levels, and I can't let her do that. I don't have a clue how to change her mind."

The reality of the situation sinks in. *Maybe I'm overstepping my boundaries here.*

Before I can stop myself, I verbalize my doubts. "Am I crazy for even thinking I can make a difference? Who am I to do something like that? Not to mention I have no idea how I could stop her or even if I have the power to do so."

"Maybe *you* don't have to."

"What do you mean?" Scratching my head, I try to decipher her statement. I love my mother dearly, but sometimes she doesn't make sense.

She laughs. "I'm sorry. I should have been clearer. You have to remember I'm not a morning person. What I meant to say was maybe you're trying to handle this on your own when you may want to consider seeking guidance from someone else. Someone with an incredible amount of power."

I crease my forehead. "Who would I know in China who would have that kind of power?"

"Not human power, Nic. I meant, maybe you need to pray and see what God can do about the situation. I know it sounds so passé, but I've found that when I'm at rock bottom and don't know what else to do, He's a pretty good listener and advisor."

"That may work well for you, but this is a huge problem. If I have trouble trusting God with the little things of life, how could I trust Him with the larger ones? Plus, how would I even approach Him on a topic like this?" My face warms at my confession. "What would I say? 'God, please stop Ms. O'Connor from shutting down the orphanage?'"

"Sometimes the simplest prayers are the strongest ones." Mom's words come through the phone on a gentle wave. "If you don't feel comfortable saying your prayer out loud, you could always write it."

I quickly scan the room for my backpack containing a journal I intended to use to record everything I experienced on this trip. I hop off the bed, the phone call having re-energized my tired body, and remove the leather-bound book from my carry-on.

"So just write everything, huh?" I reach for a pen on the desk before returning to the bed.

"Yes, just pour out your heart to Him on the written page, just as if you were talking aloud. God doesn't care if you write or speak your prayers. He's just happy you're talking to Him about what's on your heart."

I study the journal cover and the words embossed on it.

All journeys have secret destinations of which the traveler is unaware. (Martin Baber)

Instinctively I trace over the cursive lettering with my fingers. It's as if God knew exactly what I was facing. That knowledge gives me the boost of confidence I need.

"Okay, I think I can do that. Thanks, Mom." Glancing over the pages, I'm anxious to start pouring out my heart over them.

"That's what moms are for, sweetheart."

Her words tear me in two. I appreciate the love and time she's giving me, but I wish she could have been that way for me when I needed it all those years ago. I shake off the thought and focus on the empty pages in front of me. "Well, I guess I'd better go, this call is probably costing me a fortune."

"Okay. And Nic, Merry Christmas."

"Merry Christmas. I love you."

"I love you too," she chimes in before hanging up.

I drop my phone on the bed next to me and crawl under the covers and sheets. Once I'm comfortably situated, I open the journal to the first blank page and begin pouring out my heart to God the best I can. I start at the beginning, from my first phone call with Heather to the encounter I had with Ms. O'Connor this evening.

Though I'm fully aware that God knows everything that's happened over these past few weeks, it feels so good to bare my soul. When I'm finished, my hand is cramped from writing. The clock on my phone reads eight o'clock. I've been *praying* for almost an hour, and tiredness pulls at my weary bones, but my mind is not ready to go to sleep yet.

With nothing else to do, I open my laptop. Perhaps catching up on email and browsing social media will allow me to reconnect with home and normalcy for a little while.

After quickly scrolling through my inbox full of spam, day after Christmas sale promotions, and digital cards from college friends, I sign on to Instagram. I spot lots of perfect families and loving couples celebrating the holidays together, a constant reminder I have no one, other than my mom, to share the special moments of life with.

Crestfallen, I close my computer.

I climb back into the bed, reeling from the roller coaster of emotions racing through me. One minute I'm up, the next I'm down. If something isn't cleared up soon, I'm afraid this ride will be a continuous loop without the option of getting off.

11

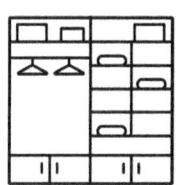

A friend made is a road paved; an enemy created is a wall built.
~ Chinese Proverb

I wake refreshed and rejuvenated. Despite yesterday's turmoil, I'd slept soundly and jump out of bed to prepare for the day ahead. When I fling the curtains open, sunshine floods the room. My feet dance across the yellow rays streaking the carpet as I float towards the bathroom. No matter what happens today, I refuse to let anything rob me of the joy welling up inside my spirit.

Not wanting to repeat my unfortunate start from the previous day, I primp as fast as I can and race out the door. Longchen had arranged for us to visit some of the more famous tourist sites around Beijing while we wait for Director Wu to return to New Hope.

Spending the day with Ms. O'Connor will likely be stressful, but I refuse to let our differing views on the orphanage ruin this once-in-a-lifetime opportunity. The excitement of all we're going to see will, I hope, overshadow any tension between the two of us.

When I arrive downstairs, I spot Longchen speaking with

the teenage girl seated next to him. His jovial manner and smile remind me of the playful grandfather type, and for a moment I think that's what my dad would have been like, were he still alive. Brushing away the thought, I wave at Longchen.

"Nǐ hǎo, Nicki," he says, rising from his seat.

"Nǐ hǎo, Longchen." I extend my hand out in greeting, and when he accepts, his calloused hand is warm.

"Are you ready to see Beijing?" He lets go of my hand.

I push my toes against the tips of my shoes, which does little to stop me from bouncing on the balls of my feet in excitement. "Oh, yes, I can't wait."

"Wonderful. I think you're going to enjoy what I have planned for you."

"I'm sure Ms. O'Connor and I will love everything you show us."

His joyful demeanor quickly evaporates, leaving him with an even more wrinkled forehead and pinched lips. "Nicki ... I apologize, but Ms. O'Connor won't be joining us today."

"What?" He must be mistaken. I scan the lobby, hoping to find her sitting in the corner drinking coffee.

When my eyes rest on him again, he's shaking his head. "I'm sorry, but I thought you knew. Ms. O'Connor called me last night and informed me she wouldn't be accompanying us today or possibly even tomorrow."

"Is she okay? Did she say why she wasn't coming?" I have my suspicions but keep them to myself.

"She seemed fine when we spoke, but she didn't offer any explanation for her absence."

"Oh." I push down my anger and disbelief, certain that her bailing on today's activities is due to our argument last night. I have to find out. "Will you excuse me for a moment, Longchen?"

"Certainly," he says, stepping back toward the chairs.

I pull out my cell phone and send a text message to Ms. O'Connor.

Longchen said you weren't joining us today. Is everything okay?

Without giving me a chance to blink, she responds.

Yes, I'm fine. Thank you for asking.

I go on the offensive.

I'm sorry you won't be going out with us today. Can we meet later to continue our discussion from last night?

While it's risky, I need to persuade her to change her mind about the orphanage. She doesn't take much time to consider my offer as my phone dings immediately.

No. I'm rather busy and need to focus. Enjoy your day.

Not the answer I was hoping for. I start to type a less than polite response, questioning my reason for even being here. Wasn't the point of coming to China to help her through this situation? I'm puzzled, angry, and confused.

While I'm tempted to run back upstairs and disregard her desire to be left alone, I delete the message. Ms. O'Connor can't be coerced, and I have no desire to act like a child who doesn't get her way, so I slide my phone into my backpack. I'll just have to find another way to convince her—one she can't decline.

Displaying the most genuine smile I can muster, I walk toward Longchen. "Well, then, I guess it's just the two of us. What's on the agenda?"

Relief washes over his face, and his eyes shine when he looks at me. "Great! I think you'll be quite impressed with today's outing."

Before I can gather more details, he motions to the young girl he was visiting with earlier. She jumps up from the chair and joins us.

"Nicki, I'd like to introduce you to Julia, your tour guide for the day."

"Guide?" I'm confused by the change of events. My eyes bounce from Longchen to Julia and back to him. "You aren't coming with us?"

"My dear," he croons, "I doubt you'd want to spend the day with an old man like me. I'd just slow you down." He turns to Julia. "That's why I asked Julia to show you our beautiful city. You'll have more fun with her youthful energy. I hope that's okay with you."

I glance back over at Julia, who stands like a statue next to him. Her long black hair, which is pulled back in a tight ponytail, plays a stark contrast to her porcelain complexion, and her oversized sweater hangs below the hips of her whitewashed jeans. She can't be more than fifteen years old.

"Uh, sure, that will be fine." While I'm sure Julia is harmless and kind, I'm not all that great with younger people, so I worry this may not work as he'd believed. Plus, she's not Ms. O'Connor.

Despite the age difference and my discomfort, I stretch out my hand toward her. "*Nǐ hǎo,* Julia. It's a pleasure to meet you."

She unclasps her hands from in front of her and places one inside mine with a light touch. "*Nǐ hǎo,* Nicki." She grins then quickly removes her damp hand. Perhaps she's as nervous about this outing as I am.

Hoping to put her at ease, I divert my eyes back to Longchen. "I'm sure Julia and I will have a wonderful time together. So, where are we heading today?"

"I've arranged for you to visit the Wall."

"That sounds wonderful." I mean the words. Although the morning hasn't gone as I'd hoped it would, I need to put the issues with the orphanage out of my mind and enjoy this remarkable opportunity. I'll probably never come back to China, so I need to take in as much of this historic and storied country as I can.

Perfectly Arranged

"I'm so glad." Eyes wide and glowing, he directs us to the restaurant. "Let's eat some breakfast, and then you ladies can be on your way."

THE DRIVE to the Great Wall is similar to the one we took yesterday—crowded city streets swarming with cars, people, and animals, including a donkey pulling a cart of bricks and a young man cooking potatoes on a metal barrel.

When our driver slows down thanks to the logjam of cars, laughter spills from my lips at the difference of this world compared to my life back home. It's so unlike anything I've ever experienced, and I never imagined a place as unique as this.

"Do you see something funny?" Julia must be confused by my amusement.

"No. Well, yes." I search for the words to explain my awe and euphoria of the scenery passing by. "Life here is so unlike life in America. All the sights, sounds, and smells I'm experiencing fascinate me. I hope I never forget them."

"Oh." She hesitates for a moment, curiosity brimming behind the hesitancy in her eyes. "Do you mind if I ask how it's different?"

A snort escapes from my nose. *Honey, there aren't enough adjectives in the dictionary to describe the divergence of our two worlds.*

"I wouldn't know where to start," I tell her in all honesty. "But let me give you one example I know I'd never see back home." I shift in my seat, recalling the memory. "Yesterday, we passed a toddler whose backside was in plain sight for everyone to see."

Julia frowns, and her eyebrows furrow. "Backside?"

"I'm sorry, I should have thought about that." *Another rookie traveler mistake.* "It's a slang term for your rear or your bottom." I point to my own less-than-stellar backside for extra emphasis.

Watching me illustrate my point, Julia's eyes light up with

recognition. She laughs, and I'm not sure if she's laughing with me or at me. "Oh, I see. But why is that funny?"

"Well, uh ..." There must be words I can offer that won't offend her, but nothing seemed adequate. I'd just have to go for it. "It's just that babies back home usually wear diapers."

"Oh, I see ..."

Sensing that she's willing to talk, I inquire about the open-air clothing choice. "Why do Chinese babies walk around with slits in the backs of their clothes and no diapers? Is that normal?"

Julia's broad grin brightens her youthful face. "Yes, it's traditional. The pants are called *kai dang ku*, and they help children with the potty-training process. When the child needs to relieve themselves, they just sit down and do so without having to worry about pulling down their clothing or finding a water closet in time." She pauses her rapid-fire explanation.

Thousands of questions spin in my mind.

"It's most popular among the older generation and is considered a healthier option than having children sit in soiled diapers," Julia continues. "I have noticed that Westerners seem less than excited by the idea. From the looks I've seen on their faces, they find it disgusting."

"Yes, I can see how that would be a problem." I clench my lips, concentrating on the honking horns outside my window instead of the absurd notion Julia had just presented.

Despite my feelings on the topic and that many people I knew back home would be repulsed, I wanted to learn as much as Julia could tell me. That required not offending her. "I'm not sure it would work where I'm from, but it's interesting and a great story to tell my mom when I get home."

Julia nods, and I sense she's more confident in conversing with me than when we first met. Hoping to keep the dialogue going, I switch topics to see if I can learn more about her.

"Your English is excellent. Did your parents teach you, or did you learn in school?"

Her eyes sparkle behind her oversized, *Harry Potter*-style

glasses. "That's kind of you to say. I've spent a lot of time practicing my English. I've taken classes, watched many TV shows, and attempted to speak with as many foreigners as possible to master the language."

"Wow, that's impressive." Most kids today wouldn't go to such lengths to be fluent in another language. Mastering a video game? Yes. But becoming bilingual? Probably not. "Your parents must be proud of you."

The color drains from Julia's face. "I don't have any parents." She averts her eyes away from mine but not before I catch the pain in them.

"I'm so sorry." I reach over and place my hand on hers. "I had no idea."

"It's okay. How could you have known?"

While I want to wrap her up in my arms, I lean back in my seat to give her some personal space. "Do you live with your grandparents then?"

"No." She hangs her head. "My parents abandoned me when I was three days old. I live at an orphanage."

I'm stunned by her confession. An orphan? What were the odds?

"Oh," I manage to say. There are so many other things I want to ask her, but I don't want to be rude or upset her further, so I take a subtler approach. "How old are you, Julia?"

She cracks a smile. "I'm twenty."

"Are you serious?" My mouth drops open. "You look younger than that. Please, tell me your secret to your youthful appearance." We burst out laughing, and I'm grateful we navigated that sensitive topic without too much drama.

"So, at what age are you able to leave the orphanage and go out on your own?"

A loose thread hangs from her sweater sleeve, and she twines it around her finger. "Well, when children in Chinese orphanages turn fourteen, they can legally leave, but I chose to stay and help with my—with the children, mainly."

My admiration for this amazing young lady swells within my chest. "That's kind, considering how smart you are. You could be attending college or studying abroad, you know."

"I hope to do that someday." She pauses. "For now, I'm content to stay at the orphanage and do what I can. Despite what people think about orphanages, I was fortunate to be raised in such a loving environment. It's truly a special place, so I can't imagine leaving it anytime soon."

Stories I'd heard back home about orphanages and foster homes flash in my memory. She is so fortunate to have been placed in a facility that provided such great care. Based on what I'd heard, not all orphanages are safe havens.

"I'm glad to hear that." I contemplate telling her about my trip to the orphanage yesterday but figure there are hundreds in the area and the odds that she would know about this particular one is slim. "So, what exactly do you do at your orphanage?"

"It varies. Mostly I assist with the younger children, teach English to the older ones, and act as a liaison with the foreigners who visit as part of the adoption process." Her posture straightens, and her voice projects more confidence as she continues to speak.

"It also allows me to share my ..." She stops when the car slows down. "Oh, we're here. Excuse me, Nicki, I need to give the driver some directions." She leans forward in the seat and speaks to him, pointing to a particular area.

I glance out the window and notice that we've arrived at a tourist location. Large charter buses are parked along the side of the street, and people are milling around, chatting and taking pictures.

Once the car comes to a complete stop, Julia pours out more instructions to the driver then turns to me. "Sorry, I hope you won't think I'm rude, but I want him to park as far from the tour groups as possible. You'll be glad I did."

In the distance, I spot a large number of colored tour flags hoisted among clusters of people with cameras and guidebooks.

Julia knows what she's doing, and I'm glad to have her navigating the way.

"Are you ready to go?" She situates her bag over her shoulder and grabs the door handle.

"Yes, I can't wait," I pull my backpack off the floor and sling one of the straps over my shoulder. "Before we go, though, can you finish telling me what it is you share at the orphanage?"

She hesitates for a moment, studying me. Pushing her glasses up the bridge of her nose, she leans away from the car door and draws closer to me. "I don't tell this to many people, but I feel that I can trust you." She glances at the driver and, when the man remains face forward, smiles at me and whispers, "I'm a Christian. When I'm at the orphanage, I find ways to share my faith with the children even though it's forbidden here in China."

I gasp, and my eyes grow wide. "You're a Christian? Really? That's amazing! So am I."

"I'm so glad to have a Western sister in the faith." Julia reaches for my hand and squeezes it, then grabs the door handle again. "Let's finish this conversation later. I want to beat the tourist crowds to the cable car line."

Like a child, I do as I'm told and follow her lead.

As we head toward the main entrance, hawkers sell Great Wall memorabilia, promising to make a good deal for their *Western friends*. I scan the selection and notice I have my choice of T-shirts, hats, books, cups, and other trinkets that will let everyone know I climbed one of the world's greatest wonders..

Confident any eye contact will have me surrounded by salespeople, I keep my gaze glued to the ground and stick close to Julia's sneakers.

At the top of the stairs, I'm hit with a strong smell of Chinese cuisine, and my stomach starts rumbling. I hadn't eaten much breakfast, and the thought of rice and noodles pulls me in that direction.

"Nicki, where are you going?" Julia calls out after me. "The ticket office is over here."

I nod in the direction of the vendors lined up in a straight row. "I thought I'd check out the food stalls. If we're going to climb a wall, I'm going to need something to give me energy."

She laughs. "Okay, but be careful and stay there. I'm going to buy the tickets and be right back."

I wave and rush over to the street cooks. Their pans sizzle from the oil and spices mixing with the noodles, vegetables, and meat. I find a stall without a line and smile at the diminutive Chinese woman standing behind the hot stove. "*Nǐ hǎo.*"

The friendly chef flashes a toothless smile at me and starts rattling a string of words I cannot in any way decipher. I point to the rice and some beef, and she nods her head in understanding.

As if performing a sacred ritual, she combines the requested ingredients then stirs them with the utmost care. When she passes me the small bowl of browned meat and white rice, sprinkled with some colorful vegetables, my taste buds water. I happily take it from her, hand her some money, and take my first bite.

Flavorful spices, juicy beef, and crunchy onions and peppers explode in my mouth. This authentic street cuisine is nothing like the standard Chinese fare I eat back home. It's so much more delicious! I give the sweaty-faced cook a thumbs up to let her know how much I'm enjoying her efforts.

Julia returns just as I'm swallowing my last bite.

"Oh my, this is so good." I wipe my mouth with my napkin. "Chinese food doesn't taste like this back home, that's for sure."

"There's no substitute for food from the motherland." She takes the empty bowl from me and passes it back to the cook. "Let's get going. The tour groups are right behind us."

I take one last look at the lady and wave goodbye. "*Zài jiàn,*" I tell her as best as I can.

"*Zài jiàn.*" Her voice lilts with joy.

Walking at a break-neck speed, Julia stops in front of a

crowded queue. "We'll take the cable car up the mountain so you can get an overall view of the Wall. Then we'll walk a few kilometers along it before heading back down. It will probably take us about two hours."

"That sounds wonderful." Having never experienced anything like this before, I don't have many expectations. For me, every adventure is a treat.

Once inside the rickety cable car, Julia fills me in on all the essential facts about the Wall, including how it was built, the material used, its exact length, and why it was important to the Chinese that they created such an enormous structure. I'm mesmerized by her knowledge and soak it all in.

As the cable car rises higher and higher, I'm able to get a bird's-eye view of the wall. The structure reminds me of a snake slithering through the mountains, with no beginning and no end, just continuing on and on in both directions.

I'm stunned at how beautiful it is. "Wow, this is amazing! The pictures I've seen in books don't do it justice."

"Yes." Julia grins. "It is truly one of our country's greatest achievements."

When the short ride finishes, we begin walking the ancient wonder. I assumed it would be a flat walking surface, but different stairs and pathways lead us up and down and to the sides. It isn't an easy trek, but I try not to let the difficulty of the task rob me of the moment. Now I understand why those T-shirts said, *"I climbed the Great Wall."*

After we pass through several towers and over several bridges, I ask Julia if we can take a short rest. Despite the cold December temperatures, I'm working up a sweat and in desperate need of a break. We find a spot in one of the watchtowers, and Julia buys some water for us from one of the vendors camped nearby.

As we rest and discuss the defensive purposes of the Wall, a Chinese boy dressed in jeans and a hoodie approaches us. He doesn't look older than ten, but the stubble on his chin says different. Julia strikes up a conversation with him, and I assume he's asking for money or directions. When she turns to me and says otherwise, my eyes widen.

"He wants to have a picture taken with me? Why?"

"In his province in the west, he doesn't see many foreigners, so it would be a great memory for him to have his picture with you." Her tone is so matter-of-fact, my defenses lower.

"Okay, sure." I stand next to him. As I lean in and place my arm over his shoulder, he looks at me and smiles like a kid sitting on Santa's lap for the first time.

"Say *nǐ hǎo*," Julia instructs while pointing his phone in our direction.

After taking a variety of different shots, all of which include him posing with his fingers in a V-shape, she hands his phone back to him, and they continue their earlier conversation. I wish I knew what they were saying as they keep looking at me and talking. At least they aren't laughing.

A few minutes later, Julia backpedals towards me and makes a request. "He wants to know if he can invite his family over to take pictures with you as well."

"Very funny," I say.

"I'm not joking."

I glance back at the boy. The hopeful look on his face tells me his request is genuine. "Sure, I'd be honored."

Julia conveys my answer, and the teen races off to find his family.

"That is very kind of you. You didn't have to do that. But I should warn you—you've probably opened the door for others to ask for a picture with you too."

Curious as to why she would say something like that, I scratch my head. "What do you mean?"

Before she can reply, the boy returns with his family, and I start taking individual pictures with each person in his group. Standing next to each of them, I look like a Western giant.

When Julia hands the phone back to the boy, I assume our

photoshoot is over, but as I turn around, I see more locals have lined up to take their picture with me. So, this is what she meant about opening the door. My heart rate increases about double to what it was beating while I climbed the Wall. Now I know how the celebrities back home feel when the paparazzi chases them down.

Ten minutes later, my face hurts from smiling so much, and Julia rescues me from the crowd that has surrounded us. She shouts out a few sentences in Mandarin, and my entourage quickly disperses.

"Thanks for putting a stop to the madness." I massage my cheeks. "I should have had you take a picture of all of that for me. My family and friends back home would have found it funny." We both chuckle and resume our trek.

To ensure I don't miss any more magical moments, I pull my phone out of my pocket. When I do, I notice a text message from Ms. O'Connor.

Nicole, I have made formal arrangements to stop funding for the orphanage. We will need to stay longer than expected to meet with Director Wu to process all the paperwork. I hope the delay in returning isn't a problem for you.

I cram my phone back into my pocket and storm off.

"Nicki," Julia shouts. "Where are you going?"

I lean against the edge of the wall and exhale. I don't have a problem staying longer, but if I were going to do so, I'd fight as hard to keep the orphanage open as she would to shut it down.

12

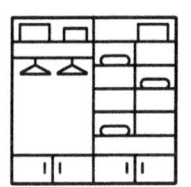

Experience is a comb that we receive just when we are going bald.
~ *Chinese Proverb*

The stones of the ancient wall pinch my taut fingers as I fight to stabilize myself. I can't believe she's going through with her plan. I'd thought she was reacting emotionally and would just snap out of it, but she's responding with typical determination.

There must be a way to stop her outrageous plan, but it's like I'm pushing a boulder up a steep mountain. The longer you climb, the harder it is to keep pushing ... *Stop funding ... Process all the paperwork ...* It all seems so final.

I survey the gray and barren terrain around the Wall. Inhaling deeply, I turn my eyes to the mountaintops, where baby blankets of snow cover the peaks. From there, I shift my focus upward to the heavens and call out to God.

"Lord, how am I supposed to do this? Ms. O'Connor's allowing a powerful emotion to dictate her actions, but I can't let her. I don't know what I need to do. Please show me how."

Tick-tock, tick-tock. My perspiring skin dampens my shirt while I await an answer from the Almighty, but despite the need, nothing comes. "Lord, please. I'll take anything you offer me, really—a gentle breeze, a bolt of lightning, a burning bush ..."

"Nicki! Nicki!"

I startle from my prayer but try to ignore Julia's calls for a little longer, certain God will give me a sign if I can just be still.

A tap on my shoulder breaks the tranquility. Julia, red-faced and breathless, stands before me. "Nicki, are you okay? Did I do something to upset you?" A forlorn look crosses her face, settling more shame on her shoulders.

Laden with guilt at the worry I must have caused her, I muster the best upbeat tone I can. "Just a bit of bad news, that's all." I flash my phone up to her as proof.

She pushes her hand to her chest, a look of relief washing over her. "Oh, I'm so glad. I mean, not about your bad news, but that I didn't do something to upset you. I thought maybe taking so many photos with strangers bothered you. I would have stopped them if I'd known you weren't happy. I—"

"Julia, slow down." I grab her arms to calm and reassure her. "Everything is okay."

"You're sure?" Her eyes dart back and forth, searching my face for evidence.

"I promise, it's not you." I grin. "It's just something I need to figure out. I apologize if I worried you."

"It's okay. Is there anything I can do to help you?"

I've only known this woman for a few hours, but I love her sweet and caring spirit. "Thanks for offering, but I don't think there's anything you can do." I gaze back out across the barren terrain, my heart heavier than before, and wonder if there's anything *anyone* can do. "Honestly, I'm not sure I know how to fix the situation. I'm praying for a sign to show me the way."

Her eyes sparkle, and she takes hold of my hand. "When the time is right, God will show you the way. In the meantime, I know something that will help you feel better."

Without giving me time to ask any questions, Julia drags me along the uneven walk path. On our way to our mystery destination, we pass numerous tourist groups listening to their guides share the rich history of the Wall in their native tongues, colored umbrellas where vendors sell cold water bottles to weary visitors, and families with crying children. Our fast-paced trek finishes at a long queue, both of us breathless and sweating.

"What is this?" I doubt a line will remedy my problem.

"You will see." A sly grin tilts one side of her mouth.

After five minutes of curious waiting, we reach the front of the line. My eyes widen as I take in the view of an alpine slide transporting riders on small toboggans down the mountain.

"Why is there a slide here?" I thought twisting, scare-you-out-of-your-pants rides like this were only found at amusement parks, not on steep mountainsides.

"It's how we're going to get back to the base. It's easier than walking." Julia bounces ever so slightly to point toward a couple partway along their journey down the mountain. "It's also more fun." Their vocalization did little to ease my increasing nerves. Were those screams of laughter or terror?

"You want me to go on this?" I point to the open-air cart, which contains nothing more than a handle and seat cushion.

Quivers shoot down my body from head to toe. I highly doubt the fun factor in all of this. Where's the seatbelt and protective helmet? Or the certificate verifying the safety of this metal apparatus? Peering down the track, I think a body harness might be a better option for me.

"I think I'll pass." I take a few steps back. Death by slide was not on my list of activities to experience here in China.

Julia reaches for my hands and pulls me forward. "Trust me, Nicki. Not only will you have a good time, but you'll also forget about whatever's bothering you for a few minutes."

Before I can refuse, a young Chinese boy waves me over to the next available cart. I look at Julia one last time for mercy and a Plan B, but she's busy taking pictures with her phone and giving me a thumbs up.

"Julia," I shout. The attendant pushes me down in the seat. "I don't think I can do this—"

"Enjoy! I'll see you at the bottom."

The next thing I know, the attendant runs like a Jamaican bobsledder behind me, and then there's nothing but the whooshing of the slide forming in my ears. I squeeze my eyes shut and grip the bar for dear life. *Lord, don't let me die, please.*

At first, my body is tense and a bundle of nerves, but within a few seconds of zigzagging my way along the metal track, I burst out laughing. This *is* fun!

I loosen my death grip on the handles and relax. Opening my eyes, I see flashes of tree limbs, and in the distance, I can make out parts of the Wall. I strain my ears for the cries of those who went ahead of me, but all I hear is the clacking of the cart's wheels against the metal track. Whizzing along at such a high speed, I don't have time to think of possible dangers or even be afraid.

A rush of adrenaline surges through my body. Before I can stop myself, I let out a shriek of delight, "Woohoo!"

Julia was right—this joyride is lifting my spirits and helping me forget my worries. Just as I'm embracing the ride and its therapeutic benefits, another attendant flags me down, cautioning me to slow the toboggan as the track finishes.

When the cart comes to a complete stop, I rest my head on the handles and laugh. What a thrill! Rising from my seat, I turn back toward the mountain just in time to see Julia coasting in behind me.

"Nicki!" she squeals and waves at me. "Wasn't that great?" She raises a hand toward me, and I help her out of her coaster.

"That was incredible!" I hug her in appreciation. "Thank you so much for suggesting I do this. I can't remember the last time I laughed so much or so hard."

"I'm glad you enjoyed it." Julia drapes her messenger bag over her shoulder and loops her arm through mine. "Did it help take your mind off your troubles?"

Perfectly Arranged

"What troubles?" I laugh.

Julia catches on to my joke. We walk in arm-in-arm to the car. As we pass back by the vendors and food stalls, I recount my ride with her, not just for her sake but for mine as well.

OVER A TRADITIONAL CHINESE LUNCH, referred to as *Hot Pot*, I learn how to dip my meats, vegetables, and desserts into steaming pots of spicy broth. I was initially wary about the entire concept, but after a few bites of savory food, I'm hooked.

Julia and I spend the lunch break getting to know one another better. She shares more about growing up in the orphanage, how she longs to find her parents, and her secret obsession with *People* magazine.

"Please don't tell anyone about the magazine," she whispers to me over the table. "It's frowned upon to have Western propaganda in your possession."

My curiosity piques at her last words. How could a nice girl like Julia obtain *black market* items? I grimace at the thought of what people would say or do to her if they discovered her secret collection. "How do you get them, then?"

"Sometimes I get them from the foreigners visiting the orphanage." She pushes her glasses up the bridge of her nose. "I also have a friend at church who works as an *ayi*, cleaning and cooking for an expat family, and she brings them to me." She giggles at the thought.

"My friend always tells me I shouldn't be reading things of 'this world.' I know she's trying to make me feel bad, but I read my Bible almost every day. Plus, if God were upset with me reading that stuff, He'd let me know."

Without blinking, she snatches the last piece of meat floating in the pot with her chopsticks and quickly devours it. As I watch her fluid movements, I envy not only her gracefulness with the pointy utensils but the ease of her relationship with

God. Perhaps my earlier unanswered pleas mean I'm struggling in this area.

After searching the pot for any last lingering food items, Julia places her chopsticks next to her plate and looks at me intently. "So, where would you like to visit next? Tiananmen Square, the Forbidden Palace, Pearl City?"

"If it's okay with you, I'd like to go back to the hotel." I point to my phone. "I still have some things I need to handle. And with so much on my mind, I don't think I'd be able to focus on anything else."

"Of course." Julia nods. She pulls a gold cross necklace from underneath her sweater and shows it to me. "Some days, faith is all that carries me." When the waitress returns with the bill, Julia quickly hides the jewelry back beneath her clothing.

Once our empty plates and bowls have been cleared from the table, Julia keeps sharing. "I'm a fairly new Christian and still learning, but I cling to God's Word to help me in difficult times. I'm sure it does the same for you."

"Thank you for the encouragement, Julia." I squeeze her hand. "You're just what I needed today."

"You're welcome." She pulls out her wallet to pay.

But I quickly grab the check from the bill tray. "Oh no." I wag my finger at her." You've done enough for me today. Paying for lunch is the least I can do to show my appreciation."

"Really, I insist on paying." Her face turns as red as the Chinese flag. "Longchen would be furious with me if he discovered you paid for the meal."

I lean closer to her. "Then I guess it will be our little secret, won't it?" We sputter out soft giggles, and the worry eases from Julia's face.

After paying the bill, we make our way to the exit. When I'm sure that it's safe to talk, I ask Julia one more question. "Do you have a favorite Bible verse?"

She tilts her head and pauses. "Hmm ... no one has ever asked me that before." She pushes open the door and steps into the sunlight. Despite the privacy we have as we venture through the parking lot, she remains quiet, leaving my mind to wander with various possibilities of how I might have offended her.

When we're buckled up in the backseat and maneuvering our way back through the hectic streets of Beijing, Julia breaks the silence. "I've been thinking about your question, and it's not an easy one for me to answer. As I said, I haven't been a Christian long and haven't read all of the Bible."

Don't worry, my friend, neither have I.

"But if I had to pick a verse that has meant the most to me, it would be the first chapter of James, verse twenty-seven."

Before I can ask her to elaborate, she begins reciting her favorite words of Scripture in her native tongue. I have no clue what she's saying, but thanks to her sincere heart and love of the Lord, the foreign words emanate in a lyrical manner that reduce the language barrier to nothing.

Finishing her recitation, she exhales. "Sorry, I only have a Chinese Bible and don't know how to say it in English very well."

"Oh, don't apologize. It was a privilege for me to hear the verse in Mandarin. Thank you for sharing it."

Once again, her cheeks turn rose red, and I hope I haven't embarrassed her with such a heavy compliment. While there may be amazing historical sites for me to experience while I'm in China, hearing Julia share her favorite passage of Scripture with me will be something that will stay with me long after the other memories fade. It's as if an angel were speaking directly to me.

When the car stops in front of the hotel, I open the door and look back at Julia. "Thanks again for a wonderful day."

"It was my pleasure." Her voice grows bubbly. "Are you sure you don't want to see anything else?"

"Not today. I need to spend some time alone figuring things out. From the looks of it, I'll be here a little bit longer, so maybe we'll have time to do more sightseeing later."

"I would like that." Reaching into her purse, she pulls out a business card. "Here is my phone number. Call or text me if you need anything. I know you said you have to handle this on your own, but I've often found the people who don't want help are the ones who need it most." She places the card into the palm of my hand. "I'm here for you, no matter what."

Grateful for our time together, I give her a long hug. She wasn't at all what I'd expected, but she was exactly what I needed.

A few moments later, I step off the elevator onto the penthouse floor and face Ms. O'Connor's room. Though I need to spend some time thinking of a way to change her mind, I'm pulled toward her door like a magnet. I tap lightly on the door and wait for her to open it.

Silence.

Maybe she's taking a nap. I check my watch—4:30 p.m. I knock again, this time a little harder. Still nothing. She's either good at playing the quiet game, or she's ignoring me. Neither one leaves me in a good place.

Deflated, I walk back to my room. I didn't think anything could diminish the joy blossoming in me earlier today. I was mistaken. Whatever warm fuzzy feeling had overtaken me disappeared with Ms. O'Connor's silent treatment. As much as I'd love to revive that spark of joy, it has fluttered away. I doubt even Marie Kondo could help me find it again.

AFTER A SHOWER and change of clothes, I plop onto my bed. Hugging my knees, I sink into the plush mattress, letting the memories of the day wind through my mind. While it was great, the text message from Ms. O'Connor overshadows everything positive that happened.

I bury my head in my knees. What can I do to stop her? Nothing comes to mind, so I spring from the bed and start pacing the room. My mom's Bible, poking out from the top of my backpack, grabs my attention. Julia's words about clinging to

Perfectly Arranged

Scripture flash in my mind's eye, so I pull the Bible out of my bag and sit down with it at the desk. *Lord, please let the answer I'm looking for be in here.*

The spine hangs on by a thread. Running my hand over the cover, the worn brown leather flakes onto my palm. Despite her many challenges, my mom cherishes this Bible and values the truth hidden in its pages. Unfortunately, because of the time difference, I can't call my mom and ask her where to look for answers, so I do what any novice might.

I close my eyes, turn the pages, and let my finger land on the thin paper, hoping divine intervention will lead the way. My finger lands on Deuteronomy 14:21. "Do not eat anything you find already dead. You may give it to an alien living in any of your towns, and he may eat it, or you may sell it to a foreigner..." *Not exactly what I had in mind, but thanks for the heads up on being careful what I eat while I'm here, Lord.*

Determined to find an answer, I flip over a few more pages. My eyes find 2 Kings 9:20. "The lookout reported, 'He has reached them, but he isn't coming back either. The driving is like that of Jehu son of Nimshi—he drives like a madman.'" While that describes the driving conditions here in China and is a good reminder to always buckle up, it still doesn't provide me with the solution I need.

Apparently, random Bible reading isn't the most effective way to discover God's will.

Strumming the pages of my mom's Bible like a stringed instrument, I recall that Julia mentioned her favorite verse was from the book of James and quickly turn there. As I scan through the first chapter, words jump out at me like never before.

"*Count it pure joy, my brothers and sisters, when you encounter trials of many kinds...*"

"*If any of you lacks wisdom, you should ask God, who gives generously to all without finding fault, and it will be given to you ...*"

"*But when you ask, you must believe and not doubt.*"

The words are a salve to my weary soul, and a wave of energy flows through me. I keep reading, absorbing every word. When I reach the last verse—Julia's favorite—my heart beats faster, as if wanting to leap out of my chest. I rub my eyes and refocus on the page before reading it, intending to finding something I can use to change Ms. O'Connor's mind.

"Religion that God our Father accepts as pure and faultless is this: to look after orphans and widows in their distress ..."

Closing my mom's Bible, I push back from the desk, too excited to sit still. My heart pounds, my blood pumps in a quick staccato beat, and I can't help but jump up and down. The answer I've been looking for is right here in front of me.

I had it all wrong.

My mind reels as ideas bombard me. With so much pent-up energy, I pace the room until I've worn a path in the plush carpet. If I proceed with what I believe God is leading me to do, Ms. O'Connor will be upset with me. No, not upset. Livid.

And at what cost?

Calculating the risks, I continue my internal debate. 'Trust me, Nicki.' Those were the words Julia had whispered before I got on the slide this afternoon but not her voice. Could it really be? I close my eyes. *What other choice do I have, Lord?*

Certain of what needs to be done, I pull out my phone and Julia's card from my purse and dial her number.

"*Wei, nǐ hǎo.*"

"Julia, hi, it's Nicki." I reposition myself back on the bed in an effort to remain calm.

"Nicki, is everything okay?" A tinge of worry fills her voice.

"Yes, it's fine. Great, actually." A wide smile expands across my face. "Remember how you said to call if I needed help?"

"Of course."

"Wonderful. Because I know what I need to do and how you can assist me."

13

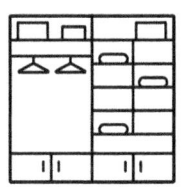

You can't tell whether or not a stuffed bun has meat inside just from looking on the outside.
~ Chinese Proverb

A loud chorus of voices and musical instruments comes over the phone line.

"Hold on, Nicki," Julia shouts over the chaos. Muffled sounds and movements fill my ears. Maybe this isn't the best time for a phone call.

Julia returns to the line, out of breath. "Sorry about that. I'm at church, and the music was starting right when you called. What were you saying?"

I feel bad for interrupting her worship, but this can't wait. "I'll keep it short, I promise. Remember when you invited me to visit the orphanage where you live?" Her acknowledgment encourages me to continue. "Well, I was wondering if we could go there tomorrow?"

Beyond being in a noisy church, the phone is silent on Julia's end.

"Julia, are you still there?"

"Yeah ... I'm here. Nicki, I'm happy to take you to the

orphanage, but are you sure that's what you want to do? There are so many wonderful sites I could show you in Beijing instead."

I know my request seems strange, and this isn't the time for a detailed explanation, but it's imperative that she take me to the orphanage even if she doesn't understand why. I have to convince her, and soon. "It may seem like an odd thing to ask, but you said you'd be willing to help me any way you could. Taking me to the orphanage will help me more than you know."

"Okay," she concedes. "I'll make the arrangements and meet you in the hotel lobby tomorrow at 9:00 a.m."

I clap my hands in excitement. "Thank you, Julia! I'll explain everything when I see you tomorrow."

After I hang up, I'm too hyper to sleep. Plus, it's only seven o'clock. I consider watching TV but doubt there's much on I would understand. Instead, I open my computer and check my email.

My inbox is full of personal emails, but there are no responses from any of the other companies I applied to last month. While the job with Emerson is waiting for me when I return, I'm afraid the offer will be rescinded once Ms. O'Connor finds out what I'm planning.

To be on the safe side, I consider following up with my original applications and sending out new ones as well. If things go awry here and other employment options are no longer available to me, I'll be starting my new year by finding space for myself among the piles in my mother's house. Not the most auspicious way to kick off a new career, that's for sure. But I'll do it if I must.

I set my laptop aside and reach for my journal.

As if I'd been doing so all my life, I speedily record the day's events, including not being able to talk with Ms. O'Connor, meeting Julia, and our adventure on the Great Wall. It's not until I reach the part about the slide that a light bulb goes off.

... I had no desire to get on that metal death trap when I first saw

it. I was certain I'd never see anyone again if I rode down the mountain in that flimsy contraption. But with Julia's encouragement and gentle prodding, I found the courage to get on.

At first, I refused to open my eyes for fear of watching myself fall to my death, but after a few minutes, something changed. I started enjoying myself and relaxed. It wasn't as terrible as I thought it would be! Halfway through the ride, I found myself laughing and not wanting the ride to stop. When I reached the end, I hated to get off.

Isn't it funny how we're so unwilling to do something for fear that it will hurt us or be too difficult, but once we get going, we realize it's not as bad as we thought, and we enjoy ourselves? I can look back over these past few months with my work and the different opportunities presented to me, including this trip with Ms. O'Connor, and see how true this has been.

As I embark on this new path to keep her from shutting down the orphanage, I'm again faced with the same fears and doubts. But like with Julia at the slide queue, I hear God asking me to trust Him. I'm trying to be obedient to that call. I pray that I can be.

I massage my cramped hands, the pressure of gently rubbing my fingers against my underused muscles relaxing and painful at once. Tired from the long day, I close my journal, which is quickly becoming a precious commodity, and promise to return to it tomorrow.

Here's hoping a new day will bring positive news to share within its pages.

WHEN I ARRIVE in the lobby the next morning, Julia is waiting for me. I wind around the tables and chairs and take in her outfit, which I assume is hand-me-down yet showcases her more stylish side. For a quiet girl like her, I wouldn't have expected her to be so fashion-forward. Her messy-bun hairstyle, ripped jeans, puffy sweater vest layered over a hoodie, and canvas sneakers remind me of a look straight out of *Seventeen* magazine.

"Good morning, Nicki." She beams at me and opens her arms.

"Hi, Julia." I accept her embrace. While I'm not usually a touchy-feely kind with people I've just met, the gesture is natural with Julia.

She releases me. "Did you eat?"

"I ordered room service." I quickly scan the lobby for any sign of Ms. O'Connor and don't see her. "Are you ready to go?"

"Yes, I have a taxi waiting outside."

After we climb into the cab, Julia rattles off our destination. The driver's eyebrows scrunch into his lined forehead by the time she finishes, but he shrugs his shoulders and maneuvers the car into the congested traffic.

"Nicki, you're sure this is what you want to do?" Julia leans back in the seat.

I nod. I need to understand firsthand about orphanages—how they operate, what they're like, exactly what happens to the children in their care, and what happens if they are not cared for—so I can show Ms. O'Connor the consequences of shutting one down. Visiting Julia's home is crucial to gaining the information I need.

First, though, I must ensure Julia understands what I'm doing and why. Repositioning myself in the seat, I search for just the right words to explain my strong desire to see her home. "Remember at the slide yesterday how you asked me to trust you?"

"Yes, but what does that have to do with spending the day at my orphanage?"

"Because I need you to do that today. Trust me." I take a deep breath before sharing everything with her. Carefully choosing the best words I can find, I explain what I feel called to do and sum up Ms. O'Connor's affiliation with New Hope and her intentions to stop funding it.

"Then last night, God showed me that I needed to stop talking and instead show her what will happen if she goes through with her decision. For me to do that, though, I need to spend time in an orphanage."

Her eyes widen, and a look of sadness covers her face. "Your boss wants to shut down an orphanage?" Her voice cracks as if she's about to cry.

"I'm afraid so." I bite my lip.

Without saying another word, she turns away and stares out the window. My heart breaks for what she must be feeling, but I stay silent in the hope that time, rather than me, will give her what she needs.

After a few minutes, she clears her throat, wipes her eyes, and turns toward me. "Why?" Her question comes out a whisper.

I release a heavy exhale. "My boss is upset and allowing her emotions to dictate her actions."

"I'm surprised you would be willing to work for someone who would do something so cruel."

I jump at her harsh tone. "That's just it. Ms. O'Connor isn't normally like this. In fact, she's quite generous. A few weeks ago, she hosted an event in her home so underprivileged teens could shop in her closet for a dress to wear to their social event and then keep the dresses. If they don't fit, she pays to have them altered or buys them something of their own. A person who does that is someone who, at their core, is unselfish and kindhearted."

"Then why does she want to shut down the orphanage?"

"She's hurting, and her gut reaction is to have others suffer along with her. I know deep down she doesn't want to do this, but she thinks closing the orphanage will take her pain away."

"But it won't!"

"You're right, and that's why I need to change her mind. But talking to her isn't going to do anything. I've tried. However, actions speak louder than words, so I'm hoping that I can show her why her decision is wrong rather than arguing with her about it."

Julia nods as if contemplating my words. When she finally speaks, her voice is soft again. "I think it's wonderful that you are willing to go to such great lengths to help the orphanage. Most people wouldn't bother."

Leaning my head back against the seat, I stifle a laugh. I wish I could take credit, but none of this is my doing. Had it not been for Julia, I don't think I would have ever looked at that Bible verse last night. It was as if our paths were meant to cross.

"You give me too much credit," I tell her. "It was actually the Bible verse you quoted yesterday that inspired me. Well, that and God." We both laugh as the car pulls into a driveway and stops.

"We're here." Julia unbuckles her seat belt, pays the driver, and opens the car door.

Before I exit the taxi, I close my eyes and focus my heart on God. *Lord, if a story about disadvantaged, low-income teens not going to prom moves Ms. O'Connor to open her closet and donate her gowns, then I pray you'll show me something here that will open her heart to these orphans.*

STEPPING OUT OF THE CAB, I wrap my jacket tighter around my chest. Despite the glaring sunshine, there's a chill permeating the air. Julia's hoodie and vest combo seem to be enough to keep her warm, so perhaps what I feel is just fear creeping its way into my head and heart.

As the taxi driver pulls away, I look up to survey the building. Compared to the buildings on either side of it, there's nothing special that identifies this as an orphanage. Just like the one Ms. O'Connor and I had visited, there are no kid posters, bright colors, or playground equipment advertising this as a home for children.

It's simply a white brick multilevel high-rise that one would find in any downtown skyline. A casual passerby might think it was a bank, shopping center, or commercial property of some kind. But an orphanage? I highly doubt it.

When my eyes return to street level, I see Julia waving to me from the entry doors.

"Nicki!" She is barely audible over all the street noise. "This way."

I take one last look up and down the congested street, then walk to the building and push through the revolving door. Once again, my heart sinks at the sparse and sterile environment that comprises what should, in my opinion, be a warm and colorful space. Sadly, the lobby houses nothing more than a few chairs and a central information desk. Is every place in China like this?

When I arrive at the desk, Julia hands me a lanyard. "This is your guest badge. You'll need to wear it at all times at the orphanage."

Not wanting to stir up trouble, I drape the plastic card with nothing but Chinese characters over my neck and wait for further instructions. "Is that it?"

Julia nods and directs us to the elevators. "We'll start on the third floor." She pushes the elevator button. "That's where the babies and toddlers are. I figured we'd start there and work our way up."

"Does every floor have a different age group?" I ask as we step inside the elevator.

"Yes. The orphanage takes up the majority of the building, with kids ranging from newborn to teens. They spread them out for obvious reasons." The elevator dings with our arrival.

The sweet aromas of baby lotion and powder hit me upon the doors opening. Accompanied by the sounds of competing cries and squeals of delight from little ones, I have no doubt this is the nursery.

"Nicki, welcome to Mother's Love Children's Home." Julia opens her arms wide, introducing me to the orphanage and all that it encompasses. "Come. I'll show you everything there is to see." She leads me down the hall to the room from which the baby noises and smells emanate. "Would you like me to tell you what I know about the orphanage?"

"That would be great."

Like a walking encyclopedia, Julia rattles off a slew of details about Mother's Love, including when the orphanage was founded, the number of children taken in each year, and why there are more girls than boys. As I listen to her recite the information from memory, my eyes remain glued to my immediate surroundings.

The beige walls and white tile flooring exude an environment more conducive to business than childcare. At least a series of windows shine additional light into the dimly lit space. On each side of the hallway are Dutch doors that open on top and close on the bottom. In all, there are five rooms on this floor.

Julia stops at the first one on our right. "The nursery. These are the youngest babies we have," she says, leaning against the door. "Some are a few days old and some a few months."

Curious, I crane my neck to look inside. Unlike the nursery at my church back home, the room is filled with rows of cribs crammed side-by-side in the small room. At least fifty baby beds must fill the space.

Scanning the cribs, I see tightly wrapped blankets with tufts of black hair sticking out of several of them. On each end of the beds is a laminated index card with Chinese characters, presumably the baby's name. Wooden clipboards dangle next to them.

Six women dressed in matching sunshine-colored aprons race around the room. They acknowledge our presence with a smile but keep focused on their tasks. No doubt they're busy feeding bottles, changing diapers, and doing their best to shower love on these infants from sunrise to sunset.

"Wow, I had no idea an orphanage would be like this." My body tenses at the sight in front of me. While I didn't expect it to look like a play place created by the Imagineers at Disney, the room's sparse set-up and limited functionality take me by surprise. I clutch my chest and resist the urge to make a quick escape.

"There are more children than caretakers, so there's not much individualized attention," Julia says as if reading my mind. "They do their best, and I try to help when I can, but there's only so much we can do."

A sudden heaviness pierces my heart. For whatever reason, these children were unwanted or abandoned by their parents. What a terrible way for their lives to have started. But at least at the orphanage, someone was caring for them.

Was the setup at Ms. O'Connor's father's orphanage the same? Most likely. And now she wanted to have it shut down? I close my eyes at the sounds of mewing and crying infants. No, it was just too horrible to imagine.

"There's much more to see. Let's keep going."

Julia's voice pulls me out of my thoughts. I hesitate at the door, unable to move. The emotions welling up inside of me after watching these babies are unlike anything I've experienced before. It's as if a tiny crack has burst through the thick wall I've built around my heart. I didn't think that was possible.

"Nicki," Julia calls out to me from down the hall. "Are you coming?"

I take one last look at the helpless infants and wonder what my heart is trying to tell me. My emotions don't usually run amok like this. Whenever it comes to children, I'm hard as flint. But for some reason, I can't deny the strange tenderness gripping me. Worried that I'm growing soft, I quickly push the thoughts and feelings aside and run to catch up with my guide.

As we move from room to room on each floor, everything looks the same except the kids become bigger and the beds larger. The top floors, which the older children occupy, are eerily quiet.

"All the kids are at school right now," Julia says as we quickly make our way through those levels.

"School?" I'm confused. "Aren't they on holiday?"

"Why would they be?" Julia grins. "The Chinese don't celebrate holidays as you do in America."

"Oh, that's right!" I smack my palm against my forehead. "I forgot."

"No worries." Julia laughs. "You're not the first foreigner who's come here and asked that question."

I appreciate her sense of humor and understanding of my cultural ignorance. I have a lot to learn about the world outside my little Connecticut bubble.

"Now that we've seen all the floors, what would you like to do next?" Julia asks as we walk back toward the elevators. "It's almost lunch and naptime here, so there won't be much going on."

My mind processes everything I've seen over the last two hours, and I'm not sure how to answer her question. None of it will help me persuade Ms. O'Connor to reverse her decision.

If I'm going to convince her how important it is to continue funding the orphanage, I need more. Something so emotionally charged, it will tug on her heartstrings, and hopefully her purse strings, so she can't say no.

"I don't know," I tell her, downtrodden. "Don't get me wrong. Everything you've shown me so far has been great. But simply telling Ms. O'Connor about the day-to-day operations won't be enough to make a difference with her. She understands what needs to be done for a business—an orphanage—to succeed, so I doubt that approach will work with her."

The sparkle in her eyes diminishes. "So understanding the vital role orphanages have in these children's lives isn't enough?"

"Sadly, no." I shake my head. "I think it will take more. Something like the girls from the gown event, where she stepped in when no one else would because she felt responsible for looking after those whose parents couldn't or wouldn't." I exhale in frustration, uncertain such a thing even exists.

"Oh." Julia turns pale and quiet.

"But I appreciate you bringing me here today." I glance back down the hallway at the rooms we left behind. "I guess I was hoping for a miracle of some kind. Maybe I just misunderstood."

Pushing up on her glasses with one hand, Julia presses the elevator button with the other. "Nicki," she finally speaks up. "There's one more part of the orphanage I'm going to show you where we don't often take outsiders." The elevator doors open for us to step inside. "I think once you see it, you'll think differently."

14

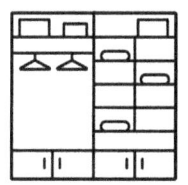

Water spilled can never be retrieved.
~ Chinese Proverb

The elevator stops two floors above where we got on. When I step into the hallway, there's nothing notably different about the space—the flooring, walls, and windows that decorated the lower levels of the orphanage look identical to this one. I look for clues that would offer some idea of the room's purpose, but as with most things in the building, there aren't many.

My curiosity is piqued. "What's on this floor?"

Julia stops in front of one of the only two doors in the hallway. "Do you remember when you asked me yesterday why I stay here at the orphanage?"

"Vaguely," I say in all honesty. A lot has transpired since then, and I'm still a bit jetlagged.

"Well, when I said I stayed because I want to give back, that was only half the truth." She looks down at the floor, and her shoulders sag.

"Okay, so what's the other half?" I place my hand on her shoulder.

When she glances up at me, her eyes are moist. "My sister."

"Your sister?" My eyebrows rise toward my hairline. "Why didn't you tell me you had a sibling here?"

"I ... I wasn't—" Julia hesitates and fiddles with the zipper on her vest. "I wasn't sure you'd understand her condition."

"What condition?" I can't imagine anything so terrible that Julia would be ashamed to tell me the truth. What could it possibly be?

"My sister ... well ... she's *different*."

I want to tell her most sisters think that about their siblings, but this probably isn't the right time for a joke. "What do you mean *different?*"

Julia clears her throat. "My sister and I are at this orphanage because she was born with a condition that keeps her from looking or acting the same as other children. The workers said my parents were embarrassed to have a child like that, so they abandoned us both here."

"Oh." My brain processes the information then quickly floods with questions. I open my mouth to begin asking them.

But Julia holds up her hand. For the first time since arriving on the floor, she smiles. "I knew you'd have questions."

We giggle, and I'm grateful for the lightness of the moment.

"Let's go inside, and I'll explain everything."

While she knocks on the door, I anxiously wait and wonder what's on the other side of it. Why would the orphanage have a special wing they keep separate from everything else? What could Julia possibly show me that would affect Ms. O'Connor and persuade her to forgo her decision?

I try not to let my mind wander too far with speculation and remind myself that I'm not home anymore. Just because it seems unusual for me doesn't mean it is for them.

The door opens slightly and a petite young Chinese woman answers. Julia quickly takes charge, and the two talk like old friends. Despite the friendliness between them, the nurse looks at me with suspicion the entire time. Finally, she opens the door wider and lets us in.

"*Xièxie*," I say, thanking her as I step inside. She smiles at me, and the tension in my stomach and shoulders releases a bit. The room is surprisingly different than the ones below. Soft, playful music fills the space, and bright colors are splashed across the floor, from toys to carpet squares. Toward the back of the room, a small cluster of children and workers are gathered in a circle on the floor.

Julia waves me over to the side of the room. "They're having story time right now." She sits on one of the few beds in the space and invites me to join her. I walk around the various-sized mattresses and sit down next to her.

"What is this place, Julia?"

She presses her finger to her lips and doesn't answer me.

Once the music stops, the worker at the center of the circle closes the book and speaks slowly to the children. When she's finished, they rise from the floor and head toward us. Eight children, some appearing to be teenagers, make their way closer to me, and my heart races. The almond-shaped eyes are different from their Chinese counterparts. Flat facial features and tongues that seem too large for their mouths tell me all I need to know.

"These children have Down Syndrome," I whisper.

"Yes." She rises from the bed.

Stuck in place, I watch her race to the group. When she does, loud shouts of joy erupt, and the children fight to embrace her. Within seconds, Julia is lost in a sea of black hair.

I can only sit and smile at the beautiful scene unfolding in front of me, trying not to disturb or disrupt it.

The workers quickly rush to Julia's aid and manage to restore order. The smaller children are taken to one side of the room while the older children walk in my direction. I leap up off the bed and smile at the teenage girl who takes over the seat I just vacated. She smiles and waves at me before wrapping herself under the covers. As I return the sweet gesture, the lights suddenly dim, and I realize it's naptime.

Squinting in the darkened room, I search for Julia. She's kneeling next to a bed a few down from where I'm standing. Tiptoeing over to her, I watch her rubbing a girl's back and whispering into her ear. Julia peeks up from her task and acknowledges my presence when I sit in silence on the bed but doesn't say anything.

When the room is filled with nothing more than heavy breathing and sleep-inducing music, Julia scoots closer to me.

"Is this your sister?"

She looks over her shoulder. "Yes. Her name is Mingyu."

"Mingyu." The name blends with ease on my tongue. "That's a beautiful name."

"It means bright jade. I gave her a jade bracelet to help her remember." She points to a sparkly deep green bangle wrapped around her sister's slender wrist.

We fall silent and watch Mingyu's chest rise and fall as she sleeps. I inch closer to Julia, anxious to know more.

"Now that I understand more about this space, can you answer some questions for me?"

"You can ask me anything." Julia glances back over her shoulder one more time. "What do you want to know?" Her voice barely rises above a whisper.

"Well, for starters, I thought Chinese families were only allowed to have one child. How did your parents manage to have two?"

"It's true that China had a one-child policy, but despite their efforts to control the population, they can't control a woman's ability to produce only one child at a time."

My eyes widen. "You're a twin?" Without letting her answer, I peek around Julia to get a better look at Mingyu. Although her condition has caused most of her facial features to differ from her sister's, a few resemblances stand out. They share the same nose, jawline, and shiny black hair. "Did your doctor say why your sister was born with Down syndrome and you weren't?"

Julia shrugs and looks down at her hands. "We don't know why or how it happened."

"I'm sorry." I place my hand over hers. "This can't be easy."

"It's not. I feel guilty knowing—" Tears pool at the corner of her eyes. "That's why I told you at lunch that my faith is so important to me. It's the only thing that helps me endure the physical and emotional challenges we face."

Wanting to encourage her sweet heart, I touch her lightly. "You're a wonderful sister."

"I try, but some days are harder than others." Julia's eyes rest back on her sister.

I squeeze her hand, hoping the small gesture will communicate my empathy. I often feel the same way about my mom and her issues.

As anxious as I am to ask my next question, I give Julia a moment to regroup. In all likelihood, it won't be an easy one to answer, but I must ask. "So, if you weren't born with special needs, why didn't your parents keep you?"

"That's a good question." She tilts her head to the ceiling. "When my parents dropped us off, the workers asked them why they didn't want to keep me. They said they were worried over time I may become like Mingyu and that they couldn't handle having children who were different." Heat creeps into her cheeks.

"In China, we always worry about *mianzi*—saving face. If anything can disgrace or humiliate your family or your name, you hide it to avoid shame. So, they brought us here." She exhales a deep breath. "While I'm mad at them for abandoning us, I'm grateful they chose this particular orphanage and didn't leave Mingyu alone. It's better that I'm here to help take care of her and the others."

I'm startled by her last sentence. "They're good to her here, right?"

"Oh, they're wonderful!" Julia says vehemently, before quieting herself. "I just meant I can't imagine not being part of Mingyu's life."

"I figured." I smile at her again. "So that's why you never left? Because of Mingyu?"

"That's the main reason. In our culture, family is the priority, and I couldn't leave her here to follow my own desires. I hope to study or live abroad someday, but not any time soon."

"I can understand why you'd be hesitant to leave. Your sister or this place."

"Mother's Love is special." Julia lifts her chin. "It's one of the few orphanages that care for special needs orphans. Not all of them are willing to accept children with their conditions."

"Really?" I balk at the thought. "Not all orphanages have designated spaces for these kids?" I scan the room and note how homey it is for them.

Julia shakes her head. "No, they try to keep them together in one place. It's what makes this home unique."

"I had no idea ..."

"That's why I wanted to bring you up here. Like I said, we don't let many outsiders on this floor unless they want to adopt a child like Mingyu. But I thought seeing the room may encourage you."

"Encourage me how?" I tilt my head.

"Well, maybe like Mother's Love, there's something special about New Hope Orphanage. That's fairly common. Perhaps you could visit and discover if there's something there that would change Ms. O'Connor's mind, something special like this, so she's moved to keep funding it."

I let her words sink in. Could there be something so special about New Hope?

"Thank you for sharing this with me. It means more to me than you can know." I lean over and hug her.

Just then, a worker approaches us and talks with Julia in hushed tones.

"She asked if we could leave and have our conversation elsewhere." She stands, indicating I should do the same.

"Of course. I'm sorry."

Rising from the edge of the bed, I take one last glance at Mingyu. "I can see why she's named after a stone. She's precious."

"She is." Julia leads me out of the room.

When we close the door behind us, another question pops into my mind. "Julia, what's your given name in Chinese?"

She grins. "I was wondering if you were ever going to ask." She loops her arm in mine as we walk down the hall toward the elevator. "It's Mingzhu, which means bright pearl."

Bright pearl. I couldn't think of a more appropriate name for Julia. Like her namesake, she shines beautifully in a world that isn't always so pretty, and her warm inner glow helps others feel like they're special. Although her parents may never see the gem she's become, they must have seen something in their daughter to give her such a name.

"I love it." I squeeze her arm. "But if it's okay with you, I'm going to keep calling you Julia. I don't think Mingzhu rolls off my tongue as easily."

She throws back her head. "You can call me anything you like as long as you don't call me Al."

I chuckle at her knowledge of pop culture and one of Paul Simon's greatest hits. "How do you know that song? For someone your age, I didn't think you'd know much about the eighties."

"I have a secret stash of *People* magazine, remember?"

As we giggle our way to the elevators, I make a note to add *witty* to my list of descriptors for her. When I tell others about her, I want to make sure they know how wonderful she is.

Waiting for the elevator to take us back downstairs, I watch Julia as she plays with her phone. If it weren't for her, I would have just given up after today.

But not now. I'd been led to Julia's orphanage, after all.

Now I know exactly what I need to do.

AFTER VISITING THE ORPHANAGE, I walk to a nearby Starbucks. The short trek takes only a few minutes, and while the scent of coffee alone rejuvenates my tired mind and body, the walk didn't satisfy my desire to see and hear more of my surroundings. I love mingling with the Chinese along the crowded sidewalks, looking at the everyday city life up close, and noting the details of the people and places unable to be seen from a car window.

When I arrive at the coffee shop, Longchen is talking with a ruggedly handsome guy with blond hair and tan skin at a table by the window. I'm hesitant to intrude on their intense conversation, but the clock is working against me. I remove my coat and head straight for their table, hoping the blond won't find my presence bothersome.

"Hi, Longchen."

Both men stop talking and look in my direction. Longchen smiles, then leaps from his seat and extends his hand. "Nicki, so nice to see you." His warm hand encases mine with a firm yet gentle touch.

I breathe a sigh of relief, grateful my timing isn't an issue. "I hope I'm not interrupting you." I steal a glance at Longchen's companion. Fortunately, he doesn't seem upset by my sudden appearance either.

"Oh, no." Longchen smiles. "Ben and I were just finishing." He cocks his head toward Ben. "Nicki, this is Ben Carrington."

I nod at Ben, and he flashes a friendly smile back.

"Hi, Nicki. It's a pleasure to meet you."

"Hi, Ben. Is Longchen showing you around Beijing as well?"

"I didn't realize he offered that service." Ben chuckles then gazes at Longchen. "Have you been holding out on me, friend?"

The older man shakes his head at Ben and turns his attention back to me. "Ben and I were just discussing the progress he's making teaching English to Chinese students. I volunteer there, and that's how we met."

"Oh, I see." I turn my attention to Ben. "Well, that's a shame because Longchen arranged my visit to the Great Wall, and it was wonderful."

"Is that so?" Ben rubs his chin.

Longchen belts out another of his deep laughs. "Ben, you are too much." He holds out his chair to me. "Nicki, have a seat and visit with Ben for a moment. I need some more tea to get me through the afternoon."

Before I can protest, Longchen vanishes through the crowd of people, leaving me alone with Ben.

With no other choice, I do my best to gracefully settle in the tall bar chair without embarrassing myself in front of this stranger. Once I've accomplished my mission, I focus on him. "So, you teach English here?" I brush my hair behind my ear. "That's an interesting job."

"Yeah, not quite where I imagined myself to be a few years ago, but it's been a blessing." Ben spins his coffee cup and stares at the dark brown liquid swirling in front of him. "I can't imagine leaving."

Touched by his dedication to his work, I'm curious to know more. "How long have you been here?"

He squints his eyes, calculating. "Almost five years."

"Five years, really?" I shake my head. "I don't know if I could be away from home that long."

"Where's home?" he asks, turning his gaze on me.

Eyes as dreamy and as green as the jade bracelet I saw earlier on Mingyu's wrist.

A girl could easily get lost in them if she weren't careful. Not me, of course. Just a girl, in general.

"New England ... Bridgeport, Connecticut to be exact," I say, somewhat tongue-tied.

"Ahh, a northern girl." One side of his mouth tilts upward. "I admire people who can handle the cold like that. I'm having a hard enough time adjusting to the dreary weather here, even after five years."

"I take it you're from the south then?"

"Born and raised in Texas." He places his hand on his heart.

A chuckle bursts from my mouth. "What's a cowboy like you doing in a place like this?"

"Well, that's a long story." He lets out a long sigh. "Basically, a broken heart and a door of opportunity that only God could orchestrate."

I fall silent at his words. They sound eerily reminiscent of my reasons for being here.

"Yeah," Ben picks up the conversation. "That's the common reaction I get when I tell that to all the girls." He laughs. "Guess I'm going to have to work on that."

"Oh, I'm sorry." My face heats up. "It's just that, well, it sounds like the reason I'm here."

"And what brings you to the land of dragons and tea leaves, Nicki?"

Lifting my shoulders to my ears, I refrain from repeating that an opportunity only God could orchestrate landed me in a country around the world from my own. "I guess you could say I'm on an expedition of sorts."

"An expedition, huh? You've piqued my interest." He leans forward, close enough to me that the soft lines on his face come into full view. "What is it you're looking for?"

If only I knew.

At one point, I thought finding the address on Mr. O'Connor's business card was it, but now I realize it's so much more than that. At the moment, I feel like I'm throwing darts blindfolded and hoping they land close to the bullseye. Sadly, that's not a good answer. But it is nice to have someone interested in the things that matter to me.

"Nicki?" Ben waves his hand in front of my face. "I'm sorry if I was pushing you to talk. I get it if you're uncomfortable telling your story to a stranger. Maybe you can share it with me another time."

"Thanks for understanding, Ben." I exhale. "I don't have all the answers yet, and I'm not sure if I ever will. That's why I need to talk with Longchen. Maybe I can at least find one or two."

As if on cue, Longchen sidles up to the table. "I'm at your service, Nicki." He gestures with his hands as if he were Vanna White displaying letters on *Wheel of Fortune*. "Now that I have my afternoon green tea."

"Here ya go, Longchen." Ben jumps out of his chair and offers it to Longchen. "I wouldn't want you to keep the pretty lady waiting."

I blush at his compliment. I can't remember the last time a guy my age referred to me as attractive.

"Thanks, Ben. Can we finish our talk at the school later this week?"

"Sure, no problem. I'll see you there." He pats Longchen on the back.

Slipping on his coat, Ben looks in my direction. "Nicki, it was great talking to you. Enjoy your time here in Beijing, and I hope you find what you're searching for." He pulls a beanie on. "And maybe someday I'll get to hear the whole story."

"It was great meeting you too, Ben. Keep working on that line." I chuckle. "And if our paths cross again, you can practice it on me."

"Will do. Take care." He winks at me.

I watch him as he makes his way out the exit and onto the sidewalk. While it's unlikely I'll ever see him again, if I did, I have no doubt he'd be a great listener.

"Ben's a nice young man, isn't he?" As if he could read my mind, Longchen interrupts my thinking.

Slightly embarrassed at being caught staring, I turn my attention back to the man seated across from me. "Yes, he is."

"I'm sure we could talk more about Ben, but I have a feeling you asked to visit with me for another reason." Stirring his drink, Longchen looks at me with hard intention. "Why don't you tell me what's so important that you had Julia arrange this meeting for us?"

I lock my fingers together to keep them from trembling. Even though Julia called Longchen for me, I was adamant she did not disclose to him why I wanted to meet. It was a conversation I needed to have with him myself.

Because so much is riding on this meeting, I decide to be honest with him and not play games. "Well, you know I spent the day with Julia at Mother's Love, right?"

"Yes." He arches his eyebrows. "She told me you asked to tour the facilities. I was a little surprised, but under the circumstances of your visit, I figured you had your reasons. What did you think of the orphanage?"

Just remembering the beauty of the place and people makes my heart flutter. "Oh, I loved it. The place is amazing." Emotions rise in my throat, attempting to inhibit my ability to speak, but I swallow the lump and push them away. "I have to be honest with you, I'm not that fond of children, so I had no idea what to expect when I went in there."

Longchen lets out a small laugh. "May I ask ... why don't you like children?"

Since his tone was so kind, I was compelled to answer him. "Let's just say the reason is messy." Or, more specifically, they are, with all the equipment they require. And the toys. Lots and lots of toys. All of that translates to clutter for me, and after living in a house filled to the brim with stuff, I refuse to let a little person destroy the order I've worked so hard to create in my home and life.

Plus, I'm not the nurturing type, which after witnessing the sweet exchange with Julia and Mingyu, I think is an important quality for a parent. A thought intrudes. *Can you learn to be nurturing?*

Longchen leans toward me. "Children aren't meant to be

complications. They're meant to be blessings, even if their situations remain complex. Or messy."

"I'm sure they are. I just don't see them that way right now."

"I understand that you may feel that way now, but perhaps you'll change your mind someday. I, myself, did not always understand that they truly are one of God's greatest gifts." His eyes light up as he talks, and again I see the fatherly qualities that I miss so much in my dad.

"So, you have children?" Despite the time I have spent with Longchen, I don't know much of importance about him. His kind demeanor and gentle approach draw me into wanting to change that.

He beams with pride. "Yes, I have a son and a granddaughter. They live in the city near me and my wife."

"That's so nice." I look away and try to hold back the tears filling my eyes, wishing I had that same loving family unit in my life. While I know my mom loves me and I love her, it's just not the same without my dad. Perhaps it never will be.

"Nicki"—Longchen's voice permeates my thought—"as much as I'd love to keep talking about my family, I don't think that's why you asked to meet with me. What is it you need my help with?"

I turn back toward him. "W—well, I was wondering if it would be possible for me to visit New Hope Orphanage tomorrow." I pause before revealing my final wish. "Without Ms. O'Connor?"

"May I ask why?"

Averting my eyes, I purse my lips. I want to tell him the truth, but like the lion in *The Wizard of Oz*, the courage I need to share my reasons with him eludes me.

"It's an unusual request, Nicki," he says when I don't respond immediately. "As much as I'd like to help you, without Ms. O'Connor accompanying us, I don't think I can take you there."

"What? No!" Pairs of eyes from around the room focus on

me, so I lower my voice. "Longchen, I need to visit the orphanage. It's critical that I go there—alone."

He leans in closer to me. "If it's so important for you to go, why not take Ms. O'Connor with you? What could you possibly do there that she couldn't help with? From what I understand, she's powerful and influential."

Yes, but just not in the way you're thinking. I rub my neck and take a deep breath. I have to tell him the truth, but the thought of saying it, especially after being at Mother's Love today, sounds so cruel.

While exhaling, I consider my next words. "It's just that ... well, the truth is, Ms. O'Connor is not happy about the orphanage or the fact that her father had been a major funding source of it."

"I see." Longchen keeps a straight face that matches the solemn tone of his voice.

"And I have a strong feeling that she's going to remove all financial aid from the orphanage. If she does, I'm afraid it will cause the orphanage to shut down."

His forehead wrinkles, and the corners of his mouth turn downward with his pinched lips. "Yes, that would definitely cause a problem."

"I didn't want to tell you because it sounds so terrible. But you have to understand she's not a cruel person. I think it's a knee-jerk reaction to discovering the orphanage and her father's involvement in it. They had a complicated relationship, which I think is motivating her actions. But if she could understand how important the orphanage is to the children there, I think she'd change her mind." My heart races with every word.

If I don't slow down, I'll be lucky if Longchen can follow any of my reasoning. I clasp my hands in front of me, letting my heart settle while Longchen sits in silence across from me.

"And that's why you want to visit?"

"Yes, I need to find something—anything—about the orphanage that will convince her to change her mind. I can't do that without knowing more about it. I need to see firsthand what's going on if I hope to save it."

Longchen pushes his drink aside and rests his arms on the table. "I know that my country has a terrible problem with unwanted children. It's an issue that is not getting better. That's why the orphanages we have here are so important."

"Then you know better than anyone why I need to go there." I keep the pleading from my voice but am sure it's coming through my eyes. "So, you'll make the arrangements for me to visit tomorrow?"

I force down a sick feeling as I search his scrunched-up face. "Longchen, you'll help me, won't you?"

"I admire you for what you want to do, and I'd be happy to call and make the arrangements." He rubs his fingers against the table. "However ..."

"However, what?" I stand up and then sit down again, just as quickly.

"Well, I'm willing to help you, but I have to let you know that I must inform Ms. O'Connor of your plans."

My heart drops into my stomach. "Why? Why would you tell her what I'm doing when you know what she intends to do?"

"Because she has hired me. Just like you, she's my boss while she's here." Frustration tinges his voice. "To not tell her would be dishonest and could compromise my reputation."

Despair crawls across my skin, leaving pinpricks of perspiration on my hands and brow. *This can't be happening.*

I lean over the table toward him. "Longchen, you can't tell her. If you do, it will ruin everything for me."

"I'm sorry, Nicki. As much as I want to help you—and I do—I have to tell her. Otherwise, you can try to think of another way to convince her that doesn't involve you visiting the orphanage. It's your decision."

Resignation sits on my shoulders with the weight of an overstuffed box filled with junk. I understand why he feels it's necessary even if it complicates my plan, and I admire him all the more for it.

What do I do now? I gaze out the window, biting my thumbnail. If Ms. O'Connor finds out about my visit to the orphanages, she'll be upset. She's already warned me to stay out of the situation. And there's no telling what she'll do when she finds out what I'm up to, including firing me, revoking her endorsement of me with Emerson, and abandoning me here in China to get home on my own. Am I willing to take that risk?

I contemplate my options before blurting out my answer. My mind is muddled with conflicting images of the orphanage today, the verse from James, my mother's cramped house, and my dead-in-the-water business.

Yet so much is riding on this. I close my eyes. *Lord, help me make the right decision.* As soon as the prayer escapes my lips, Mingyu's sleeping face flashes in my memory, and my eyes pop open.

Confident of what I must do, I turn to Longchen. "Please, make the call."

15

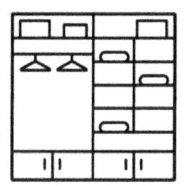

One will not jump into the river until the boat overturns.
~ Chinese Proverb

The following day, I arrive at New Hope with my trusty sidekick. I don't need just Julia's translating services for this trip. Her support has been essential these last few days, and I'm not sure how I could have made it without her.

For this visit, I don't plan on just touring the facilities as I did at Mother's Love the day before. If this visit is going to cost me everything, then I have to be all in. I intend to spend as much time as I can doing hands-on work to unearth the one thing that will change Ms. O'Connor's decision.

As we wait for Assistant Director Chang in the lobby, I pace the room.

"Nicki, why don't you sit down? You're making me nervous with your fidgeting." Julia pats the seat next to her.

"I can't." I crane my neck toward the door leading to the back. "So much is riding on what I discover. If I can find something that will appeal to Ms. O'Connor's sense of giving and her desire to help those she feels are being neglected or forgotten, then I may have a chance of changing her mind. If I don't, well ..."

"Wearing yourself out here won't do you any good. Keep your energy. You may need it."

I surrender and sit. Julia's hand pushes down on my knee, and I realize my leg is bouncing.

"Sorry." I cross my legs.

Ten minutes later, the door opens, and Assistant Director Chang waves us over. After the formal introductions and greeting, we settle into her office.

"I'm surprised to see you back so soon after our visit the other day. I didn't think you'd come back until Director Wu returned." She pours herself a cup of tea from a traditional Chinese teapot. "Care for a cup?"

"No, thank you," Julia and I say in unison.

Unbothered by our refusal, the assistant director takes a sip, places her drink on the saucer with a light touch, and smiles. "How can I help you today?"

I scoot toward the edge of my chair. "Julia and I would like to spend some time here at the orphanage to get a better feel for the place."

Still smiling, she locks her fingers together and leans on her desk. "I see. And will Ms. O'Connor be joining you on the tour as well?"

My back stiffens. "No, actually, she won't."

"Well, that's too bad." She takes another sip of tea. "When she left here the other day, she seemed a little agitated. Perhaps a tour of the facilities would put her at ease."

"Yes, that sounds like a great idea." I fake a smile. "I'll be sure to suggest that to her."

"Wonderful." Ms. Chang reaches for her phone. "Let me inform my secretary that I'll be out of my office for a while as I show you around."

"No." My sharp response resounds in the otherwise quiet room, and I cringe inside.

She takes her hand off the receiver. "I'm sorry." Her fingers intertwine as confusion laces her brow. "I don't understand. I thought you wanted to spend some time here."

"No—I mean, yes." I glance at Julia to calm myself. *Cool it, Nic. You can't mess this up.* "What I meant was I don't just want a tour of the facilities. I was thinking that we could spend some time in one or two of the rooms, observing everything that goes on."

"That's an unusual request, Miss Mayfield. It's not often people, especially foreigners, ask to stay in a room with the children. Unless, of course, it's a parent in the middle of the adoption process." She tilts her head and smiles at us. "I'm sure you can understand why, for security reasons, I won't be able to allow that."

Upon hearing her words, my entire body tenses. Every fiber in my being wants to throw a fit, but that won't help the situation. From what I remember of my pre-trip research, the Chinese aren't fond of emotional outbursts. I'll have to try a more rational approach.

I take a deep breath. "I understand your concern and your safety protocol, and I applaud you for being so diligent in protecting the children. But I can assure you I'm not a danger to anyone. I simply want to sit in the room and observe."

"Again, Miss Mayfield, I'm sorry, but the answer is—"

Before she can finish, Julia confronts the assistant director in their native tongue. Their sharp tones and raised voices contradict the calm and rational behavior preferred between professionals. My eyes dart back and forth between them as if watching a tennis match. After several minutes of sparring, Ms. Chang pushes back from her desk.

"Well, Miss Mayfield, it seems that your friend here is convincing." She walks toward another door directly behind our seats. "Please, follow me."

Shocked by Ms. Chang's words, I rise from my seat and fall in step behind her.

Walking out of her office, I lean over to Julia. "What did you say to her?"

"The truth," Julia whispers back to me.

I stop dead in my tracks and try not to lose it. "What truth?"

"Nicki, I didn't have a choice." Her shoulders droop. "I had to tell her about Ms. O'Connor's plans to withdraw funding. I'm sorry."

"What?" My voice level goes up a notch. "Why would you do that?"

"I had to, or you wouldn't have gotten in."

"How do you know that? I could have worn her down until she caved."

"*Bù tū guòbā chi, bù zài guò biān zhùan.*"

I rub my forehead. "Julia, you know I don't understand what you just said."

"It's an ancient Chinese proverb that says if one were not planning to eat rice crusts, one would not be circling the cooking pan."

"Now I'm really confused."

She touches my arm. "It means people don't hang around without a purpose. She knew you weren't here to be an extra pair of hands. If I didn't tell her the truth, you weren't getting in."

"Great." I run my fingers through my hair. "So now what?"

"Now, let's see if she can help us. Knowing that the funding is at risk, I'm sure she'll be more than happy to point us in the right direction. We don't have time to play games. Too much is at risk."

I tilt my head back and let out a deep breath. She's right. I should have been honest with Ms. Chang in the first place.

"All right." I squeeze her hand. "Thanks for getting us in. I don't know what I'd do without you."

"You can thank me once we find that special thing, or special someone, Ms. O'Connor can't resist."

AFTER A SHORT TREK through the orphanage, Assistant Director Chang leads us to an outdoor area where a group of young toddlers play.

"What are we doing out here?" I lift my hands to shield my eyes from the sun.

The woman's black hair shines in the bright light as she turns toward me. "Based on the circumstances, I thought these children may be a good fit for you."

Squinting, I look at the children milling around on the playground. Twenty kids bundled up in coats, gloves, and hats dig in the sandpit, chase after an assortment of balls, or giggle as they fly on swings through the air. A few outsiders wander around in circles entertaining themselves. *This is definitely not a good fit for me. Kids making messes.*

Ms. Chang calls to one of the workers pushing a child on the swings. The petite woman, dressed in corduroy pants and an oversized green sweater, rushes over to us.

"This is Fei-Hung," Ms. Chang informs us. "She's in charge of our young toddler room."

I smile and bow in the woman's direction.

"She'll let you know what you need to do. I'll come to check on you later." She spins around and marches back towards the orphanage.

As Julia and Fei-Hung talk, I walk to the edge of the playground to see what I've gotten myself into. These children are much younger than I'd thought. Many of them stumble to stay upright, and the slits in the back of their overalls indicate they are potty training. Despite the cold temperature, beads of sweat form on my lips. *These are just babies!*

"Nicki." Julia's voice cuts across the sounds of young laughter and yells as she walks my way. "Fei Hung asked if we can gather the children and take them inside. It's time for lunch."

"Uh-huh ..."

With unbridled force, Julia grabs my hand and pulls me into the play area.

"I don't think I can do this." I wiggle out of her grip. "I'm not good with children, remember? And I'm *really* not adept with babies."

"Nicki." Maneuvering around toys and tiny bodies, Julia marches back to me. "The only way we're going to find what we're looking for is to get our hands dirty." She rests her hands on my shoulders. "Don't worry. You're not alone."

"I'm not?" I look up at the sky, willing Mary Poppins to swoop in with her umbrella and save the day. No such luck.

"No, you're not." Julia's voice is a mix of compassion and sternness. "I'm here, and God's always with you."

Deflated, I drop my shoulders. Despite my spiritual epiphany a few days earlier, I haven't leaned on God much. I've relied on myself for so long that it's all I know. But this situation is so much bigger than me, and I can't do it alone. As the gentle pressure from Julia's hands lifts from my shoulders, I'm reminded I don't have to.

Lord, give me the strength. I close my eyes and plead with the Almighty. When I open them, my insides are still squeamish, but I am determined to see this through. "What do I need to do?"

Julia flashes a smile at me then turns toward the playground. "There." She points to a little girl sitting on the grass. "Why don't you get her and bring her inside? I'll wrestle the two little ones next to her."

Before I can change my mind, she runs off in the vicinity of two boys chasing each other in circles. I watch her lovingly tackle each of them, whisking one under each arm and pretending to fly away with them. Uncertainty and nervousness battle determination while I watch the boys squeal in delight as she carries them inside. Julia makes it looks so easy.

Maybe it is.

I amble toward the little girl I've been assigned to, wondering why she isn't playing with the other kids. When I reach her, I squat down to her level and wave.

"Nǐ hǎo." I open my hands, inviting her into them. "Are you ready to eat lunch?"

Ignoring me, she pulls up clumps of grass and filters them through her fingers. I look around for help, but everyone else corrals other children. I'm on my own.

I ruffle the young girl's short black hair. "Okay, sweetheart, it's time to go inside." I reach over and pick her up by her armpits.

"*Bu!*" The child screams as if I'd pulled her away from her favorite toy, her arms and legs flailing.

Despite my best efforts to comfort and calm the girl, she remains uncooperative. I set her back down. As soon as her feet hit the ground, she runs off laughing.

"Get back here!" I laugh, too, and race after her.

My long legs outrun her stubby ones, so I catch up to her in a few seconds. Being the amateur I am, I engage in a game of chase with the toddler, who zooms in every direction just out of hand's reach. Short of breath and patience, I'm finally able to scoop her up before she can dart off again. Struggling to wrap my arms around her flailing frame, I grin at my efforts. If this is what parenthood requires, I'm clearly not cut out for the job.

"I've got you now." I straddle her legs over my hips the way I've seen mothers carry their babies. It's not as easy as I thought it would be, especially with her hands pounding against my chest. Once I have her settled, I hold her hands together and head inside.

Although I've managed to calm her body, her voice is another matter. She screams so loudly I'm certain glass is breaking somewhere close by.

"There, there," I soothe her. But she belts out another scream, her plump red cheeks and soaked bangs letting everyone know just how she feels about me taking her away from her playtime.

I quicken my pace, praying I can make it inside before the child passes out or my eardrums burst. Her howling drifts across the playground, but with each step I take towards the building, the wails diminish. *Good, we're making progress.*

When I reach for the door handle, I'm shocked by sudden silence. I look into the girl's chocolate brown eyes and am met with a loud hiccup and a single teardrop.

While I'm not usually affected by little ones, my heart softens.

Stepping inside, I pull the girl closer to my chest and look over my shoulder for a final peek at the playground. "See, it's not so bad." *Am I talking to myself or her?*

A warm sensation floods over me, and I'm proud of myself for handling the difficult situation. As I'm contemplating the big step I'd just taken, the warm, fuzzy feeling from within moves outside, and a foul odor permeates my nose. Looking down at my chest, my eyes scan the vomit covering my sweater.

"Eww!" I hold the toddler at arm's length.

A caretaker, speaking rapid Mandarin, rushes to my side. She plucks the toddler out of my hands and passes me a towel. I take it and stalk off in search of a bathroom.

When I locate one down the hall, I soak the towel with water and attempt to remove the toddler's breakfast from my clothes.

Yuck. *Why* did I ever think I could do this? Children and I are not meant to be.

As I'm scrubbing an unpleasant brown color from my sweater, Julia walks into the bathroom with a navy-blue sweatshirt she tosses to me. "How did you know I needed a new top?"

"Word travels fast in China." Julia chuckles. "One of the workers said you could borrow it."

"Great." I retreat to the stall to change. "That's not embarrassing at all." With my vomit-laden sweater pinched between two fingers, I exit the stall and face the mirror. The borrowed clothing was a bit small for my frame but would do.

"I'll have them wash this for you." Julia takes the dirty sweater from my hands.

I grab it back. "Thanks, but I'm not staying."

"What? Why not?"

"Kids and I just don't mix." I squeeze the excess water from my sweater and ball it up in my hands. "I was crazy to think I could help with them. I'll just go back to the hotel and think of something else to persuade Ms. O'Connor." I scramble for the exit door, but Julia runs ahead of me.

"Are you really going to let a one-year-old and a little vomit stop you from what you came to do?" Her eyes glare at me with all seriousness.

Paralyzed by her question, I wrestle with my fears before answering. "It's just more challenging than I expected."

"Things worth fighting for usually are. And if it were so easy, then we wouldn't need God's help, would we?"

I tug at the sweatshirt crushing my ribcage, and exhale. She's right. Even if I listed out a hundred reasons why I shouldn't be allowed anywhere near children, there's no point arguing with her. If I'm willing to succumb to a bit of puke, then I'm allowing Ms. O'Connor to win.

And these children don't deserve to lose so easily. Someone has to fight for them.

"Fine." I raise my hands in surrender. "I'll give it another shot. But if I end up with anymore vomit on me today, I'm holding you responsible."

"Challenge accepted." Smiling, she takes the dirty sweater from me.

Lunchtime is wrapping up when we arrive in the young toddler room, which is bustling with activity. Several kids roam around the room unattended and carefree while others wait in their highchairs to be released from captivity.

Similar to the spaces I saw at Mother's Love, this one is also filled with rows and rows of cribs, with just a small section allotted for toys and games. In the middle of the play area is a large, faded rug with cars, dolls, and books scattered over it.

Without considering otherwise, I begin cleaning the mess. Abandoned toys are stored on a small shelf. It takes me a while to figure out where to place things since no organizational systems are set up. Just laying the toys haphazardly makes my skin crawl, but I do my best to put like items together.

When I turn around to pick up more toys off the floor, a pair of familiar eyes meet mine. *Oh no. Not her again.*

I freeze. I don't want to upset her or her stomach. Sucking her thumb, she waddles over to one of the books on the floor, picks it up, and holds it out to me.

"You want to clean up too?" I'm impressed by her desire to organize at such a young age.

She stares at me without moving, the book still in her hand.

"I think she wants you to read to her," Julia says while making her way toward us.

"What?" I blink.

"Read. To. Her."

"How am I supposed to read to her?" I bite my lip. "I don't know Chinese."

"Make it up. She doesn't know the difference. She just wants a book before naptime." Julia removes the book from the little girl's hand and offers it to me.

I hesitate. Make stuff up? My right-brain personality doesn't do that. Those round eyes peer at me with sweet belief. How can I say no?

Snatching the book from Julia's hand, I drop to the floor and sit cross-legged. I move the remaining toys away so the little girl can sit next to me, but she bypasses the empty spot I cleared and plops down into my lap.

"O ... kay then."

Impatient for me to begin, the girl flips open the board book and resumes her thumb sucking.

Here goes nothing. The first page is full of strange

symbols and a spotted dog with a bone. "Once upon a time, there was a dog named Spot." I speed through the short book, making up a narrative that would never win a Pulitzer Prize.

A short distance away, Julia beams at me.

"Shh." She holds her finger to her lips. "She's asleep."

I gaze down at my lap and see only long eyelashes. "My stories are so boring that I put people to sleep."

"Isn't that the point?" Julia peeks at the little girl before returning her attention to me. "Looks like you're not as bad with kids as you thought you were. You have a magic touch."

The little girl's weight warms my torso as she breathes in a soft rhythm, even though her thumb is still encased in her mouth. "Maybe I do." I brush her hair with my fingers. "I wonder what her name is."

"Lei Ming."

My eyes dart to look upon her face. "How do you know?"

"I asked Fei Hung because I knew you'd want to know." She chuckles.

"I'm the curious type, that's all." I snicker, then press my cheek against Lei Ming's head and listen once again to her steady breathing. "Do they know much about her?"

"Not really. She was dropped off a few months ago, left at the front door."

Tears fill my eyes. How does a parent do that? I pull Lei Ming closer to my chest.

"Here, give her to me." Julia reaches for the toddler. "I'll put her in her crib."

I surprise myself by clutching Lei Ming tighter. "No, that's okay. I'll let her sleep here awhile."

"Are you sure?" Upon my confirmation, she leaves me alone with Lei Ming.

Sitting on the floor with a toddler on my lap is the last thing I expected to happen on this trip, yet here I am. Despite the rocky start, a fondness for this little girl fills me with something

I've never experienced before. I tremble at the warm rush of affection melting my heart.

Instinctively I lift Lei Ming's hand into mine and rub my thumb over her smooth skin. Is this what mothers do with their children—sit in awe of the amazing creation in front of them?

But caring for a child for an afternoon is not the same as full-time parenting. I'm not sure I'm cut out for that. Or if I ever will be.

A caretaker taps me on the shoulder. From her hand motions, I surmise she wants to put Lei Ming in her crib. I rake my fingers through her soft hair one more time, then slowly release the young girl into the caretaker's arms. They disappear into the darkness, and once they're out of sight, I look around my immediate surroundings as if I've lost something.

Or someone.

I rise from the floor on wobbly legs, jiggling them to get the blood flowing again. Despite the shaking, I can't escape the question haunting my mind. Why is it I can't feel my legs but can feel the hole that's so quickly formed in my heart?

JULIA and I finish our day at the orphanage folding laundry, helping with baths, and keeping the children from choking on rice cakes during snack time. It's not much to write home about but fulfilling in its own way.

Upon arriving at my hotel room, I'm exhausted physically and emotionally. I order room service, fill the bathtub with water, and check my email. There's only a note from my mom asking when I'll be home and about her souvenirs.

Since I haven't shopped for a single gift yet, I decide to email her about my day with Lei Ming instead. She'd be overjoyed and somewhat surprised to know that I spent quality time caring for a little one and didn't despise it completely. Although it might give her false hope, at least it will distract from souvenirs for a while.

Before I can hit the send button, a knock sounds at my door. I check the clock, where bold red numbers confirm nowhere near enough time has passed for my meal to make it to my room. Curiosity piqued, I untangle my legs from my sheets and walk to the door. Maybe the kitchen staff didn't have a lot going on tonight.

"Wow, that was quick." I smile as I open the door, my stomach rumbling in excitement for the earlier-than-expected meal. But it's not room service.

It's Ms. O'Connor.

She strides past me. "We need to talk."

16

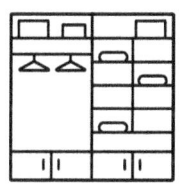

If one does not cast a big net, one cannot get big fish.
~ Chinese Proverb

My eyes widen in surprise and my brows reach for my hairline. "It's nice to see you, too."

Ignoring me, she proceeds straight to the living room.

Her unwelcome presence causes my body to shake uncontrollably. I knew I'd have to confront her eventually, but the situation seems much more intimidating now that we're face-to-face. I close the door, lean my head against it, and try to gain my composure. No matter the backlash or the consequences, I must stand my ground.

After a quick prayer, I follow her into the living area where she's pacing the Oriental rug. It's only been three days since I last saw her, but she looks paler and more tired than ever before.

"Are you feeling okay?"

She stops pacing and frowns at me. "What kind of question is that?" Her voice snaps with fire. "And if anyone's going to ask questions around here, it will be me."

While I'm curious as to her wellbeing, any inquiries will only infuriate her and escalate the situation. I take a seat on the couch instead. "What would you like to ask me?"

"How dare you go behind my back and return to the orphanage?" Her nostrils flare and a vein bulges from her forehead.

"I didn't go behind your back." I stiffen at her accusation. "Longchen told me he was going to inform you of my plans." *Even though I wasn't willing to be so honest.*

"And what exactly did you hope to accomplish by going there?" She takes two steps toward me.

Swallowing, I debate how much I should tell her. Until I have something concrete to present to her, I'm unsure she'll understand my reasons for visiting the orphanage.

"I just thought it would be interesting to see. That's all." I hide my hands under my legs to stop them from trembling. I'm not sure what I'm more afraid of—my dishonesty, the Almighty, or her.

"Let me get this straight." She scoffs. "You have an entire city of ancient ruins and history at your doorstep, and all you want to see is the inside of an orphanage?"

"That—that sounds about right."

She narrows her eyes and stares at me. "Nicole, I'm highly disappointed in you."

"I know you're not happy with me right now, but I'm equally disappointed in you as well." I stand up and look her straight in the eyes. "This is not the Ms. O'Connor I know. A woman who is caring and compassionate to those in need."

Her mouth drops open. "You do remember that I brought you here at my expense, don't you?"

"Yes, of course, but—"

"Based on your actions, I have no choice but to send you back home immediately. Your services are no longer"— she turns away to cough—"needed here."

"What? No!"

She clears her throat. "I will have Longchen arrange for you to fly home as soon as possible. You may stay here at the hotel until your plane departs."

"I can't leave just yet."

"Also, I'm withdrawing my recommendation for your job with Emerson. I can't endorse someone who betrays me, both professionally and personally, in good conscience."

"Betrays you?" I raise my voice. "I'm trying to keep you from making a mistake."

"That's your opinion."

A knock interrupts us, and she glances at the door. "It looks like your dinner has arrived."

When I open the door, the hotel attendant carries a tray of food into the living room and sets it on the coffee table. "*Xièxie*." The man bows at my thanks then leaves the room as quickly as he entered.

The smell of chicken and garlic permeates the room. Ms. O'Connor lifts one of the metal covers. "Fried rice with chicken. Nice choice." She sets the lid back on the plate. "I suggest you get your fill of authentic Chinese dishes before you leave. The food just doesn't taste the same back home." She turns to leave.

"Ms. O'Connor, wait!"

She hesitates at the door before spinning around. "Yes?"

"Please let me explain."

"I doubt there's anything you could say that will make me change my mind." She lets out a heavy sigh. "But I'll give you a few more seconds of my time."

I swallow and muster up as much courage as I can. "I went to New Hope today to see if I could find something that would help you think differently about what you're doing, and what I saw was amazing. The caretakers are wonderful and shower as much love as they can on those kids, and the children ... the children are happy and playful even though they've been abandoned." I pause to keep myself from tearing up.

"None of them deserve to be there, but despite that, they're finding a way to thrive, hopeful that someday someone will choose one of them to be part of a family and take them to a real home. Why would you want to shut that down?"

Her eyes bear down on me, and her mouth twitches as if she's going to answer the question. Instead, she just shakes her head. "Have a nice flight home, Nicole."

As the door slams shut, numbness infuses my body, and I sink into the couch. Going to the orphanage had been risky, and I'm paying the price. I should be grateful Ms. O'Connor was generous enough to fly me home and let me stay at the hotel in the meantime.

But with this turn of events, I'm unemployed, broke, and will be living with my mom by the end of the week. I have no regrets. What kind of person would I be if I just stood by and did nothing? A guilty one. And I certainly couldn't live with myself knowing that I turned the other cheek to save my own skin.

Staring at the ceiling, my mind tosses around everything that's happened the past few days. What had Ms. O'Connor been about to tell me before wishing me farewell? Is it possible she was going to tell me what it would take to reverse her decision? I rack my brain for a few minutes and give up on the futile effort. Regardless of what I want to believe, Ms. O'Connor made her choice, and there's nothing I can do about it.

Might as well start packing.

In the bedroom, I set my luggage on the bed and throw in my stuff pell-mell. My mom's Bible lands inside the suitcase with a loud thud. I cringe, then retrieve the worn-out leather book and sit down with it on my bed.

After opening it to the page where I'd left the bookmark, I find the verse from the book of James that Julia shared with me and read it aloud. "Religion that God our Father accepts as pure and faultless is this ... to look after orphans and widows in their distress."

I close my eyes and bow my head. *Lord, did I misunderstand what I was supposed to do? Or did I simply fail at what you called me to do? Either way, I'm sorry. I pray you'll be with Ms. O'Connor and those children in the days to come. And by some miracle, please keep the orphanage open.*

With less fury, I shut the Bible and lay it gently inside the suitcase this time. Leaning back on the bedframe, I stop fighting my feelings and let the tears flow. The phone rings as I'm alternately praying for and thinking about what might happen to the children in the orphanage. I wipe my cheeks before answering the call.

"*Nǐ hǎo*, Nicki. This is Longchen."

A sour taste forms in my mouth. "Longchen, I was expecting your call."

"Yes, Ms. O'Connor asked that I change your flight. I'm sorry to hear that."

"Me too."

"Well, I've made the arrangements and thought I'd call you with the details." He waits as I look in the nightstand for something to write with, then proceeds in a matter-of-fact tone to tell me the date and time of my flight.

I write as quickly as I can. "Wait, did you say December 30th?"

"Yes, I did."

"But that's two days from now." My heart beats faster.

"All the other flights were fully booked. This was the only one I could get you on with such short notice."

"Longchen, I don't understand. Ms. O'Connor said—"

"Ms. O'Connor said as soon as possible. Two days from now was the best I could arrange." He pauses. "I hope you'll find a good way to use your extra time."

Processing his words, a huge smile covers my face. "Thank you, Longchen, thank you."

"You're welcome. I pray your remaining days are prosperous and productive. Good night, Nicki."

Setting the phone back down in the base, I squeal and leap in the air. I have two more days to change Ms. O'Connor's mind.

Her hesitancy at the door earlier leads me to believe there's a small window for me to present her something that will appeal to her sense of responsibility for the neglected and abandoned.

I place my luggage back on the floor—there's no need to pack tonight.

God's not done with me yet.

A WET AND overcast sky greets me the next morning, but I refuse to let the cold and dreary weather bring me down. After taking a warm shower, I eat a hearty breakfast and spend some quiet time with God. Then, with the few minutes I have to spare, I open my inbox. It's full of new emails waiting for my attention. I scroll through the list for anything urgent. There's just one.

Uh-oh.

Clicking on the message from Emerson, I brace myself for the worst.

Dear Miss Mayfield,

Thank you for your interest in the project manager position at Emerson. While your skills were a match for the position, we unfortunately need to rescind our offer for employment. We will be in touch if anything suitable becomes available in the near future. Best of luck.

I close my eyes and exhale before shutting down my computer. Ms. O'Connor meant what she said and isn't wasting any time following through with her promises.

Disappointed, I amble over to the window and look down at the city shrouded in gray. Leaning my forehead against the frigid pane, I debate the cost of my decision. This email was the last nail in my coffin.

Out of the corner of my eye, I spy my mom's Bible in my suitcase. The verse I'd read last night and the sliver of hope I'm holding onto about Ms. O'Connor and what she didn't say comes to the forefront of my memories. Armed with my faith and a heart full of purpose, I grab my bag and head out. I must get to the orphanage as quickly as I can. Ms. O'Connor's decision could be detrimental not just to the children but to her as well.

I ARRIVE at the orphanage early and alone. Julia had called to say she thought it would be best if she stayed at Mother's Love today since her sister isn't feeling well. I'm a little nervous to visit the orphanage by myself, but trust that with God I'm never truly on my own.

When I walk in, the secretary directs me to the waiting area. While sitting in the cold, metal chair, I question why I can't go in and start helping. With time a precious commodity, I can't afford to sit idly by.

The clock ticks at a snail's pace. Impatient, I wrap my feet around the chair legs to keep from fidgeting. With each move of the hands, worry gnaws at me as I realize time is slipping away. Finally, the door to the office area opens, and an elderly Chinese woman greets me.

"Miss Mayfield?"

"Yes, I'm Nicki." I rise and walk across the room to meet her. She extends a wrinkled, spotted hand. When I place mine in hers, her skin is cold and thin to the touch. If I squeeze too hard, I may just break her.

"It's a pleasure to meet you, Nicki. I'm Director Wu."

"Oh, I wasn't expecting you to be here for a few more days." My mouth curves upward at the grandmotherly figure in front of me. "It's a pleasure to meet you as well."

She fingers the strand of iridescent pearls layered atop her magenta turtleneck. "Under the circumstances, I felt it would be best if I came back from my Christmas celebrations early. Would you care to join me in my office?"

Christmas celebrations? I thought the Chinese didn't observe the Christian holiday. Did that mean Director Wu was a believer? I'd be interested to know and discuss it more with her. Later, of course.

After a short trek down the familiar hallway, I gasp when I reach the doorway of her office. It's a room unlike any other I'd seen since arriving in China. While most spaces I've been in thus far have been sparsely furnished, Director Wu's personal space is on overload.

The perimeter of the room is lined with rows of binders stacked two feet high off the floor. A corner bookcase is crammed with a mix of magazines and books. In the opposite corner stands a large file cabinet with more papers poking out of it. And in the center of the room is a large wooden desk covered with piles of assorted papers and manila file folders.

Breathe, Nicki. I tell myself before entering the room. *Stay calm, Nicki. If you can handle your mother's house, you can handle this.*

Director Wu empties one of the two chairs stuffed with clutter and adds it to the overflowing mess on her desk.

"Please have a seat, Nicki."

With light steps I scurry over to a cracked cushioned chair and sit down. The director stays rooted at her desk.

"Assistant Director Chang tells me you requested to help here at New Hope yesterday. Alone."

"Well, I wasn't really alone." I gulp. "My friend Julia was here with me."

"But without Ms. O'Connor." She pauses. "And without her permission, I'm assuming."

How did she know?

Sensing my discomfort, she pats my arm. "Chinese people are notorious for sharing information rather quickly." She laughs before continuing. "Assistant Director Chang also told me Ms.

O'Connor wasn't too happy to discover our lovely orphanage and of her plans to stop funding it."

"I'm sorry, but yes." I sigh. "On both accounts."

"I can see how she'd be surprised to discover the orphanage and her father's involvement in it. But that still doesn't answer why you're here without her."

"Because I believe I can change her mind."

"And exactly how do you plan to do that?" Director Wu raises one eyebrow. "I'm sure that once she makes a decision, she isn't likely to back down from it."

"You're right. She's a determined woman, but I think I can persuade her to reconsider."

"What do you mean?" The director tilts her head.

"Ms. O'Connor is withdrawing funding because she's emotionally wounded." I shift in my seat. "She's upset that her father would care for children he didn't even know yet seemingly neglected her, his only child. So out of her anger and personal hurt, she's doing the unthinkable."

Absorbing the information, Director Wu sits down in the cluttered chair next to me. "I see. So, what do you think will cause her to reconsider?"

I bite my lip. My need to help the director see Ms. O'Connor's true nature without divulging too much of her history—even though we're at an impasse—brings tension to my insides. Still ...

"Because of her personal history, she feels particularly drawn to children who have been neglected or abandoned because of their parents' issues."

"And the hundreds of orphaned children living here at New Hope won't do it?"

"You'd think it would." I perch on the edge of my seat. "I think it has to go deeper for her. If I can show her something, even if it were just one child, with whom she felt a personal connection on some level, I think it would touch her heart and push her to reconsider her decision."

"Well, that's a bold ambition, and I admire your efforts." She leans closer to me. "But why do you feel like this is something you need to do? I can't imagine Ms. O'Connor is supporting you in this."

"No, she's not." I shake my head. "I can only tell you that I feel called to do this. I can't explain it fully, but I'm walking by faith and doing what I think I'm supposed to do." I take a breath for courage, but I must be honest. "The rest I'm leaving up to God."

Director Wu smiles at me, clearly not offended by my mention of God. "I appreciate your efforts, Nicki. I can't imagine this has been easy for you."

"No, it hasn't. It's cost me dearly. But I'm learning that sometimes that's what faith and obedience require."

"Yes, I know firsthand how true that is." Director Wu puts her hand on my arm.

Her statement piques my curiosity. I'd love to know more, but time is ticking, and I need to move on.

"Director Wu, please don't think of me as rude, but as much as I've enjoyed our talk, I'd like to see the children if you don't mind."

"Yes, of course. I heard you made a new friend here yesterday."

"New friend?" I furrow my brow as I run through memories from yesterday. Something clicks. "Oh, you mean Lei Ming. Yes, we had quite the bonding experience." I laugh. "I'm not sure we're friends, though."

"Little Lei Ming is a character, isn't she?" Director Wu throws back her head, her cropped silver hair shining under the lights. "Her name means 'thunder rolls.'"

"Oh, that's a perfect name for her strong spirit." I think about our tumultuous meeting and smile. "I was sad to hear about her family just leaving her on the doorstep here, though. I can't understand how anyone could do that."

"Unfortunately, it's not uncommon in China." Director Wu's

tone turns serious. "Many parents are too poor to take care of a child, especially if the child is sickly, so they drop them off at an orphanage hoping to give them a better chance—"

"Sickly? I don't understand."

Director Wu stares at me then rises from her chair. "Why don't we take a walk?"

Surprised by her invitation, I spring from my chair and follow her into the hallway. I'm grateful for the opportunity to leave her office. Had I stayed much longer, I would have been tempted to start decluttering and organizing.

"Is something wrong with Lei Ming?" My chest tightens against my rapid heartbeat as I consider the possibility.

She places her hands behind her back as we traverse the hallway. "Sadly, Lei Ming suffers from a heart condition. We assume her parents discovered she had the defect and couldn't afford the surgery. Knowing that our orphanage takes in children with heart issues, they likely left her with us so we could do what they couldn't."

"What do you mean, you could do what they couldn't?" Confused, I stop walking.

"Well, part of our mission is to help children who suffer from heart conditions to receive the treatment they need. We supply the funds needed for the operation then provide a recovery space for the children." She turns and enters another hallway.

Taking in the information, a million questions form in my mind while I catch up to her. But there's only one that matters most.

"Is Lei Ming going to die?" I'm not certain I want to hear the answer.

"It's a possibility. She's on the waiting list for surgery, but it may be some time before she's admitted, especially if Ms. O'Connor goes through with her plans." She hesitates. "Without the funds the O'Connor estate provides, we may not be able to continue doing the work we do or even stay open to accept children."

I stop and lean against the wall as I process everything Director Wu has told me.

Lei Ming.

An orphanage for heart issues.

Surgery.

A nagging feeling that I'm missing something pokes my mind. What could it be?

The elderly woman rushes to my side then grabs my arms to keep me from falling over. "Nicki, are you okay?"

Before I can say anything, she calls out in Mandarin for what I assume is help.

Think, Nicki, think.

A young girl quickly hands me a glass of water. I take it from her and close my eyes. Squeezing them tightly, I strain to jog my memory.

Blackness overtakes me for a few seconds before realization hits. My eyes open wide.

I turn and look straight at the director. "It's a matter of her heart."

17

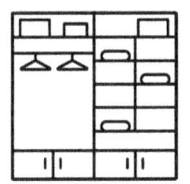

A great fire may follow a tiny spark.
~ Chinese Proverb

Removing the water glass from my hand, Director leads me to a nearby bench. "Nicki, please sit down. I'm worried you're not feeling well."

I do as she asks, but my mind whirrs. Could this be it? Could the heart connection be what influences Ms. O'Connor to change her mind? I run my hands through my hair and think hard. Ms. O'Connor had admitted to her own health issues when she was young. If I'm right, then I might have the ammunition I need to convince her.

"Director Wu," I say once my brain has slowed down a bit. "Would it be possible for me to visit the area where the heart recovery patients are?"

"Yes, but why would you want to go there?" She studies me carefully as if she's not completely convinced I'm straight in the head.

"Because"—I smile—"I think it's what may change Ms. O'Connor's mind."

"Nicki, are you sure you're feeling okay?" She directs her gaze on my head now, searching for any signs of a brain injury.

I appreciate her grandmotherly concern and take her hands in mine. "I'm thinking more clearly than I have been in days." There's so much more I want to say, but it will have to wait. Time is running out—for me, the orphanage, and the children. "I promise, I'll explain everything, I promise. Right now, I need you to take me to the recovery wing."

Knit eyebrows and downturned lips mar her composure. She scans me from head to toe one last time then nods. "Okay, follow me."

We walk down a maze of corridors until we reach a set of swinging hospital doors covered in warning signs. The director pushes a button on the intercom next to the door and speaks into it. After a short conversation, she looks at me and confirms our entry.

"One of the nurses will bring us gloves and masks." She lifts a stern smile in my direction. "While we're waiting, why don't you share with me why you're interested in our recovery unit?"

While it would be preferable to wait until I'm a hundred percent certain of the connection I think I've made, I can't hold out on her for my comfort. She's waited patiently and done all that I've asked. The least I can do is explain myself. I take a deep breath and start from the beginning. "A few weeks ago, I learned Ms. O'Connor was born with a heart condition.

"She didn't have any complications growing up because of it, but I know she's sensitive about the way it affected her relationship with her father and how it kept her from doing the things she wanted to do when she was a young girl. If I can tell her about the work that you're doing here on behalf of children who suffer from similar afflictions, she may just change her mind."

I expect Director Wu to be elated with my idea. I have, after all, unearthed the one thing that might save her orphanage.

Instead, she stands in front of me, nodding her head and tapping her index finger against her lips. "Interesting."

Not just interesting—it's game-changing! Does she not understand the significance of it all?

Her lack of excitement deflates my sense of purpose, so I decide to go full force with convincing her.

"You see, Ms. O'Connor is deeply concerned for those who can't afford to overcome the obstacles they face because of financial duress, whether it's a teenager who can't afford a dress for a special occasion or an organizer who isn't all that business savvy." I laugh and place my palm against my forehead. *She even helped me, and I didn't realize it.*

I continue my explanation. "I believe, now more than ever, that this"—I point at the hospital doors—"is what will touch her heart and reverse her decision."

The swinging doors open with a whoosh, and a nurse in purple scrubs greets us and holds out two sets of masks and gloves.

"Well, Nicki," the director says while slipping her mask over her face. "I hope this is what you're looking for." She motions to the nurse, who leads us through the doors and into the recovery unit.

My eyes slowly adjust to the dim lighting. The recovery unit is an oversized hospital room with three beds and two cribs. The only noise in the room comes from the beeping monitors next to each patient's bed.

While I take in my surroundings, Director Wu walks over to one of the cribs and talks with the nurse stationed there. They whisper to each other, and once they finish, Director Wu waves me over.

My stomach lurches at her signal. I'm not sure if it's the strong sterile odor that lingers in the air or my unease at seeing a young child hooked up to a bunch of machines, but I'm unable to move for a moment.

I bite my lip and inhale before walking over to the director, then stop in front of a crib lined with a lamb-covered sheet. A swaddled baby sleeps inside.

"This is Qing Shan." Director Wu points at the pink index card with symbols hanging at the top of the baby bed. "She was brought to New Hope when she was just a few days old. Two expats found her abandoned in the back of a truck. When they had her checked out, they were told she had a heart condition.

"The doctors told them of the work we do here raising funds and providing surgery for children with heart conditions, so they brought her to us." Leaning against the crib, she bends over to pick up the sleeping infant. "Because of the surgery, she has a better chance to have a full life."

Afraid of all the tubes and lines connected to the fragile child, I reach out and finger the only part of her untouched by medical equipment—the charcoal patch of hair sticking out from the blanket. "What a terrible beginning for someone so little and innocent." I swallow and choke back the emotions rising within me. "But how wonderful that there was a place like New Hope to help her."

Director Wu holds her out to me. "Here, would you like to hold her?"

"No, I couldn't." I shake my head. "I shouldn't."

Grabbing my arm, the director pulls me closer. The smell of baby powder and lotion tickles my nose. She places the baby into the crook of my arm.

"Don't worry, she won't bite." She chuckles. "Just breathe and relax. If she senses your tension, you'll upset her."

I hold my breath, afraid to move. Looking down at Qing Shan, I notice how adorable her smooth skin, small nose, and pouty lips are despite all the medical equipment. I can only imagine what beautiful eyes lie behind those closed eyelids. Pulling the infant closer to my chest, I grin. *Are all babies this precious? Would my own children be so captivating?*

Instinctively, I start rocking back and forth. Swaying with her in my arms, an overwhelming anxiousness fills my heart. While I haven't always been fond of children, Qing Shan's story, her battle at such a young age, and her beauty rock me to my core. At this moment, nothing else matters but her well-being. Not only do I want this little girl to survive, I want her to thrive.

From somewhere deep within me, I find the courage to voice my question to a possibly painful answer. "Will she recover fully?"

"Lord willing, yes." Director Wu's solemn tone settles over us. "But with heart surgeries, there are no guarantees. We have had many success stories here, but not every child makes it."

Qing Shan twitches and cries.

"Oh, what did I do?" I look at Director Wu for help and guidance.

"Nothing, she's just a little restless."

I thrust my arms toward the older woman. "Maybe you should take her."

"No, you're doing fine." She pats me on the back. "Just keep rocking, and she'll calm down."

Although I doubt my ability to soothe her, I relax my shoulders and follow Director Wu's instructions. "Hush, little baby," I whisper into Qing Shan's ear. While I'm no radio superstar, my off-key tune seems to work. Within minutes, the baby's peaceful demeanor returns.

I relax my lips into a small smile. *Maybe I have a maternal side after all.*

Not wanting to press my luck, I settle her back down in her bed.

Afterward, I stand and watch her tiny chest rise and fall in sync with the monitors. Without thinking, I place my hand over her torso, wanting to feel her small heart beating within. *One, two, three.* Once I'm satisfied with her strength, I remove my hand.

Teary-eyed, I turn my back to the crib. A cold chill runs through me. If it weren't for this place and the life-saving surgery provided, who knows what would have happened to her?

Director Wu brushes up against me. "It's not easy watching these children, or any of the kids for that matter, knowing how hard life is for them. I constantly question God about it. While I don't have all the answers, over time I've learned to trust that He created each of them just as they are and that He is caring for them by having a place like this available to meet their needs."

I notice small tears forming at the corners of her eyes. Moved by her compassion, I want to ask her about her faith.

"Director Wu!" a small voice interrupts our conversation.

The director and I look across the room to see an excited young boy skipping toward us.

"Wang Wei," the director squeals. She wraps her arms around him in a big hug.

The boy can't be more than eight years old. Whatever Director Wu is telling him brings him to hysterical laughter, and I chuckle as he hops up and down. They talk for a few minutes more before he races back to his bed, his portable monitor trailing behind him.

"That is Wang Wei," she tells me while watching him crawl back into bed. "He had surgery a few weeks ago and should be back with the other children soon. He is a strong boy."

I look over in his direction and see him staring at me. Wanting to be friendly, I wave in his direction. He hides under the covers then quickly reappears. Giggling, I cover my eyes. We exchange joyous shrieks back and forth as the horseplay between us lasts for several minutes.

When Director Wu taps me on the shoulder, indicating that playtime is over, I frown. I was enjoying our impromptu game of peek-a-boo, and I'd like to think Wang Wei was too. It's been a while since such giddiness had surged through me.

"Have you seen enough?" She glances at her watch.

Knowing I need to act like the adult I am, I wave once more to Wang Wei then nod at the director. "Yes, I have. Thanks."

At the exit, I linger at the doors and take one last look at

Qing Shan and Wang Wei. While it's difficult to see young children confined to hospital beds and intricate medical equipment, my heart is full of gratitude for the help they've received. It's comforting to know they'll no longer suffer from debilitating conditions. But what about the others who still need help? *Like Lei Ming.* I shiver at the thought.

On the other side of the hospital doors, Director Wu pauses. "So, what now, Nicki?"

Lowering my gaze, I ponder her question. There's only one thing left for me to do.

I look up at her, determination burning inside me. "I need to bring Ms. O'Connor here."

"And what if she doesn't want to come with you?" A worried look crosses the director's face.

"That's not an option."

ALTHOUGH THE CLOCK is working against me, I stay at New Hope long enough to take pictures of the children. With Director Wu's permission, I snap photos of them playing, resting, and eating. I want to have as many memories of them as I can to share with everyone back home. Plus, I plan to hang them up when I get home to have a visual reminder to pray for them—that is, if I can find any available wall space in my mom's house.

Upon returning to the hotel, I head straight to Ms. O'Connor's room. Relief settles over me when she answers right away.

"Nicole, what are you doing here? I thought you'd already be on a plane back to the States."

The muscles in my chest tighten at her remark, so I pray for the same courage Daniel held when he walked into the lions' den, that David used when fighting Goliath, then face her. "Longchen couldn't get me out right away."

Her expression remains stoic, but annoyance flashes behind her eyes. "Well then, what can I do for you?"

"May I come in?"

"I don't see the point." She places her hand on her hips. "There's nothing more for us to discuss." She pushes the door closed.

"Please, listen to what I have to say." I brace my hand against the dark wood to keep her from shutting me out.

She blows out an air of frustration. "There's nothing else you can tell me that will change my mind." She pushes hard on the door. "Good night, Nicole."

Before it closes completely, I hold up my phone in the small crack that's left. "This ..." I push my phone further through the door, flashing a picture of Lei Ming in front of her. "This is why you can't stop funding the orphanage. Do you want this little girl's suffering on your conscience? To know you could have done something to stop it but chose not to?"

"Who is that?" Her tone turns angry. "And of what concern is she to me?"

"Let me in and I'll tell you."

Ms. O'Connor hesitates for a moment then opens the door with the slowest possible movement. "Come in."

"Thank you." I smile at her as I enter, but she doesn't reciprocate.

"You have five minutes." She scowls at me.

Once we're situated on the sofa, I reopen my camera roll and locate the picture I'm wanting. "This is Lei Ming. She's one of the children at New Hope who will suffer greatly if you insist on going through with your plan."

"There are other orphanages in Beijing that will take in the children." She glances at the photo then looks away. "Or they can find someone else to provide the funds. It's not my problem." She plucks a piece of lint from her stylish sweatsuit. "Now, if that's all, you can find your way out."

"No, it's not all." I scoot closer and place the photo directly in front of her. "If you go through with your plan, this little girl will die."

"Don't be ridiculous." She pushes away my hand. "No one is going to die just because I stop funding the orphanage. The administrators will figure out something else. They always do." Her gaze shifts toward the large open window where streaks of lightning illuminate an ominous black sky.

My heart beats faster. All the emotions I've experienced over the last few days— anger, sadness, sorrow, and grief—bubble to the surface. "No, they won't."

Despite my soft tone, Ms. O'Connor whips her head around. Her eyes are wide with surprise, but she doesn't say anything, so I do.

"This little girl suffers from a heart condition. She's on the waiting list for surgery. Surgery that your family funds provide."

"A heart condition?" She clutches her throat and lowers her voice. So low she's almost inaudible. "How do you know that?"

I look at the picture I took of Lei Ming then turn my attention back to Ms. O'Connor. My heart aches, knowing what could happen to the little girl if this conversation doesn't go well. I must stay calm. "Director Wu told me. She knew that I had spent some time with her the other day and informed me of her condition. Then she told me about the work they're doing there."

"What work?"

"New Hope not only houses and cares for children waiting for adoption but is known for taking in children with heart issues. Because of the children's fragile conditions and the large expense it takes to care for them, most orphanages are unwilling to take them in. It's also difficult to find new donors. So, they use the funds provided by your family to give these children the life-saving surgeries they need."

I stop talking to give Ms. O'Connor some time to process everything I've said and the opportunity to respond. While she doesn't say anything, her creased forehead and pinched eyebrows indicate she's listening to every word I say.

"I spent some time in the recovery unit of the orphanage today, where the children who just had surgery stay until they are healthy enough to go back with the other children. It's amazing." I open my photo album, find a picture of Wang Wei, and hold it up to Ms. O'Connor. "This fiery eight-year-old is recovering nicely. He has an infectious laugh that makes everyone smile."

I scroll through the pictures again until I locate the other one I want to share with her. "And this sleeping beauty just came out of surgery. They call her Qing Shan." My voice quivers when I say her name.

"For someone who's managed to avoid kids as much as I have, well, my heart was touched in places I didn't think any child ever would reach." I close my phone with a quick snap before I lose my composure. "So, you see, Ms. O'Connor, the funding your family provides is critical in ways you didn't even realize."

She shakes her head. "That doesn't make sense."

"But it does! And you're the perfect person to support this place, considering your history."

"What do you mean, my history?" A look of confusion covers her face.

"Well, you know, since you had a heart condition, I just thought maybe ..."

"A heart condition?" Her face pales as she sinks farther into the couch cushions. "How do you know about that?"

"You told me a few weeks ago when we were eating lunch, remember?"

She narrows her eyes as if trying to recall our conversation. "Even if I did tell you, then I'm sure I also told you not to mention it ever again."

"I'm sorry." I'm taken aback by her sudden change in disposition. Why was she so angry that I knew about her heart condition? "I just thought under the circumstances you wouldn't mind me talking about it."

"Wouldn't mind?" Her voice rises. "My heart condition caused my father to pull away from me. I was broken in his eyes, and he couldn't stand the thought that the only child he'd ever have wasn't perfect. Why would I want to discuss the one thing that hurts me the most?"

"I know it's a sensitive topic, and I'm not trying to cause you any more pain." I reach out to her, but she pushes back against her seat. Despite her rejection, I forge ahead. "I just thought that of all people, you would understand the difficulties these children are facing. Director Wu and I agree that you are the perfect person to—"

"You discussed my heart condition with Director Wu?" Her eyes burn with rage.

Uh-oh.

As much as I'd like to revoke my confession, I can't. "Yes, I had to."

"That's where you're wrong. You weren't supposed to tell anyone that I'm broken and nothing more than damaged goods."

"Please don't talk about yourself that way, Ms. O'Connor. You aren't broken or damaged. Not then, not now, not ever." I cringe at the thought that she sees herself that way. I certainly don't. And neither does God.

"We're done, Nicole." She turns away from me. "Please leave and don't bother me again."

"Ms. O'Connor, please—"

"Go!"

I pick my phone up and do as she asks. I know without a doubt that I've crossed the line with her and ruined any chances I had to reverse her decision. If anything, I've given her more ammunition.

Opening the door, I take one last lingering look at Ms. O'Connor. I'm tempted to march back in there and try to convince her once more that what she's doing is wrong, but from the outline of her quivering figure and the soft whimpers filling the room, I know I can't.

I lean against the doorframe and stifle my tears. My heart aches for her, not only for the pain she's enduring but also for the hefty weight of her decision and the consequences it brings.

While I want to keep fighting for all the children of New Hope, I force myself to slip out of the room.

When I hear the soft click of the door behind me, I shudder. Any hopes I'd had of saving the orphanage had just disintegrated.

With no hope left, I return to my room. I don't bother turning on any lights and climb straight into bed.

While there are things I should be doing, like packing and emailing my mother about my sudden return, I can't move. I curl up under the covers in a fetal position with my phone. Opening my camera roll once more, I scroll through all the photos I took this afternoon. As I gaze on each sweet face, a heavy sadness bears down on me.

The reality is that I failed everyone.

The children of New Hope.

Director Wu.

Lei Ming.

Julia.

Ms. O'Connor.

Myself.

And, ultimately, God.

Burying myself deeper under the covers, I let exhaustion overtake me. I'm mentally, physically, emotionally, and spiritually spent. There's nothing left for me to give.

Closing my eyes, I decide to stop fighting and wave the white flag. In the morning, I'll pack and say my goodbyes to the people and places that had so quickly captured my heart. And then, I'll go home.

18

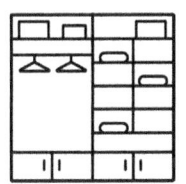

A bridge never crossed is like a life never lived.
~ Chinese Proverb

After a restless night of sleep, I roll out of bed. The grumbling in my stomach reminds me that I never ate dinner yesterday and beckons me to find suitable sustenance. Following its call, I decide I'll indulge in one final authentic Chinese meal—noodles.

I shower, then open my email to let my mom know of my impending departure. For the sake of my heart and my head, I keep my note short.

> *Sudden change of plans. I'm flying home tonight and will be landing tomorrow morning. I'll explain everything when I see you.*
>
> *XOXO, Nic*

When I finish, my attention lands on the message from my mom reminding me about her souvenirs. My eyes roll a full 360 degrees. With all the craziness of the past few days, I'd forgotten my promise to bring back some Chinese memorabilia. Without replying, I close my browser and head out to find everything I need.

The hotel concierge recommends a nearby market for shopping and a popular noodle house for my stomach. Rather than hail a taxi, I exit the hotel and join the other pedestrians, bicyclists, and cars fighting the concrete jungle of downtown Beijing.

Men, women, and children of all ages surround me as I walk shoulder to shoulder among them.

Some talk with each other in rapid Mandarin while others gaze straight ahead, lost in the world streaming out of their headphones. In the distance, car horns blare and bicycle bells ding every few minutes in frustration and warning. Street vendors call out to those passing by, encouraging us to stop and check out their meat on a stick or their blanket of housewares for sale.

After a short five-minute walk, I find the noodle house and order a bowl of beef, vegetables, and noodles to satisfy my hunger. The spiciness of the sauce, the crunch of the vegetables, and the softness of the noodles combine into the perfect send-off meal.

"Goodbye, my friend." Smacking my lips in satisfaction, I bid the delicious cuisine farewell. "I will miss you. You won't be the same back home." Determined to complete my mission, I head back out onto the sidewalk with the masses.

I locate the gift market a few blocks over from the restaurant. Walking into the building, I'm overwhelmed by the sheer size of it. On either side of me are endless rows of shops crammed full of clothes, purses, shoes, and jewelry. In the middle of the building, an escalator carries people to what I can only presume are more floors jammed with more goods to buy. It's an organizer's worst nightmare.

Rather than shut down mentally from all the choices available to me, I enter the first store I see.

A salesman pops out from behind a merchandise stand. "Nĭ hăo. How can I help you?"

"I need a few souvenirs to take home with me."

"What did you have in mind?" He follows me around the store as I browse the gift selections.

"My mom asked for some chopsticks, a straw hat, and a silk robe." I stop at a display of hand fans. "Oh, she'd love this."

He digs through the large bin and shows me five differently designed fans. "Which one would she like best?"

It's my mother. She'll want all of them.

"Um, I'll take all five." While I know her overly crowded house doesn't need any more clutter, I also know that this will be my last time in the Land of Dragons and Tea Leaves, so I splurge. I just hope the nice salesman doesn't think I'm a hoarder too.

After securing my mom's requests, I treat myself to a few goodies, adding a traditional Chinese dress, known as a *cheongsam*, and an onyx and jade chess set my dad would have loved to my basket.

When I plunk down my bulky stash of items at the checkout, a display of pearls behind the counter catches my attention. Had I promised to bring pearls to someone? While the cashier rings up my items, I stare at the jewelry, trying to remember what it is about the beautiful pearls that has me stumped.

Beautiful pearls. Isn't that what Julia's Chinese name means?

Without hesitating, I ask the salesman to show me a few pieces. I slip on several styles and colors until I find just the right one. When I'm finished, I know where my next stop will be—Julia. I type out a text message.

> Coming to Mother's Love. See you in a few minutes.

She instructs me not to come, but I can't leave without saying goodbye to her. While I didn't arrive in China looking for a friend, I'm grateful I found one in her. Despite her refusal, I respond.

Too late, on my way.

As the taxi pulls into the orphanage, Julia's waiting for me in the lobby. A worn and weary disposition lays heavy across her from head to toe, and dark circles shine under her eyes.

"Are you okay?"

She yawns. "I'm fine, just a little tired." She points to some chairs and we sit down. "My sister has been having asthma issues and I was up most of the night watching her to make sure she wasn't having any difficulty breathing."

"I hope it's nothing serious."

"It's not." She yawns again. "She's had this all her life. But I finally got her settled and thought it might be better if we didn't disturb her. That's why I came down here to meet you."

"Oh." I slump into the chair.

"Is something wrong?"

"No. I mean, yes." I gnaw at my bottom lip. My intention in coming here was to wish Julia farewell, but now my chest tightens as if a vise were clamping down on it. "I wanted to see you one last time."

"One last time?" Julia pushes up her glasses, her brow puzzling above the frames.

Afraid to look at her, I lower my gaze. "Julia, I'm going back to America tonight."

"What? Why?" Panic laces her words.

Over the next fifteen minutes I recount the last two days in detail, including my surprise visit with Director Wu, my discovery of the recovery wing at New Hope, and my final confrontation with Ms. O'Connor. When I finish, I taste the tears that have poured out with my frustration, sadness, and hopelessness.

"I'm sorry, Nicki." Julia reaches into her pocket and passes a

Kleenex to me. "I know you're upset you couldn't persuade Ms. O'Connor to change her mind."

Clogged up like a dirty drain, I take the tissue from her and blow my nose. "She's determined and she's hurting. I tried everything I could to convince her, but not even the connection to the heart patients would sway her. There's nothing else I can do." I yank at the tissue. "But I didn't come here to talk about Ms. O'Connor." I pull a small red box with gold ribbon out of my jacket pocket. "This is for you."

She carefully removes the box from my hand. "What's this?"

"A little something to say thank you"—I pull a heavy swallow around the lump in my throat—"and goodbye."

"You shouldn't have bought anything for me." She looks up at me with moist eyes, then rubs the ribbon through her fingers. "I don't have anything for you."

"Julia." I place my hands on hers. "You have given me encouragement, support, and strength these past few days, and for that, I will always be grateful." I wipe a tear from my eye. "Mostly, you have given me the gift of your friendship, which I will cherish more than any present you could have given me." I reach over and give her a hug. "I'll miss you."

"I will miss you, Nicki, so, so much." She squeezes me.

When we end our hug, I pull away and point at the box. "Open it!"

Julia twists her mouth and looks away. "Well ..." She bows her head.

"Is something wrong?" I tilt my head and try to make eye contact.

She looks up at me. "In China, we don't usually open gifts in front of others. It's not a common practice for us. You know, that whole saving face thing."

"I'm sorry. I didn't know." My face burns with heat.

"It's okay." Her chuckle releases on a soft lilt. "I guess traditions can be broken." She unwraps the ribbon, her eyes widening as she opens the box. "This ... is for me?"

I remove the pearl bracelet from her shaking fingers and slip it onto her right wrist. "A tribute to your given name, Mingzhu."

"No one has ever given me anything so wonderful." Her face lights up as she thumbs the individual beads. "Thank you so much."

"*Bu ke qui*," I say, offering a response to her gratitude while returning her embrace.

"Wow! You're almost fluent."

After a few more minutes of giggling, Julia turns serious. "You know, Nicki, you still have time to go to New Hope and say goodbye to everyone there. It would probably do your heart good."

While I know she's right, I don't think I'd be able to handle it because I know what lies ahead of those kids. But I also know that if I don't go, I'll never be the same. To not say goodbye to Director Wu, Lei Ming, and the other children would leave a large void in my heart. A regret I'd live with for the rest of my life.

Determination courses through me, pushing me to fulfill one final act greater than myself before leaving for home. "You're right, let's go to New Hope. I'll wait in the taxi for you while you go get your jacket."

Julia rises from her seat, more downcast than when I'd arrived. "I wish I could go with you, but I need to stay here with my sister."

"Oh, of course." In my excitement to return to New Hope, I'd forgotten about what was going on with Mingyu. My heart drops, knowing what's coming. The sooner I leave for New Hope, the sooner I have to say goodbye to her. Still, I can't ask her to leave her sister just because I want to avoid the inevitable.

I hate goodbyes.

Taking a deep breath, I reach for Julia's hands. "Well, I guess this is so long for now. Thank you for everything."

"Will I ever see you again?" She shifts from side to side.

"I hope so." It's highly unlikely our paths would ever cross again. But perhaps someday ... "Take care of yourself and your sister. And don't forget to email me, okay?"

Tears pooling in her eyes, Julia simply nods.

I give my sweet friend one final hug, walk toward the exit, and climb into the waiting taxi. After telling the driver where to go, I lean my head back on the seat and close my eyes. Who would have thought your heart could become so attached to a place and a person so quickly that when you left them it felt like a part of you died?

A loud banging on the car window brings me out of my reverie. I open my eyes to find Julia standing next to the taxi and power down the window.

"Julia, what are you doing?"

"I changed my mind. We haven't come this far for me to abandon you now. Plus, you need a translator, right?"

AS THE TAXI pulls into the long gravel driveway at New Hope, my stomach lurches. I swallow hard to keep my meal from reappearing.

"Nicki, are you okay? You look pale." Julia studies my face like a doctor might.

"I'm fine. I'm just nervous to go in, that's all."

Julia rests her hand on my shoulder. "It'll be all right."

After a few seconds of content quietness in the backseat, without warning, the taxi swerves off the narrow driveway into the grass to avoid colliding with another car. I upright myself then glance at the other vehicle. Could it be?

"Julia!" I shout once the car passes us. "I think I saw Longchen in that car."

"I can't see." She turns and looks out the back window. "The car is too far down the drive." She situates herself back in her seat. "Why would Longchen be here?"

My mind races with possibilities, none of which are good.

"Do you think he brought Ms. O'Connor here?" Julia asks what I'm thinking.

I shake my head. "Knowing how upset she was yesterday, I highly doubt it. Unless ..."

"Unless, what?"

"Unless she's here to officially remove her funding and explain her decision in person." I wince at the thought. "I'd hoped she'd change her mind, but there's no telling what she'll do from one moment to the next." My bottom lip wobbles and I shift away from Julia and stare out the window.

We remain quiet until the taxi stops in front of the main doors of the orphanage. When the driver tells us the cost of the ride, we pay him and exit the car.

"Nicki," Julia says as we walk toward the main entrance. "You can't be certain that was Longchen. Therefore, you can't be certain Ms. O'Connor is here. Don't let misguided assumptions ruin your goodbyes."

How did she get so wise at such a young age?

"Yeah, it probably wasn't him," I concede. "But the clock is ticking, so let's get inside."

When we walk through the doorway to the orphanage, an immediate sense of foreboding comes over me. The unusual busyness in the lobby and the staff's tension-filled inflections offer a stark contrast to the normally serene environment.

Julia must notice it too. Before I can ask her to find out what's going on, she heads to the information desk. When she returns, her pinched lips form a straight line across her otherwise pretty face.

"Well, what did they say?"

"Not much." She shrugs and passes me a security lanyard. "Just that some VIP is with Director Wu, and they were making sure everything was in order."

"Did they say who the VIP was?"

"No, they didn't. I don't exactly work here, you know."

"Do you think it's Ms. O'Connor?" I tighten my grip on my

jacket. "Is it possible that was Longchen in the car, and she's here to remove the funding?"

Julia pries my coat from my fingers and hangs it next to hers on the rack. "Relax, Nicki. VIPs are always visiting the orphanages. I see them all the time at Mother's Love. It's what they do." She places a hand on my shoulder. "It doesn't necessarily mean Ms. O'Connor is here."

I roll my neck, which is stiff from anxiety. "Okay, I'm going to quit thinking about her and enjoy my time with the kids." I open the door. "After you." I lead Julia to the young toddler room in hopes that by the time we're finished there, Director Wu will be available to see us.

When we enter, the room bursts with activity. Young children play, roam around, or are tended to by the caretakers. A mixture of crying and laughter fills the air.

I stand at the door and take in all the commotion. Although I've never been fond of kids, my heart jumps at the sight of all these little ones. Their sweet faces tug my heart toward a maternal instinct I'd never experienced.

Perhaps I was wrong to say I never wanted children of my own. Maybe I could give a child the love and attention he or she deserves, even if I'm not a perfect parent. These kids, after all, seem happy enough despite the fact they don't have any.

Julia taps me on the shoulder. "Nicki, the caretakers asked if I could help get the snacks ready. Will you be okay on your own?"

"Sure, go ahead. I need to find someone anyway." I part ways with Julia and search the room for Lei Ming, finding her in the middle of a group of children on the rug where we'd read. She rocks a baby doll in one hand while sucking the thumb of her other.

It doesn't take me long to snake through all the chaos and plop down beside her. With quick movements that take me by surprise, she crawls with her doll into my lap. I lean my head down on top of hers and inhale the combination of baby shampoo, Goldfish crackers, and slobber.

It's a smell I hope I never forget.

Despite the language barrier between us, we do our best to converse and play. Lost in her world, nothing else matters to me—that is, until a familiar voice shatters it.

"Nicole, I thought you weren't fond of children."

Ms. O'Connor.

I squeeze my eyes shut to fight the fear that overtakes me upon hearing her voice.

When I raise my head, my former boss towers over me. "Ms. O'Connor, what are you doing here?"

"I could ask you the same thing." She smirks at me.

Shaking, I set Lei Ming on the rug. Goldfish drop to the floor as I stand up, but despite the appeal of keeping my attention on something other than Ms. O'Connor, I don't pick them up. "I'm here to say goodbye. As you're well aware, I'm leaving tonight."

Before I can inquire about Ms. O'Connor's reason for being at New Hope, a crying Lei Ming pulls at my pants. I bend down and pick her up. Once she's happily situated on my hip, I introduce her to Ms. O'Connor.

"This is Lei Ming." I hold up her tiny arm and wave it in Ms. O'Connor's direction.

Ms. O'Connor takes Lei Ming's hand in hers. "Hello." She stares at the child for a moment. "This is the little girl you showed me last night, isn't it? The one with the heart condition who's waiting for surgery?"

"Yes, it is." With nothing to lose, I gather my courage to drive the point further. "Does she look broken to you?"

Something sparks between us in the air. I touched a nerve. When Ms. O'Connor lets go of Lei Ming's hand, there's a softness in her eyes that I haven't seen before.

"Why are you here, Ms. O'Connor? If I remember correctly, you aren't fond of children either."

Perfectly Arranged

"Yet here we are." Ms. O'Connor makes a sweeping gesture. "Ironic, don't you think, that two women who've avoided them for so long now find themselves surrounded by children?"

"I'd say more destiny than irony." I scan the room, taking in colorful toys, scampering feet, bedhead, and food stains on clothes. "You still haven't said why you're here at New Hope. Or do I already know?" I look down at Lei Ming, who's rubbing her fingers over my knit sweater.

"Nicole, I know you think I'm a monster, but you're wrong." Ms. O'Connor pulls down on the hem of her suit jacket. "In fact, I'd like to—"

My head jerks up. "I don't think you're a monster."

"Please, let me finish. I need to apologize."

Goosebumps appear on my skin. "Apologize?"

"Yes, for my behavior last night. It was wrong of me to be so harsh with you, and I'm sorry." She raises her chin. "I hope you can forgive me."

I've never seen her look as vulnerable as she does right now. While there are so many things I want to say, her words temporarily strike me speechless. Could this really be the Ms. O'Connor who's accompanied me on this trip? I blink away the cobwebs after a few seconds and refocus on her. Yes, there she stood.

"Apology accepted."

"Thank you, Nicole. Now, I must get back to Director Wu." She points to the door where the director is speaking with one of the caretakers.

"Um, before you go, I owe you an apology. Ouch!"

Peering at the floor, I see a young boy jamming his metal truck into my ankle. "Hey, stop that." My raised voice startles Lei Ming, and she begins to cry. The truck-wielding toddler continues pounding my flesh, but with Lei Ming in my arms, I can't stop him.

I turn to Ms. O'Connor. "Will you hold her for a minute?"

Her eyes widen. "What? No, I can't." She puts up her hands and steps backward.

Another scream emanates from Lei Ming just as the sinister toy smashes into me again. I thrust Lei Ming into Ms. O'Connor's arms.

Juggling the toddler and her purse, my former boss struggles to stay upright. "What am I supposed to do with her?"

"Just bounce up and down a bit." Eyes watering, I grit my teeth against the pain. If that toy strikes my ankle bone one more time, I might be going home with one less foot.

Ms. O'Connor awkwardly bounces Lei Ming in her arms while I grab the lethal truck from the toddler's hands and replace it with a less dangerous jack-in-the-box. Once I know he's situated and not likely to inflict any more harm, my attention returns to Ms. O'Connor.

Despite her uncoordinated movement, she's managed to calm Lei Ming. Together, they make an unlikely pair—the crotchety older woman with so much power holding the sick toddler with so little. I can't help but smile as I watch them relax into each other.

"Ms. O'Connor? I can take her now."

Pulling the young girl closer to her chest, Ms. O'Connor shakes her head. "No, I'm fine."

"Watching you with her, I'd say you're not too shabby with kids either." I stuff my hands into my pockets and swallow my pride. "Look, Ms. O'Connor, like I was saying before, I'm sorry too. I shouldn't have told Director Wu about your health issues without your permission. I hope you can forgive me."

"Thank you, Nicole. I appreciate that." Holding on to Lei Ming, she walks around the rug, pointing to different toys and talking as if the toddler understands every word she says.

With every fiber of my being hoping this softer side of her will work to my advantage, I ask the question burning within me. "Does your being here mean you've changed your mind about withdrawing the funds?"

"I'm considering all my options." She shakes a stuffed animal in front of Lei Ming, who quickly embraces it in her arms, then sighs. "After you left, I realized I was behaving like my father. I promised myself never to act that way."

"What do you mean?"

She makes a funny noise with her lips, entertaining Lei Ming before answering me. "My father was obsessed about keeping up appearances and what people thought of him. Why do you think he never told me about this place? He must not have wanted people to know he had a charitable side, probably worried that if people knew that about him, they'd ask for money for every good cause under the sun."

Like a grandmother, she cradles the playful toddler closer to her chest. "He always had to keep up that hard exterior, to let everyone believe he could fix everything while deep down he knew he couldn't. I hated that about him. When you told me you'd shared my heart condition with Director Wu, I reacted the same way my father would have." She bows her head. "Coming here was the only way to right my wrong."

Behind us, someone clears their throat. I look over my shoulder to find Director Wu in my line of sight. Tension radiates to my right, where Ms. O'Connor stands with Lei Ming still in her arms.

"I already knew about your heart condition." Director Wu's grave tone sends chills down my spine. "It's all in the letter."

19

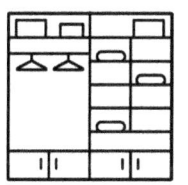

There's nothing as heavy as a secret.
~ Chinese Proverb

"How did you know already?" Ms. O'Connor takes a step back, her body rigid.

"Your father told me."

Wait, what? My curiosity level piques even further. "How is that possible? I thought Mr. O'Connor had never been here."

"No, he never visited New Hope that I'm aware of," the director states.

"Then how did you find out?" Even though it's not my place, I ask anyway.

"As I mentioned, he wrote to me when I first took the position as head director. In it, he shared Ms. O'Connor's heart issues."

Ms. O'Connor balks. "I highly doubt that. My father was a private man and would never disclose personal issues with anyone. Ever."

"This must be shocking news to you, but it's true." Director Wu offers Ms. O'Connor a sympathetic glance.

"I don't believe you."

Director Wu stands a little taller. "Are you accusing me of lying, Ms. O'Connor?"

Fire shoots from Ms. O'Connor's eyes. "I'm a businesswoman, Director Wu. I've learned you can't always take people at their word. Even honest people act dishonestly under pressure. You're fully aware of my intention to remove funding, so how can I know you're not just saying these things to thwart my plans?"

"Ms. O'Connor!" Multiple pairs of eyes look my way, and I cringe. *Oops.*

Director Wu steps closer to us as her eyes shift to the caretakers who are staring at our threesome. "Why don't we move to my office and continue this conversation in a more private setting?"

"Yes, let's do that." Ms. O'Connor sets down Lei Ming, who's been wrapped in her arms this whole time, on the floor.

Sensing the distress in the air, the young toddler speeds away. Without giving us a second thought, she joins the other children playing on the rug.

Watching her, I almost don't hear Ms. O'Connor. "Nicole, are you coming?"

I stutter. "You ... want me ... to join you?"

"You opened this Pandora's Box. You may as well see it to the end." She walks toward the doorway where Director Wu waits.

"Okay, but I need to do something first." Knowing Ms. O'Connor's limited patience, I run over to where Lei Ming is playing and sweep her into my arms. She giggles and squirms, the sound of her joy melting my heart.

Once she's calmed down and settled in my arms, I whisper into her ear, "I couldn't leave without saying goodbye, little one. Thank you for showing me the blessing of children and offering me the hope that one day I may make a good mother." I kiss her cheek. "I pray you get the surgery you need and find your forever home soon." I choke up on those last words.

The reality that neither of those things might happen for her hits me hard. As heartbreaking as it is to consider, I can't dwell on that now and brush the thoughts away. Ms. O'Connor is waiting.

Although she didn't understand a word I said, Lei Ming covers my cheeks with her chubby fingers. I'm overwhelmed by the tender reply. As the tears well in my eyes, I place her back on the rug. Without hesitating, she trots off and resumes playing.

"Nicki, where are you going?" Julia calls to me from across the room as I step through a maze of toys.

I wave her over to me. While I want to tell her about Director Wu's revelation, I don't have the time and must keep our conversation brief. "I'm going to Director Wu's office."

"Why?"

"Nicole!" Ms. O'Connor's sharp tone cuts across the baby chatter and adult Mandarin throughout the space. "Are you coming?"

I look at Ms. O'Connor and the director standing in the hallway. "Yes, I'm coming." I lean against the doorframe. "Julia, I can't explain right now, but I'll fill you in later. Just pray that everything works out."

"Nicole!" Ms. O'Connor calls again.

Without waiting for Julia's response, I race to catch up with the two ladies. Although the deafening silence and awkward tension that accompanies us as we navigate back to Director Wu's office cause my insides to quiver, I'm grateful for the few moments of quiet to collect my thoughts.

Why did Director Wu keep her knowledge of Ms. O'Connor's condition a secret from me? Why didn't she mention the letter before? Could this letter make a difference with Ms. O'Connor and her decision to remove funding?

As Director Wu unlocks her office door, my mouth goes dry. Knowing the dire state of the space, beads of sweat form along my hairline. There's no doubt in my mind that Ms. O'Connor's minimalist and meticulous style will be at odds with the director's chaotic ways. What will she make of the overflowing piles of paper, books, and clutter?

Maybe she'll be too preoccupied with seeing her father's letter and won't notice the mess.

My question is answered as soon as we walk into the untidy office. Her curled lip and wrinkled forehead quietly tell me she's not impressed with the disarray surrounding her. I can only hope she'll be able to overlook the clutter and not let that sway her decision-making in any way.

"Please, sit." Director Wu points to the chairs in front of her desk.

Ms. O'Connor and I perch on the ends of our seats—the clutter scattered upon the cushions prevent anything otherwise—then refocus our attention on the director.

Politely declining the woman's offer for tea, Ms. O'Connor says, "I'd much rather continue our discussion about my father's letter."

"Yes, of course." The director puts down her cup and places her arms on her desk. "What would you like me to tell you?"

"I'd like to know what the letter says, but I'm also curious as to why you failed to mention the existence of such a letter to me in the first place."

Director Wu tilts her head. "Ms. O'Connor, in China, we have a saying— 'yǐn shuǐ sī yuan.' It means 'when drinking water, remember the origin.'"

Ms. O'Connor's forehead creases with confusion. "And you're telling me this why?"

"It means to remember where your good fortune comes from." Director Wu laces her fingers together in front of her. "Your father was very good to us here at New Hope, and one of his requests was that we respect his privacy as our benefactor. I didn't say anything to you because I wanted to honor him and his request.

"However, when I learned you were upset with Nicki for sharing your heart condition with me, I knew there was a possibility you weren't aware of the letter. At that point, I couldn't keep it a secret any longer. For her sake and the orphanage's."

"No, I knew nothing about this place nor my father's involvement in it. I'm only here because I found a card with Chinese writing among his most valuable possessions after he died. It was then I decided to investigate."

"I see." Director Wu takes another sip of tea. "Well, now that you're here and you know about the letter, would you like me to tell you what it said?"

"I'd prefer to see it for myself, if you don't mind."

The director's face blanches from soft brown to almost colorless. "That's not necessary. It would be easier and quicker for me to tell you its contents."

Ms. O'Connor arches her eyebrow. "You do have the letter, don't you?"

"Yes, I have it, but ... I'm not exactly sure where it is." She lowers her head, and I notice the rims of her ears are splotched with red.

I'm not sure if it's embarrassment over the condition of her office or shame and the whole saving face issue that Julia was referring to before. Either way, my heart breaks for this sweet woman.

"How is that possible?" Ms. O'Connor scans the room, and I can imagine her judgmental thoughts.

I pat her arm to calm her. While we're anxious to know what the letter says, berating the poor woman won't do any good. I've worked with enough disorganized people to know that to help them, you have to work with them, not against them.

"Director Wu, I'm sure you didn't mean to misplace the letter."

"I never thought someone would ask to see it." She looks at me with sorrow-filled eyes. "Although I remember what it said, it's been a while since I actually held it."

She turns to Ms. O'Connor, whose stiff posture leaves no one in the room questioning how she feels at the moment.

"I can assure you it's here, somewhere. Nothing ever leaves my office." She chuckles, but despite her efforts to ease the tension in the room, it falls short.

Although it's critical that we find the letter, I'm determined to de-escalate the situation. "Ms. O'Connor, why can't she tell us the letter's contents now and locate the actual document for you later?"

"No, that won't do." Ms. O'Connor grimaces.

"Why not?"

"Nicole, I'm about to withdraw my family's fund from the orphanage. She knows this. With the exception of the business card, we never found anything among my father's belongings about his involvement here nor any of his correspondence with the director. The only thing I have to go on is the word of my father's accountant.

"Without seeing the actual letter, how can I be certain everything she tells us is legitimate?" Her eyes soften as she looks at Director Wu. "Plus, if she can't keep important papers straight, how can I know she'll correctly convey my father's words?"

"Ms. O'Connor is right. It would be best if I could show her the letter." She sighs then glances around the room. "But, as you can see, I'm not very good at keeping things organized around here. I had an assistant once ..."

"Maybe I can help." The words fall out of my mouth before I realize it. "I'm an expert at bringing order out of chaos and finding items others would consider hopelessly lost. I did it all the time in my job as a professional organizer. I'm sure I can do the same for you."

"Don't be ridiculous, Nicole." Ms. O'Connor waves her arm in a half-circle. "It would take days to find it in this mess. Don't you have to catch a flight soon?"

"You hired me to help you, remember?" I glare at her.

Without allowing her to answer, I address the director. "Would you mind if I asked you a few questions to see if I may jog your memory about where you put the letter?"

"If you think it will help, ask away." She smiles at me.

Ms. O'Connor exhales deeply and loudly but doesn't say anything else.

I walk around the room, figuring out my best approach. Inside, I'm giddy. I'm the Sherlock Holmes of professional organizers. "Director Wu, you're sure you never threw the letter away?"

"No, I would never do that."

"When was the last time you read the letter?"

She gazes upward, pondering the question. "Oh, about 30 years ago when I first became director."

I make my way towards the file cabinet located directly behind her desk. "Okay, if it's been that long, odds are you probably stored it in one of these before you had so many other papers to manage." I point to the metal container.

"It's possible. Once the paperwork became more than I could handle, I purchased another one." She tilts her head toward the second cabinet across the room. "Then I gave up filing, then went to a binder system, and finally a piling system."

"So, if I had to guess, I'd say the letter is somewhere in here." I open the top drawer of the cabinet to determine what type of filing system the director used, if any. After perusing the contents, I discover that she used manila file folders hand-labeled in Chinese writing.

"When you labeled these folders, would you have labeled them by specific categories or by general ones?"

After grabbing her reading glasses from the corner of her desk, she joins me at the filing cabinet.

"Let me see." The director puts her readers on and flips through the folders jammed in there. "It looks like I used general categories. Does that help?"

"Yes, it does." I wink at her. "Did you file them alphabetically by category too?"

She studies the files again. "Yes."

"Great!" I clap my hands. "Then it's likely you would have stored the letter in categories such as *Letters, Important Documents*, or even *O'Connor*." I move away from the cabinet to give her space. "Try locating folders with those labels first."

Director Wu goes to work, searching each of the files. She closes the first drawer and opens the second one. "Ah, here's one labeled *Documents—Private*." She passes it to me before returning to the cabinet. "And one I called *Letters*." She plops a thick folder on top of the first.

Like a machine, she continues sorting through the overflowing papers and folders. Sadly, the third drawer doesn't produce any files. Opening the bottom and final drawer, she fingers the papers quickly but only comes up with one thin folder. She adds it to the other two.

"This one is marked *Coalition of Medical Missionaries*. It may be in here too." She closes the drawer. "Unfortunately, there wasn't anything labeled *O'Connor*." She removes her glasses and sets them on her hair. Small beads of sweat have formed on her forehead.

"That's okay, you've given us a few places to look." I offer her an encouraging smile. "Why don't you sit and browse through these to start?"

Director Wu follows my instructions. Once she's settled at her desk, I hand her the pile of paperwork we unearthed from the file cabinet.

"Thank you, Nicki," she says as I sit back down in my chair.

When I reclaim my spot next to Ms. O'Connor, my boss doesn't look at me. Her eyes are glued to Director Wu. We sit quietly as the director sifts through the papers. Some she scans and discards, others she lingers over longer, smiling and occasionally wiping a tear from her eye.

Removing her glasses, she gathers a few of the letters into

Perfectly Arranged

her hands and fans them in front of us. "I've been head director of New Hope for thirty years now, and these letters remind me of how amazing the work really is. I can't think of a more satisfying calling than to help children who need it and to find homes for those cast aside."

She sets them back down in a pile and looks at Ms. O'Connor. "I thank God and your father for this place and for the privilege of serving these children." Without waiting for a response from either of us, she places her glasses back on and focuses her attention back to the task.

Watching her work, I'm touched by her heartfelt sincerity.

As the stack of papers dwindles, it dawns on me that the letter may not be in there. If it's not, there isn't enough time for me to search every file again, and without it, Ms. O'Connor will follow through with her plan to remove funding. I rub my sweaty palms over my jeans. *Lord, please let her find this valuable document soon!*

Just as I'm about to give up all hope, Director Wu gasps. "This is it." She holds up an old, yellowed envelope for us to see.

While I'm tempted to grab the envelope out of her hands, I show restraint. Instead, I wait for Ms. O'Connor to do something. To my surprise, she doesn't move. Rather than exhibit her usual take-charge behavior, she sits with rigid posture in her seat, her complexion paler than the snow piled up outside. I was certain she'd be excited by the discovery of the letter and to unravel the mystery that brought us here. I know I am.

But then again, I'm not about to hear from my deceased father either.

"Would you like to read it, or shall I?" Director Wu finally speaks up.

Ms. O'Connor flinches at her words. "You go ahead."

"Certainly." Director Wu opens the faded envelope and, with a light touch, removes several sheets of paper.

She looks at both of us one last time then begins reading.

Dear Madam Wu,

Congratulations on your post as incoming director at New Hope. Your impressive qualifications make you the ideal person for the position. I'm certain your skill sets will supply the orphanage all it needs to succeed in the years to come. As I do with all incoming directors, I'm writing to explain my reasons for financially supporting New Hope as well as my expectations moving forward.

During the Great Depression, my parents relinquished me to a state welfare system. There I was to stay under the supervision of caretakers until a home was found for me or my parents returned to claim me. Unfortunately, neither of those situations occurred. As you can imagine, that plus the dismal living conditions at the orphanage left me hard-hearted and hopeless.

One afternoon, I overheard some of my caretakers discussing the poor quality of care for orphans in other countries. Right then, my heart softened. I couldn't bear thinking there were children living in worse circumstances than me. I pledged that one day I would find a way to improve the quality of life for those who were abandoned, forgotten, or rejected by no fault of their own, just like I had been.

But those dreams we make as children often flee, and that's what happened to mine. Although I prospered financially later in life, I never followed through with my commitment to help the less fortunate. That is, until—

Knock! Knock!
Ms. O'Connor and I swivel toward the door.
Director Wu stops reading. "Come in."
The door opens, and a young boy peeks around it. I recognize his face but can't place him.

"Wang Wei!" She leaps from her chair to greet him.

Ah, yes, the little boy from the recovery unit! It's good to see him up and around. Through the small crack in the door, I see Julia pacing in the hallway. What is she doing here?

The two talk for a few minutes before she closes the door behind him then sits back down. "My apologies. That was Wang Wei. He wanted to let me know he'd just been released from the recovery unit."

"That's great news!" I glance over at Ms. O'Connor, hoping she'll be moved by the young child's progress. "Wouldn't you agree, Ms. O'Connor?"

"As wonderful as that is—" Despite her word choice, Ms. O'Connor's pinched tone holds anything but happy thoughts. "—I'd like to hear the rest of my father's letter, if you don't mind."

The director clears her throat. "Yes, of course. Now, where was I?" She searches the letter for where she left off. "Oh yes, here."

> *That is until the birth of my precious daughter.*

> *My world changed with Katherine's entrance into it. Her presence brought me a joy and purpose I'd never had before. But with that joy also came sorrow. Shortly after her birth, we discovered that our sweet baby girl had been born with a heart defect.*

> *I consulted the best doctors in the country until I found one who could perform the surgery necessary to save her life. Although the operation was successful and Katherine's life had been spared, I still worried about further complications that could take her away from us. I assume every parent's worst nightmare is the loss of his or her child, and I dare not think how I would ever overcome such a tragedy.*

Thankfully, her physician, Dr. Tang, calmed my fears and assured me she would be fine. He reminded me how fortunate we were to have access to such wonderful medical advancements. According to Dr. Tang, in his ancestral country of China, children who endure similar conditions aren't as fortunate.

Intrigued by his comments, I researched the situation. I learned that many children in China suffer from life-threatening heart conditions but lack the necessary funds for the operations and ongoing treatment that would offer them any hope of a long life. I also discovered that because of this, their parents feel they have no choice but to abandon their ill children to orphanages rather than watch them die.

I sympathize with their dilemma; however, I know the decision to leave their children adds an additional burden to the facilities that are already struggling to provide for the vast number of kids who have been left in their care.

This information was a turning point for me and renewed the commitment I made in my youth. Several months later, as if by divine intervention—

"Divine intervention?" Ms. O'Connor lets out a heavy sigh and wrinkles her forehead.
Director Wu ignores her and continues reading.

—I stumbled upon a missionary program that allowed me to not only support orphanages in China but to provide money for the heart surgeries. By doing so, I hoped many children would have happy and healthy lives for years to come.

While our work in China has been successful, I would like to expand our efforts and centralize the care these patients receive. Under your direction and in partnership with the Coalition of

Perfectly Arranged

Medical Missionaries, I want to create an in-house program at New Hope that offers heart patients a streamlined care process.

It will be your responsibility to determine the procedures and protocol for identifying which children qualify for surgery, arranging their surgeries, establishing post-surgical services, and finding suitable homes for them once they have fully recovered.

As always, I'm willing to provide the additional funds for this. I only have two requests: that you report to me directly on the state of the program, particularly the progress of the children's health as a result of our in-house care, and that you keep my involvement in this completely confidential. For personal reasons that I do not wish to disclose, I choose to be a silent benefactor.

When and if I tell of my involvement, it will be at my discretion. I appreciate your respect for my privacy and for taking on this program as part of your role as director. I believe we can make a difference in the lives of these children. In the next few weeks, a representative from the CMM will be in contact with you. Please have ready a report of needs and costs as well as a planning timeline to establish this program.

In closing, I trust that you will do a superb job in this role. I believe our combined efforts will not only benefit many needy children but will also become a longstanding tribute to my one and only child.

Cordially,
Thomas O'Connor
July 27, 1988

As Director Wu folds the letter and places it back in the ancient envelope, my eyes dart from her to Ms. O'Connor, who hasn't said a word. She's bent over, her upper torso trembling.

"Ms. O'Connor, are you okay?" I reach over and rub her back. I can't tell if she's crying, having trouble breathing, or both.

When she rises and looks me in the eyes, I'm shocked at what I see.

20

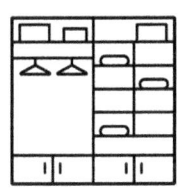

The lotus root may be severed, but its fibered threads are still connected.

~ Chinese Proverb

I stare at the fragile woman sitting across from me. Instead of the confident and tough façade she normally wears, Ms. O'Connor has dwarfed into a little girl, with wide eyes, quivering lips, and hunched shoulders on full display. It's a stark contrast to the person I've come to know these past few weeks.

Yet it's touching to see her this way. Underneath her coiffed hair, designer clothing, and hard exterior, she is a vulnerable and broken woman who's longed for her father's love just like the rest of us. Just like me. Now the heavy armor shielding her has been shattered by the words she's always wanted to hear.

"All these years, my father truly loved and cherished me, and I had no idea." Ms. O'Connor pulls a tissue out of her purse and wipes the tears from her eyes. "May I see the letter?"

"Of course." The director passes her the envelope.

With shaky hands, Ms. O'Connor carefully removes the letter from its case and unfolds it on her lap. Her fingers caress the thin paper and black script lettering as if, in doing so, she could touch her father one last time. Finally, she reads the words to herself.

In an effort to respect this sacred time between her and her father, I try not to stare while she pores over the message written so long ago, but curiosity draws my eyes back to her form every couple of seconds. My intrusiveness niggles an uncomfortable sensation in my midsection, yet I can't help but feel relieved. Her moist eyes and forlorn face mean the letter is reaching a part of her heart that's been closed off for a long time.

When I can't bear to watch her any longer, I glance at Director Wu, whose head is bowed in prayer. Caught between the two women, I'm tempted to bolt. I squirm in my chair and make every effort to remain quiet. It would be rude of me to interrupt the private connections they're making with their fathers to ease my discomfort.

After several more minutes of awkward silence, Ms. O'Connor tucks the letter into the envelope and turns her attention to Director Wu. "I appreciate you sharing this letter and its contents with me. I'm sure it wasn't easy for you to break the vow you made to my father to respect his privacy. However, I'm grateful you did."

Director Wu acknowledges Ms. O'Connor's gratitude with a nod.

"As I mentioned earlier, I had no idea about any of this. I was completely unaware of his upbringing, the effect my birth and health issues had on him, or his desire to help those who had been abandoned or forgotten." She fingers the edges of the envelope.

"Sadly, my father and I had a complicated relationship—one that didn't afford us the opportunity to share intimate details of our lives. I'm not sure if it was his pride or my hurt that built the divide between us, but it was there, and neither of us was willing to cross it." She holds up the envelope. "Perhaps this letter is the bridge that was meant to bring us back together, even if he's not here to meet me on it."

"I'm sorry to hear your relationship with your father was difficult, my dear." Director Wu offers her another Kleenex. "It seems you deeply cared for one another."

Ms. O'Connor places the tissue against her nose. "As long as I can remember, I believed my father didn't love me, that he was too busy with other things to spend time with me or that my brokenness caused him shame. No matter how hard I tried, I never felt good enough for him." She looks at me and beams. "But now, now I know none of that is true. He loved me more than I realized—so much so, it's incomprehensible."

"Oh, he did love you." I place my hand on her forearm. "He just expressed it differently than you'd have liked. Not everyone shows love in the same way, you know. Your father conveyed his love for you in deeds, even ones you didn't know existed." I grin. "And when you offer a down-and-out organizer a second chance or open your closet to underprivileged girls so they can feel special for an evening, you're demonstrating love in the same way."

Director Wu rises from her seat and stands in front of Ms. O'Connor. "Nicki's right. We can't always understand the actions of others or why they are incapable of offering us the things we desire or in the manner we desire it.

"Regardless of what your father did or didn't do while he was alive, you inspired him. You encouraged him to greater things, and because of you and his rich love for you, numerous lives have been saved." Director Wu squeezes Ms. O'Connor's shoulder before stepping back and leaning against her desk.

"Thank you, Director." Ms. O'Connor once again wipes the tears from her eyes. "I truly believe you're saying that from the heart and not in light of the circumstances."

I breathe a sigh of relief and feel some of the tension slip out of the room.

The director holds up her hand as if taking an oath. "As God is my witness, I meant every word." She puts down her hand and smiles.

A silence falls over the room. Arriving at New Hope today, I truly believed any hope of saving the orphanage had vanished. There was no doubt in my mind Ms. O'Connor would follow through with her decision to stop funding since she had the motive and the means to do so. But seeing how affected she's been by her father's words, I'm not sure what her next move will be.

My chest tightens. There's only one way to find out.

"Ms. O'Connor, now that you know your father's reasons for supporting New Hope, I'm curious ... are you still planning to remove funding?"

The ticking on the wall clock stops. The clouds drifting in the bright blue sky halt. No birdsong lilts through the open window.

Ms. O'Connor stows away the letter in her purse then stands. "Yes, I've made a decision." She looks down at me, then at the director. "Based on what I've learned here today, I will continue my father's commitment to the orphanage and those children suffering from heart conditions."

Ecstatic, I jump from my chair. "Oh, that's such good news." Without thinking or asking, I throw my arms around Ms. O'Connor and squeeze her, surprised when she returns the gesture. When we finally let go of each other, we're both crying. Again.

Director Wu claps her hands. "Yes, that is wonderful to hear. Your father would be pleased with your decision."

"I hope so." Ms. O'Connor looks directly at the director. "There's just one condition for me to continue providing the necessary money. Without it, I'm afraid I can't continue to fund in confidence."

I freeze. *What condition?*

Director Wu pushes back her shoulders and tilts her head. "And what would that be?"

If the director is nervous about Ms. O'Connor's conditional terms, her stoic figure isn't relaying that. Unlike the nausea

Perfectly Arranged

gurgling in my stomach and the wobbly knees that threaten to leave me sprawled out across the tile floor, Director Wu's relaxed posture and placid smile indicate she's ready for whatever my boss is about to dish out.

Ms. O'Connor takes a deep breath. "Over the past few days, I've been conducting research on New Hope. Surprisingly, my father left no contingencies in his will regarding future funding. Now that he's gone, the only way I can support it is through the O'Connor Foundation, the philanthropic arm of my estate.

"But I'm concerned they may not see the orphanage and heart center in a good light if they were to consider it in its current condition." She walks over to the crowded bookshelf and swipes dust from the shelf ledge. "It seems that not only are the financials a bit messy and incomplete, and as I toured the facilities this morning, I noticed that most of the rooms and offices are out of order as well."

"Unfortunately, I have to agree with you." Director Wu bows her head. "Things here aren't as orderly as they could be. While I could make excuses, I won't. I take full responsibility for the problems you've mentioned."

"I appreciate your honesty, Director." Ms. O'Connor wipes her hands, sending dust motes floating through the air, then clasps her hands together in front of her. "However, if I am to continue funding the orphanage, I insist you bring someone on board to help you get things back in proper order.

"If you refuse the assistance, I'm afraid I won't be able to present New Hope to the board for consideration. I can assure you my father would have required the same had he known."

"I'm certain he would have as well." Director Wu eyes the room with skepticism. "But I'm not sure where I will get the money for an additional employee. All your family's funds are allotted for the children's overall care and surgical treatments."

"Doesn't the government supply you with funds?" Ms. O'Connor asks.

"They do," the director says, "but the cost to care for so

many children has skyrocketed, and we continually find ourselves short on money."

"Is that why there are so few workers in each room?" I ask, trying to process everything I'm hearing.

The director looks back at me and nods. "Yes, I would love to have more help in each room. We desperately need it, but we haven't even had the resources to hire any additional caretakers for the last eight or nine months."

"That's definitely a problem." Ms. O'Connor marches back toward us.

"It is, and while I know it will be detrimental to the children, we just don't have the means to add someone else to the payroll for an audit and inspection." Director Wu's voice cracks. "So I have no choice but to turn down your generous offer."

My joy dissipates. *Lord, please don't let Ms. O'Connor change her mind again!*

"I do have some concerns with the way the money is being handled here." Ms. O'Connor straightens her back. "And while I must bring someone in for an overview, you don't need to worry about paying for it out of your budget. I'll be handling everything from financing the salary to personally hiring the person I have in mind."

I'm shocked. "You already have someone in mind?"

Ms. O'Connor looks me squarely in the eyes. "I do."

"Who?"

"Why you, of course."

"Me?" My eyes dart between the two women. "You're joking, right?"

"No. I'm not joking. You're the perfect person for the job, Nicole. You have the experience and qualifications, do you not?"

"I don't think so."

Ms. O'Connor crosses her arms in front of her chest and scrutinizes me. "Why not?"

"Because that would require me to live in China."

"But I thought you liked it here."

Perfectly Arranged

"I do, but, but ..." I stammer to find the words. *Or the excuses.* Like déjà vu, I find myself searching for valid reasons to offer to Ms. O'Connor why I can't possibly do what she's asking.

"But what, Nicole?" Ms. O'Connor crosses her arms.

"Well, I'm not sure I'm the right person for the job." I rake my hand through my hair. "I mean, yes, I can organize large shoe closets and overflowing paperwork without too much trouble, but I have no clue how to run an orphanage. You'd be better off with someone who has a human resources background and strong leadership skills. Not someone who sorts like with like or places items in a container and slaps a label on it."

I let out a laugh. "Plus, I don't know the culture or the customs, and I don't even speak the language. That's reason enough for me not to take the position."

Ms. O'Connor walks over to me and takes my trembling hand. "Nicole, what I'm looking for is someone I can trust. Despite our short-lived and often contentious relationship, I trust you." She removes her hand from mine and places it under my chin, tilting my head until our eyes meet. "Unlike most people who work for me, you didn't always concede to my demands.

"In fact, you often challenged me, which could have cost you your job. But that's what I admire about you and why I'm entrusting you to oversee and organize what my father started. I need you to conduct an independent evaluation and re-organization of the orphanage and heart center so we can make sure everything is in proper order and up to date.

"Without it, I'm afraid the O'Connor Foundation won't be willing to allocate the money. As I'm much too ... old to stay and do it myself, I can't think of anyone else better suited for the position than you." She winks at me. "And if I'm not mistaken, you seem to have a genuine love for this place and these kids."

As her words sink into my mind and my heart, her faith in me touches me more than I ever would've expected. To say our relationship has been rocky would be an understatement, but all along there's been mutual respect and understanding I've never had with any other client. Just as she hadn't known how much her father had loved her, I hadn't realized how deep her respect was for me. Or how much I've come to care for her.

Without saying anything, I walk over to the window and try to make sense of what she's asking me to do. *Can I move to China? What will my mom say? What about starting over with a new career? But if I decline her offer, what would that mean for the children and New Hope?*

My thoughts continue down this path as I stare out the window. Beneath me, a group of older children push each other on the swings, chase balls back and forth, and jump rope. There's a happiness to their lives despite their circumstances, a joy that eludes most people, even though these children face insurmountable odds. *Joy in all things*. Only children could teach a lesson so valuable.

Shouldn't someone who works at an orphanage enjoy children? Shouldn't being good with them be a requisite for the job? I consider my history on the subject—while I might have had a few good days with Lei Ming, I'm automatically ruled out.

Ready to confront Ms. O'Connor on the matter, I step away from the window and face her. "And what about the children?"

A frown lines her face. "What about them?"

"We both know that, until this trip, I wasn't fond of kids. I'm still not sure I'll ever want any of my own, and while I have seen my maternal side blossom a bit since being here, I still question my ability to be a good parent. Someone with more than three days of experience and an enthusiasm for them longer than that would be helpful, don't you think?"

"Nicki." Director Wu's interjection cuts across the conversation. "I agree with Ms. O'Connor. You are the perfect person for the job. As for the children, I've seen you with them, and I have no doubt in your growing abilities to offer them the care they need. You may not feel like a natural around them right

Perfectly Arranged

now, but with some time and guidance, I'm certain you'll develop an even more nurturing role.

"Besides, Ms. O'Connor isn't asking you to work here as a caretaker. Your job would mainly be helping me." She beams at me like a proud parent. "Plus, having someone young like you is exactly what New Hope needs. Not only could you get this place in order, but you could provide a fresh perspective that's been missing for quite some time with an old-timer like me at the helm."

I blush at her kind words. I know they were spoken in complete sincerity, but I'm still having a hard time believing I could ever be nurturing.

"Well, Nicole, that's two votes for you to take on the position." Ms. O'Connor clasps her hands under her chin.

"Make it three," a voice shouts from the hallway.

"Who is that?" Ms. O'Connor spins her head towards the door.

I giggle. "That would be Julia, my sidekick and translator. She's been waiting in the hallway for me this entire time. Obviously, she's bored and taken up eavesdropping." I say, loudly emphasizing the last word for Julia's benefit.

"So, what do you say, Nicole?" Ms. O'Connor quickly returns to the topic at hand. "Will you act as my liaison here at New Hope, assisting the director as needed, setting up systems so things run more smoothly around here, and occasionally interacting with the children?"

I bite my lip. She can't possibly expect an answer on the spot. "I appreciate the offer and the trust and confidence you both have in me, but I'll need some time to think about it."

"Of course. We want you to prayerfully consider all your options." Director Wu's gentle tone soothes my frantic state of mind.

Ms. O'Connor nods and tugs at her blazer, a telltale sign she's back to business mode. "The sooner, the better. I'm sure you can understand the urgency of the situation."

Of course I do. I also understand the repercussions if I don't take the position. The future of New Hope and children like Lei Ming hang in the balance. Unlike Ms. O'Connor, though, I'm not one to make hasty decisions and just jump onto the next plane. *Okay, maybe I do, but this time it's different.*

"Well, I'll need to talk to my mom, of course. Then I'd like to get the opinion of my friends as well." I do some quick calculating in my head. "Could I give you my answer in a couple of weeks?"

Ms. O'Connor narrows her eyes. "Although I'd prefer sooner, I do know that I'm asking you to leave your life at home behind and move to another country. That's not something you can just decide on a whim. I can give you two weeks to give me your answer, but not a moment longer." She glances at her watch. "If I'm not mistaken, you have a plane to catch, correct?"

Panic overtakes me when I look at the clock on the wall behind Director Wu's desk. The hour hand is farther along than I'd realized. "Oh, I need to go."

After grabbing my bag from the chair, I give Director Wu and Ms. O'Connor quick hugs goodbye. "Thank you both for everything. I'll be in touch soon."

As soon as I step into the hallway and close the office door, Julia jumps up from the bench where she's been visiting with Wang Wei and pounces on me. "I'm dying to know what happened in there and how you ended up with a job offer in China."

I wave at the young boy whose feet dangle off the edge of the bench.

Julia's eyes track my attention. "Oh, he's waiting to see Director Wu. She told him to wait out here." She calls him over. "Nicki, this is Wang Wei."

"Yes, we've met before." I hold my hand out to him.

He rubs his hand against his pants before slipping it in mine. When he does, my thumb rubs against the thick white gauze that covered his IV port. A dull ache for what he's gone through pricks my heart. No matter how young or how old we are, we all carry scars with us.

"He says you played hide and seek with him, sort of, in the recovery unit." Julia translates Wang Wei's message for me.

His ear-to-ear grin brings back the smile to my face.

"Yes, I did." As much as I'd love to continue chatting with these two, the ticking hand on my watch calls me toward the next part of my journey. "Julia, I'm sorry to cut this short, but I have to go. My plane leaves soon."

"Oh, okay." She says a few words to Wang Wei.

Nodding, he sidles up next to me then wraps his arms around my waist. Touched by his gesture, I lean down and hug him.

"We really should get moving." Julia's words pull me from the sweet embrace, and she starts walking at a rapid pace. "Plus, I can't wait for you to tell me everything that happened with Ms. O'Connor."

I take one last glance at Wang, who'd retreated to the bench during Julia's departure, and smile. Interacting with him was the perfect send-off gift.

ON THE DRIVE back to the hotel then to the airport, I fill in Julia on everything that happened from when Ms. O'Connor and I met in the toddler room until I shut the door to Director Wu's office.

"She had no idea about her father's past?"

"None. It wasn't until Director Wu read the letter to us that she learned the truth about his life as an orphan, the depth of his love for her, and his decision to support New Hope and the children who suffered from heart conditions."

"Wow." Julia pushes back against the seat. "I can't imagine how shocked she must have been." She looks out the car window. "Like being reunited with my parents one day. It would be life-changing."

Julia's words spark surprise in my mind and my heart. I'd never questioned whether that was something she hoped for in the future. Don't most kids who've been separated from their birth parents long to be reunited with them at some point? Or perhaps, like Ms. O'Connor, the pain of confronting the people who you believed abandoned you might be too hard to handle?

A memory of Ms. O'Connor's tears and heartfelt words as we'd sat in the office while Director Wu had read the letter flashes in vivid color before me. In her bravery to search for her father and listen to his words, she'd finally reconciled with her past and found healing. Maybe one day Julia could find that closure as well.

"So," says Julia, breaking the silence. "Do you think you'll accept Ms. O'Connor's offer?"

I lean my head back. "I don't know. It's such a big decision."

Julia bounces in her seat. "But if you live here, I could take you to all the places you didn't get to visit on this trip and to all the other interesting cities in China like Shanghai, Xian, and Hong Kong. Oh, and I could teach you Mandarin too."

Moved by her excitement, I chuckle. "We'd definitely have fun."

"Then just say yes."

I let out a heavy sigh and look back out the window. "I wish it were that easy, Julia, but it's not. There are so many advantages to accepting Ms. O'Connor's proposal, such as not moving in with my mother, not having to search for another job, and of course, getting to be here with you and the kids." I smile at the thought.

"But then there are also the disadvantages, like being so far away from family and friends and leaving the comforts of home." Until this trip, I've never been outside of the country. Could I possibly survive months in a place that's not truly my home?

My rapid heartbeat mirrors the anxiety in Julia's scrunched forehead and wide eyes. "I'm sorry for putting this on you, Julia. It's just all so overwhelming. But I have two weeks to figure out what I'm supposed to do, and I plan on using that time to make my decision."

"Airport." The taxi driver's rugged English conveys my destination.

I open the car door and place my luggage on the sidewalk. Julia says a few words to the driver then joins me.

"I guess this is goodbye," she says. "Again."

"Not goodbye." I reach out and hug her. "Just so long for now."

She pulls away from me. "Does that mean you're coming back?"

Slipping my backpack onto my shoulder, I grab my suitcase handle and make my way toward the airport doors. A few steps out, I stop and blow a kiss in her direction. "Say a prayer for me, Julia."

21

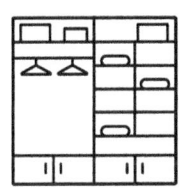

Wherever you go, go with all your heart.
~ Chinese Proverb

My plane touches down at Bridgeport International in the early hours of the morning, and a dusting of snow covers the ground. The pilot informs us we landed just ahead of a blizzard expected to hit the area within the next few hours. Despite my exhaustion, I scramble to collect my things from my seat and race off the plane so I can make it home before the snowstorm wreaks havoc on the city streets.

A whirl of emotions spin through me, battering me from every direction as I ponder my next steps. I don't have the energy to entertain the added stress of getting stuck. China had required everything in me, but the sacrifice was worth it.

I arrive at my apartment as the first rays of sunlight pierce the thick darkness of night. Before crawling into bed, I send a quick text to my mom to let her know I'm back and will call her once I've had time to rest and recover from jetlag.

As anxious as I am to see her and to share everything that happened on my journey, I couldn't begin to put together a coherent sentence even if I drank an entire pot of coffee. And to explain to others what Ms. O'Connor is asking of me, I'll need a clear mind.

I sleep for two days straight. When I finally manage to extract myself from bed and stumble to the window, the snow is piled kid-high, which means going to visit my mom will have to wait.

As will my decision about the orphanage. Perhaps that's why the image of the small child came to mind?

I can't discuss something so serious over the phone, and it would be impossible for me to make a life-changing decision like that without her input.

After I shower, collect my mail off the floor, and make myself a mug of steaming hot chocolate, I pluck my laptop from my backpack and plop down on the couch. I'm planning to google what living in China is like for an American but click on my email first. My inbox is a hodgepodge of last-minute sales, offers to help me reach my new year resolutions, and late Christmas wishes from friends. I delete all of the emails but two.

One from Emerson Technology and the other from someone who goes by the name texasbbguy. Running my cursor over both, I debate which one to open first. Having been rejected by Emerson already, I choose the mystery sender. When the full message appears, I'm pleasantly surprised.

Hey Nicki,

This is Ben Carrington, Longchen's friend from the coffee shop. I hope you remember me and don't mind that I got your email from him. Rumor has it that you might be returning to China soon (word travels fast here). I enjoyed our short visit and wanted to let you know that if you do happen to make it back, I'd love to show you around and help you acclimate to living in a foreign country.

I know firsthand how difficult it can be and if I can do anything to make the transition easier for you, I'd be happy to help. If you decide not to return, I understand and hope we can keep in touch. Either way, I'll be praying for you, asking God to give you wisdom and peace about the plans He has for you.

Take care, Nicki, and get some rest. I know how hard jetlag can be!

All my best,
Ben

I ease my laptop shut. Never in a million years did I expect to hear from Ben. A mix of excitement and uncertainty shoots through me. My arm pebbles with goosebumps as I open my computer and reread his email.

Should I reply?

If I did, what would I even say? I spend 30 minutes composing and deleting responses, none of which seem appropriate. Dropping my laptop on the cushion next to me, I chew on my thumbnail as I search my brain for a suitable reply. It shouldn't be that hard.

So why am I having trouble getting out the words? Ben's just a nice guy being friendly and helpful. That's it. I need to quit making more of this than there is and move on to the more pressing matters at hand.

Setting my computer back on my lap, I write a short but courteous response letting him know I'll keep him posted of any plans I make to return to China. If I decide to accept Ms. O'Connor's offer, having Ben's help would be another checkmark in the pro column for going back. But is that all it would, or could, be with him?

I'm not going to consider that now. Instead, I click on the email from Emerson.

Dear Miss Mayfield,

We would like to extend our apologies for the email you recently received from us. There was a clerical error, and an email rescinding our offer of employment was mistakenly sent to you. We are sorry for any trouble this may have caused you and would once again like to offer the project manager position to you. Please call us at your earliest convenience so we can discuss this matter with you further.

*Regards,
The Human Resource Department at Emerson Technology*

I cover my face with my hands. Did Ms. O'Connor convince them to take me back, or was her threat to remove her recommendation an empty one and the earlier email actually a mistake? Maybe she wanted to make sure I had an honest choice. Regardless of what she did or didn't do, this means I have a job even if I choose not to return to China.

As wonderful as this news is, it adds another layer of confusion to my already muddled mind. Earlier, the only thing impacting my decision was the fate of the children. Now it seems I have to throw my well-being, something that hadn't carried that much weight before, into the mix.

I just assumed if I didn't return to New Hope, I'd move in with my mom and search for a stable job. But that isn't the case anymore. This new email from Emerson means I can remain independent and safeguard my relationship with my mother. That's two checkmarks in the pro column for staying.

How will I possibly decide? And would it be crazy to think I could have them all?

Conflicted, I jump up off the couch and pull the cleaning supplies and the vacuum out of the hall closet. Although my apartment is spotless, when my mind is cluttered and I have no clue what my next move is, organizing and cleaning soothe my spirit like nothing else can.

So for the next three hours I polish my furniture until there's no varnish left and sweep the carpet bare of all its thread. When I'm finished, everything sparkles and shines, but my emotions are still a jumbled mess.

As I climb back into bed, an avalanche of fear crashes over me. What if I can't make a decision? Or worse, what if I make the wrong one? I bury my head in my pillow and scream. Because, honestly, I don't know what to do.

It takes two more days for me to snowplow my way, both physically and mentally, out of my house and drive to my mom's to deliver her souvenirs. I park in front of the house where a blanket of white has covered her less-than-desirable front yard. If only it were that easy to make spaces look so neat and orderly. Deep down, I know that it's not, and, truth be told, I need to offer my mother more patience and grace.

None of this is her fault. Although she may not be the mother I've dreamed of, she's the perfect one for me. Sadly, I haven't always seen her in that light. Like Ms. O'Connor, I've let disappointment and unmet expectations mar my vision of what a parent should be. Thanks to our China adventures, though, we're both seeing our parents through new lenses. Ones tinted with unconditional love.

Before I can reach the porch, she throws open the front door. "Nicki, you're here!"

Without giving me a chance to drop my bags, she wraps me in her arms and squeezes me so tightly I can hardly breathe. When she finally releases me, her eyes drop to my bags. Excitement with the wattage of the thousands of bulbs lighting the outside of her neighbor's house brightens her face.

"Are those for me?"

"Yes, they are. Everything you asked for and then some."

"Oh, let's get inside so I can see what you brought." She

dashes from the doorway. "It's like Christmas all over again," she shouts over her shoulder.

Rather than relax in the living room, my mom leads me into the kitchen.

"I'm sorting my after-Christmas sale items in the living room. It's better if we open everything in here." She pulls out two mismatched chairs for us.

I'm so happy to see her that I don't dwell on her admission that she's added more unnecessary items to her household clutter. An announcement like that usually drives me crazy but not today. I choose to ignore it and enjoy my time with her. Besides, how can I be upset when I'm presenting her with more stuff she doesn't need?

"Can I open my presents now?" She wiggles in her seat.

I smile at her. "Sure, Mom." I pass her the first bag. "I didn't have any wrapping paper at home, so I couldn't wrap them properly. Sorry."

"That's okay." She removes the fans first, opening each one and studying the intricate designs painted on the fabric. "Oh, they're beautiful. I know exactly where I'm going to hang these."

"You do know they're hand fans, right?" I pick one up and demonstrate.

Her eyes crinkle at the corners. "Of course I do, Nicki." She grabs the fan out of my hand. "But it's not warm enough here to use them that way, so I'm going to display them so that others can enjoy their beauty too."

I grimace at the thought of anyone else coming over to the house in its current state but try to stay in the moment. Perhaps with practice the niggling sensation in my belly will diminish. Plus, who knows, maybe one day Mom will be able to invite people into her home. I'll hold onto that dream for both of us.

It doesn't take long for my mother to empty the bags. She examines each item I bought with care and asks me tons of details about them. The longer we mull over her souvenirs, the longer I can delay telling her about Ms. O'Connor's request. *Yes, I'm a coward like that.*

After she slips on the Chinese silk robe, her attention lands fully on me. "So." She ties the sash around her waist. "Tell me what brought you home earlier than expected."

Since my mom already knew about the orphanage and Ms. O'Connor's plans to close it, I only needed to fill her in on the whirlwind activity of the past few days, including my visit to Mother's Love, my encounter with Lei Ming, the discovery of the heart unit, the shocking letter from Mr. O'Connor and Ms. O'Connor's surprising response to it.

Then, like a proud parent, I pull out my phone and scroll through my photo album of the kids. I hold off on sharing the most important part of the story until I know she can handle it. *Or until I can handle saying it out loud.*

"Oh, Nicki, that sounds like such an amazing experience. I'm so happy for you." She passes my phone back to me. "And these children are adorable. You really seem to have taken a liking to them, which I wasn't expecting."

"That makes two of us." I take one last look at Lei Ming before my screen goes dark.

"So, is there a chance kids might be in your future?" She tilts her head, her face flush with hope.

"Mom, don't get too excited." I resist the urge to roll my eyes. "I definitely enjoyed being with the kids, but I'm not a hundred percent sure I'm cut out for motherhood."

She throws her head back. "No one is a hundred percent cut out for the job. It's something you grow into. But who knows, maybe spending more time with kids will develop your maternal side. You could always volunteer in the church nursery for practice."

I gulp hard, knowing it's time for me to divulge the part of the story I've been keeping from her.

"Nic, is something wrong? You look pale." She places the back of her hand on my forehead. "You don't feel warm."

"I'm fine, Mom." I gently remove her hand from my forehead and wrap it in mine. "There's just something else I need to tell you."

"Okay, what is it?" Her eyes narrow.

I fidget in my seat and clear my throat. "Well, Ms. O'Connor made her continuing support of the orphanage conditional."

"Conditional on what?"

"On the condition ..." I fumble to get the words out. "On the condition that I go back to China for a while and help get things in order at New Hope."

"Oh! How did you answer?"

"I told her I'd need to think about it." I bow my head and lower my voice. "She gave me two weeks to give her an answer."

She doesn't respond immediately but instead pushes back from the table. My adrenaline spikes as I watch her cross the room. I pray I haven't upset her.

For a few moments, neither of us speak, each lost in our thoughts.

As the clock in the hallway announces a new hour, my mom whispers, "And if you say no?"

A lump forms in my stomach as I turn to face her. Looking at her frail body hunched over the sink, I'm worried the news is more than she can bear. "I don't know." I hesitate to think about what would happen if I refuse her offer. "I want to believe she'd find someone else and continue providing the funds, but there's no guarantee she'd do that. She was pretty firm on what her terms were."

My mother sighs and walks back to the table. "Then it seems you have a big decision to make."

I pick at my cuticles. "It's all I've thought about since I left New Hope."

When our eyes meet, I notice hers are filled with a tenderness I wasn't expecting.

"And?"

"How am I supposed to make a decision like that? There are

pros and cons to both going and staying, and I have no clue how I'm going to determine which one is the right choice."

"Nicki," she says reassuringly as she combs her fingers through my curls. "Do you remember Queen Esther?"

"From the Bible?"

"Yes."

"What about her?" I offer a look of confusion. While I'm familiar with the well-known woman of the Old Testament, I don't see a connection with her to my current conundrum.

My mom settles back down into her chair. "God sent young Esther to a foreign land and put her in a place of position so she could help save her people from suffering and destruction.

"I can't help but think that's what God's doing with you, too, Nicki. He sent you to China for such a time as this, to keep those orphans from harm." She flashes a proud smile at me. "And I have a strong feeling He's not finished with you there yet, either."

I'm speechless and stunned by my mom's keen observations. Not only because it shows how closely she was listening to me, but also because I never realized how deeply her spiritual wisdom flowed. Sure, I'd listen to her ramble on about things she heard during a sermon or from her Bible study, but on more serious matters, I never really looked to her for that type of guidance. How did I never notice that before?

Probably because you were too occupied with her clutter and trying to avoid it, Nic. That's something I'm going to have to work on. I wonder if Marie Kondo has any advice in her book that might help me with that?

"If that's true, then it means we'd be apart for a while." I shake my head. "I'd hate leaving you here all alone. You're my family, and family should take priority." *Isn't that what I learned from my time in China?*

My mother leans over the table and covers my cheeks with her hands. "Nicki, don't worry about me. I'll be fine. I have plenty of people who can watch out for me."

"So you'd really be okay with me going back for a short

time?" The tears that had been pooling in my eyes break their barrier and flow down my cheeks.

"I'll be happy with whatever you choose. Of course, if you decide to return to China I would miss you, but it's only temporary, right?" She removes her hands from my face and wipes away her tears. "Ultimately, though, you have to follow your heart and do what you feel God is calling you to do. In the end, that's all that matters. And if you ask me, I don't think He's done with you in China or that orphanage yet."

Hearing her words, I drop my head onto the table again.

My mother might just be right.

TEN DAYS after my hasty departure from China, I call Ms. O'Connor. While I would have preferred a face-to-face meeting, Heather asked if we could have a phone conference as Ms. O'Connor was extremely busy trying to get caught back up on work. It wasn't my ideal scenario, but there was no point in delaying the inevitable.

As I wait for her to answer, I close my eyes and throw up one final plea to God. *Lord, I hope I'm doing the right thing here. You know what an extremely difficult decision this has been, but in the end, I'm trusting in You and what I feel You've called me to do. If it's not, please let me know now!*

I pause and wait for a bolt of lightning to strike or a clap of thunder to roar. But when I open my eyes and look out my living room window, the sun is shining.

Finally, Ms. O'Connor answers. "Nicole, I've been waiting to hear from you."

Despite her desire to get straight to business, proper phone etiquette calls my name. "Hello, Ms. O'Connor. How are you today?"

"I'm fine, thank you." She coughs. "As much as I'd love to

chitchat, I'd prefer to get to the reason for this call. Do you have an answer for me?"

I bite my lip. "I do. But I have to tell you that you've put me in quite a predicament."

"Not really."

Easy for you to say; you weren't the one debating this life-changing decision.

"Well, I've weighed all my options, spoken to those closest to me, and spent a lot of time in prayer."

"Yes, I know. I've been anxious to have your answer for a while now."

"After all that, I've decided to return to New Hope and do the job you've asked me to do. I'll get things organized there and ensure everything runs smoothly so that the O'Connor Foundation won't have a reason not to continue funding." I crack a small smile. "I can't believe I'm saying this, but I think it's the perfect arrangement for both of us."

Quiet hangs over the conversation. She doesn't push back or, in fact, say anything at all. Only a sniffle and a sigh of relief come my way.

"That's wonderful, Nicole. I know you'll do an excellent job for me, for my father, and the children."

I grin at her rare compliment. "I'll do my best, Ms. O'Connor. I won't let you down, I promise."

"I know you won't. I trust you completely." She steadies her voice. "May I ask what swayed your decision to go back?"

Despite the lengthy list of pros and cons I made, the hours I spent journaling, praying, and seeking out other's opinions, and the photos I pored over every day, deep down, I just knew it was the right thing to do. But how do I explain that to a woman who bases her decisions on data and facts? She may not understand my logic or the peace that's flooded my spirit since I agreed to return to New Hope, but I do.

And ultimately, that's what matters most.

"It's what I was meant to do," I say with a confidence I've

never had before. "I may not have been able to save myself, my mother, or my business, but I truly believe I can—I mean, God can—use me and my skills and talents to help the orphanage." I choke back my emotions. "And despite my lack of maternal instincts, maybe even these children."

Another sniffle comes over the line. "Well then," her voice returns to a more formal tone, and I can imagine her tugging on her blazer as she always does when she's discussing business. "We need to get things moving as I'd like you back at New Hope right away. A lot needs done there, and I don't want to waste any time.

"For the Foundation to consider New Hope as a potential recipient, I need you to professionally organize all the rooms as you see fit, update the policies and procedures to ensure they're running everything to the highest standards, and digitize all the paperwork from the last five years so I can have the proper documentation for submissions. And, Nicole, we only have three months to do it all."

"Three months?" I'm confused by her sudden demand for the job to be done so quickly.

"Yes, the board of the O'Connor Foundation will meet in May to plan their budget for the upcoming fiscal year, so I need you to have things wrapped up by the first week of May. Then, on June first, the Foundation will announce their funding allocations."

She clears her throat. "I want to make sure New Hope is included in those allocations and receives everything it should, plus some. For that to happen, I need everything to be in order."

Despite her serious tone, I can't help but smile at her generosity and her desire to ensure New Hope's future. Definitely a change of heart since discovering her family's connection to the orphanage a few weeks ago. I'm thrilled at her new outlook.

"I'll have to work fast," I tell her. "But I promise you I'll get it done." I feel the urge to salute her, but since we're on the phone, it's pointless.

"That's what I like to hear."

"In fact, I'm already preparing to leave."

"You are?" Surprise laces her voice.

"Yes, I was thinking that if I can get things packed up and settled here in a timely manner, I might be able to make it back in time for the Chinese New Year that Longchen told me about at Christmas." My heart flutters at the idea of celebrating such a special occasion in person, with Julia and possibly even with Ben. "I'll contact Heather later today to start working on the details."

"Wonderful. Thank you for agreeing to do this. It means more to me than you can ever know."

"I'm happy to do it for you."

"Take care, Nicki," she says, her voice soft. "I'll be in touch soon." Our call ends with a click.

I pull my phone away from my ear and stare at it. While I'm not shocked by her abrupt finish to our conversation, I am floored by what she said. *She called me Nicki!*

God, you definitely work in mysterious ways.

Chuckling, I reach for a moving box on the floor. Three months ago, I was packing up my office, sad but determined to make a way for myself. Then Ms. O'Connor entered my world, and my life changed in ways I could never have imagined. We've become the most unexpected team.

Now I'm separating the details of my life into two piles—things to store until I return and things to take with me overseas. Smiling, I place my mom's Bible in with the items I want with me in China, then tape the brown cardboard flaps shut. It's time to close this chapter of my life and begin the next one—the one, it seems, God has perfectly arranged.

THE END

AUTHOR'S NOTE

In 2006, my family and I moved to Nanjing, China, for my husband's work. It was a surreal experience and one we loved and treasured. Not only did we see some of the world's most impressive sites (I visited the Great Wall and rode the sled down three different times), but we learned a lot about different people and cultures and enjoyed each and every opportunity we had while there.

The following year, my dad called and asked if, on my next visit to Shanghai (to which I traveled often), I could drive by a particular address and take a picture of what was located there. Intrigued, I agreed. Dad emailed a Chinese business card from a friend who had discovered it in her deceased father's belongings and was curious why her father kept it. The next time I went to Shanghai, I looked for the address listed on the card but couldn't find it. I decided to keep the card and always wondered what was at the location – if it still existed – and exactly how the friend's father had been associated with it.

My writer's brain thought it would make a great story someday. However, since I could never get a complete picture of how it would play out, I tucked the card away with my other

Author's Note

book ideas, figuring that the pieces would fall into place and a story would emerge when the time was right.

While I never forgot the business card, I decided to forgo my writing dreams, and in 2013 I started my own professional organizing business. I loved the idea of helping people bring order to their homes and lives, and so By George Organizing Solutions was born. From Day One, I had fascinating clients. I was captivated by the things I discovered as we worked together, not just the items themselves (old Broadway playbills of performances they had been in, novels written by their famous relatives), but also the stories that went along with them.

That's when the pieces of this novel started to fall into place. From my experience as an organizer, I knew exactly how the story could unfold using a professional organizer as my main character. Now all I needed was a protagonist. Fortunately, or unfortunately, some might say, I had a client who hired me to organize her shoe room (yes, it was a room, not a closet). She was quite challenging to work with, and I knew she would be perfect for the part. Soon I had my story's framework.

The last piece of the puzzle was to figure out the identity of the mysterious location. With no idea of what was there, I was free to base it on anything I wanted. Since writers are encouraged to write what they know, I mined my China experiences for something that might work. That's when I remembered an organization called Hopeful Hearts, a charity we supported while living in Nanjing. Their mission is to raise funds for children in desperate need of heart surgeries that could not be paid for by their parents or the orphanages in which they lived. Remembering the organization's incredible work, I decided to incorporate it into the book. I hoped to use it as a backdrop for my story and thought I might raise awareness and money for the organization and its worthwhile endeavors at the same time. To learn more about Hopeful Hearts or to make a monetary donation, please visit http://hopefulheartsnj.org.

Author's Note

Finally, in 2017, I had all the puzzle pieces figured out, and marrying them together, I started to write a book.

A well-known Chinese proverb says, "A journey of a thousand miles begins with the first steps." When we picked up and moved to the other side of the world fifteen years ago, I had no idea my writing journey would start there. While it's been a long and windy road, I know each step along the way has allowed this story to develop into what it was meant to be. Almost as if it was perfectly arranged.

And I pray that knowing the story behind the story helps you, the reader, enjoy it even more.

READER'S GUIDE

1. From the first chapter of the novel, Nicki states what she wants to do with her life. Proverbs 16:9 reminds us, "We can make our plans, but the Lord determines our steps." How can we make plans that align with God's steps, and what difference could it have in our lives?

2. Nicki focuses on her career instead of pursuing love, marriage, and a family. Will people applaud her decision or look down on her because of it? Why?

3. Disquieting parent relationships are a focus of the novel. How are Nicki and Ms. O'Connor's parent issues alike, and how are they different? How do their familial struggles help or encourage you as you review your own family ties?

4. Do you consider Ms. O'Connor's and Nicki's mom's hoarding issues to be a mental issue, a faith issue, or something completely different? How is storing up treasures viewed from a faith standpoint?

5. Ms. O'Connor believed she was broken goods in her father's eyes because of her physical condition when she was younger. How can our physical shortcomings impact our view of ourselves and the way we live our lives?

6. Nicki says she only prayed to God about the small issues

of life, certain that more significant problems (i.e., cancer) overshadowed her needs in God's eyes. How can we limit ourselves with that attitude or thinking? What have you learned about prayer from Nicki's journey?

7. As Nicki read through Scripture, one verse jumped out at her and moved her to action. Has there ever been a time when a verse or group of verses moved you to do something you might not have done otherwise? What was it, and what difference did it make?

8. The Bible says, "Two are better than one, for they get a greater return on their work." How did Nicki learn this lesson, and how does it encourage you when you are resistant to ask others for help?

9. Judging or misjudging others plays a prominent role in the story. How have you misjudged others before, and what did you learn from it?

10. After listening to her father's letter, Ms. O'Connor realizes his great love for her and how that love saved many lives. How does that truth resonate with you and your relationship with your Heavenly Father?

11. How did Nicki's willingness to say yes to new opportunities change her life? How could it do the same for you?

ABOUT THE AUTHOR

While I loved reading and making up stories as a young girl, fear kept me from pursuing a writing career. So I tucked away the dream of becoming a writer and author and became a wife, mother, teacher, and professional organizer instead. Life was good and I was content scribbling down my thoughts every once and awhile.

Then one day, an idea came to me and wouldn't leave. I pushed it aside, hiding it in the deep recesses of my mind, but it was always there calling to me. Finally, I gave in and put pencil to paper (*old-school, I know*).

Thanks to the love and support of my family, friends, and amazing writing coach, I turned that story idea into a novel. In doing so, I finally allowed myself to believe that, yes, I am a writer.

With one manuscript under my belt and a newfound

confidence as a scribe, I'm unearthing the dream I buried so long ago. I'm not sure where the road will lead, but I'm grateful to be on the journey.

A few things you should know about me:

1. I've been married to my college sweetheart, Clint, for almost 30 years. Together, we have two beautiful adult children, Kayley and Abbey.

2. The ocean and the beach are my happy place. I go there as often as I can to relax and scuba dive.

3. My other childhood dream was to be a tennis champion. When I'm not watching a tennis tournament, I'm on the courts pretending there's still a chance I can go pro.

4. I'm an avid reader. What writer isn't?

5. I love to travel. I've been to 6 of the 7 continents. Only Antarctica is left to visit.

COMING SOON FROM LIANA GEORGE ...

Coming July 5, 2022 ... Perfectly Placed
Book Two of the Hopeful Hearts series
by Liana George.

Nicki Mayfield may have hung up her label maker, but she's not done organizing yet!

Charged with the task of restoring order at New Hope Orphanage, Nicki determines to do whatever's necessary to secure its future funding. Surprised by a series of unexpected events at work, with family, and in her relationships, Nicki questions if God perfectly placed her in China after all. Resolved to find that answer and save the children, she takes on every challenge facing her. Will all be lost, or can Nicki ultimately remove all the obstacles and save what matters most?

Coming April 4, 2023 ... Perfectly Matched
Book Three of the Hopeful Hearts series
by Liana George.

Will beloved organizer Nicki Mayfield succeed at carving out a new career and building a most unexpected family, or will she end up in the one place she's never wanted to be–living with her mother?

Find out in the final book of the Hopeful Hearts Series, *Perfectly Matched*!

YOU MAY ALSO LIKE THESE TITLES FROM SCRIVENINGS PRESS

Beneath the Seams

Peyton H. Roberts

Fashion designer Shelby Lawrence is launching her mother-daughter dresses nationwide when she receives a photo of the girl who will change her life forever. Runa, the family's newly sponsored child, is a clever student growing up near Dhaka, Bangladesh. Shelby's daughter Paisley is instantly captivated by their faraway friend. As the girls exchange heartwarming messages, Shelby has no idea that a tragedy in Runa's life is about to upend her own.

Dresses are flying off the racks when a horrifying scene unfolds in Dhaka that threatens to destroy Shelby's pristine reputation. Even worse—it sends Runa's life spiraling down a terrifying path. Shelby must decide how far she's willing to go to right a tragic wrong.

Both a gripping exposé of fashion industry secrets and a heartwarming mother-daughter tale, Beneath the Seams explores love, conscience, hope, and the common threads connecting humanity.

Cake That!
Heather Greer

Ten bakers. Nine days. Only one winner.

Competing on the *Cake That* baking show is a dream come true for Livvy Miller, but debt on her cupcake truck and an expensive repair make her question if it's one she should chase. Her best friend, Tabitha, encourages Livvy to trust God to care for The Sugar Cube, win or lose.

Family is everything to Evan Jones. His parents always gave up their dreams so their children could achieve theirs. Winning *Cake That* would let him give back some of what they've sacrificed by allowing him to give them the trip they've always talked about but could never afford.

As the contestants live and bake together, more than the competition heats up. Livvy and Evan have a spark from the start, but they're in it to win. Neither needs the distraction of romance. Unwanted attention from Will, another competitor, complicates matters. Stir in strange occurrences to the daily baking assignments, and everyone wonders if a saboteur is in the mix.

With the distractions inside and outside the *Cake That* kitchen, will Livvy or Evan rise above the rest and claim the prize? Or does God have more in store for them than they first imagined?

Candy Cane Wishes and Saltwater Dreams

A collection of Christmas romances by five multi-published authors.

***Mistletoe Make-believe* by Amy Anguish**—Charlie Hill's family thinks his daughter Hailey needs a mom—to the point they won't get off his back until he finds her one. Desperate to be free from their nagging, he asks a stranger to pretend she's his girlfriend during the holidays. When romance author Samantha Arwine takes a working vacation to St. Simons Island over Christmas, she never dreamed she'd be involved in a real-life romance. Are the sparks between her and Charlie real? Or is her imagination over-acting … again?

***A Hatteras Surprise* by Hope Toler Dougherty**—Ginny Stowe spent years tending a childhood hurt that dictated her college study and work. Can time with an island visitor with ties to her past heal lingering wounds and lead her toward a happy Christmas … and more? Ben Daniels intends to hire a new branch manager for a Hatteras Island bank, then hurry back to his promotion and Christmas in Charlotte. Spending time with a beautiful local, however, might force him to adjust his sails.

***A Pennie for Your Thoughts* by Linda Fulkerson**—When the Lakeshore Homeowner's Association threatens to condemn the cabin Pennie Vaughn inherited from her foster mother, her only hope of funding the needed repairs lies in winning a travel blog contest. Trouble is, Pennie never goes anywhere. Should she use the all-expenses paid Hawaiian vacation offered to her by her ex-fiancé? The trip that would have been their honeymoon?

Mr. Sandman **by Regina Rudd Merrick**—Events manager Taylor Fordham's happily-ever-after was snatched from her, and she's saying no to romance and Christmas. When she meets two new friends—the cute new chef at Pilot Oaks and a contributor on a sci-fi fan fiction website who enjoys debate—her resolve begins to waver. Just when she thinks she can loosen her grip on thoughts of love, a crisis pulls her back. There's no way she's going to risk her heart again.

Coastal Christmas **by Shannon Taylor Vannatter**—Lark Pendleton is banking on a high-society wedding to make her grandparent's inn at Surfside Beach, Texas the venue to attract buyers. Tasked with sprucing up the inn, she hires Jace Wilder, whose heart she once broke. When the bride and groom turn out to be Lark's high school nemesis and ex-boyfriend, she and Jace embark on a pretend romance to save the wedding. But when real feelings emerge, can they overcome past hurts?

Scrivenings PRESS
Quench your thirst for story.
www.ScriveningsPress.com

Stay up-to-date on your favorite books and authors with our free e-newsletters.

ScriveningsPress.com